C000163310

THE BADGE AND THE BAD BOY

LENA HENDRIX

Copy editing by James Gallagher, Evident Ink

Proofreading by Laetitia Treseng, Little Tweaks

Cover by Sommer Stein, Perfect Pear Creative Covers

Sensitivity Reading by Chula Gonzalez

READER NOTE

This book contains adult material including references to substance abuse, child neglect (not on page), and elements of life on a rural ranch that includes the natural death of an animal. It is my hope that I've handled these topics with the care and research they deserve.

I would also like to extend a special thank you to Chula Gonzalez for performing a very thorough sensitivity read to ensure that Val and her family have been represented with proper care and accuracy. Also, thanks for encouraging me to include a little dirty talk in Spanish—holy hotness!

ONE
VAL

"Pushing those veggies around the plate isn't going to make them go away any faster," said Eric, his rumbling voice sounding behind my back.

Shooting my partner the side-eye over my shoulder, I continued to poke and prod my dinner around the sagging cardboard take-out container. It may have been well after midnight, but when you worked the midnight shift on the police force, two a.m. meant dinnertime—usually in the form of shitty takeout from Uncle Mao's Chinese Restaurant. Giving the repugnant vegetables one last scowl, I dropped the chopsticks into the container and pushed it over the edge of my desk and into the trash.

"You have the eating habits of a five-year-old," Eric teased as he approached my desk in the bullpen of the police station. The years had been kind to my partner and his salt and pepper hair and slight paunch were the only signs of his long tenure on the force.

"Well, the best thing about not actually being five is I can choose *not* to eat my vegetables. You ready to roll out?"

Eric and I had been partners in the Eleventh District of

the Chicago Police Department for the past three years. Notoriously dangerous—ironically the district with the youngest and most inexperienced police officers—an assignment in the Eleventh District meant that a break for dinner lasted only fifteen or twenty minutes before we had to be back on patrol, doing whatever we could to keep innocent people alive.

Only six miles north and my job would have meant a cushy patrol learning from twenty-year veterans, but that wasn't all that appealing anyway. I loved the thrill, the challenge of solving a case and keeping my city safe.

I stood, adjusted my utility belt and vest, and slid my chair beneath the desk. I scanned my desk to ensure everything was in place before I was ready to go. "Let's do it."

I tucked myself behind the wheel of our squad car. Eric never minded that I preferred to drive—my need for control and order. Usually on quiet nights, I had to make sure his ass didn't fall asleep on the job. Eric was a lot like the older brother that teased you, but you knew always had your back. He had a decade of experience on me—but he'd also lost the hunger. The hunger to maintain justice and order amid the chaos of the city. Mostly, he looked at his job as a cop as just that—a job. To me, it was a calling.

Sensing the seriousness in my mood, Eric cleared his throat. "You should find out any day now, right?"

I tightened my grip on the steering wheel and willed my breath to steady. "I'm hoping. So far it's been a waiting game."

Eric shook his head. "Man, I can't believe you're going to leave me to kiss ass with the ATF. You tell your folks yet?"

I huffed. "Are you kidding? They're horrified enough that I carry a gun every day."

He shrugged. "The ATF may not be all it's cracked up to be."

I rolled my eyes in his direction. Applying to be a part of the elite Bureau of Alcohol, Tobacco, Firearms, and Explosives unit, more commonly referred to as the ATF, had taken over a year, and there still was no guarantee I'd be accepted to become a federal agent. Women made up less than twenty-five percent of the entire Chicago Police Department, and even fewer had aspirations to become a special agent.

As a first-generation Mexican American woman, if that was my future, I'd have to blaze the trail myself. None of those things meant anything at all to my parents, but I could show them what it meant. Make them proud.

"You're just pissed you won't have someone watching your ass while you nap," I teased.

Eric sank lower in the seat and pulled a baseball cap farther down his brow. "Well," he grunted as he got comfortable, "you're not wrong there. Don't fuck up while I'm out."

I laughed and shook my head. I'd learned in the academy that to be a female police officer, you had to develop a thick skin and handle a certain amount of ball-busting to have a chance of surviving. It didn't matter that I had proved my skills; if you weren't one of the good ol' boys, you were *other*.

I glanced out the window and up at the passing street-lights. The rain was a slow, dreary late fall precipitation that kept everyone shuttered away from the damp cold. The twilight hours—known as *witching hours* by the most super-stitious cops—could be so calm they almost made your skin crawl. City streets were all but abandoned. Some houses were so run-down with broken windows and peeling paint it was hard to tell which ones sheltered civilians and which hid away criminals.

Sometimes the answer was both.

Adjusting the volume of the pop music thumping out of the car radio, I turned the squad car for another long loop through our section of the city. Quiet chatter on the police radio became my company while Eric dozed beside me.

Dispatch: **Squad 9522 to dispatch.**

Me: **9522. Go ahead.**

Dispatch: **We have a reported 650 in progress. Intersection of Kilbourn and Maypole. Possible 4210.**

650, home invasion. 4210, kidnapping. Shit.

I pushed the button on my vest walkie to respond as I hit Eric awake with the back of my hand.

Me: **Officers 842 and 1732. En route.**

The computer to my right lit up with information from dispatch. Apparently, a neighbor had called with complaints of shouting and glass breaking. One witness reported seeing a white male with a gun enter the home. After flipping on the lights and sirens, I whipped hard down a side street and barreled toward the address on my screen.

Tension curled up my spine and gripped me at the base of my neck. I bumped my partner again. "Wake up, E. I've got a bad feeling about this."

Eric rubbed his eyes and swung the computer his way to get up to speed. I chanced only a glance in his direction as he read through the information and relayed it aloud to me.

Eric's voice got low, muttering to himself as he scanned the words again. I couldn't catch all of what he said. "Kilbourn and Maypole. I know that house. Fuck . . ."

"What?"

Eric shook his head. His lips were in a hard line, and I'd learned his body language well enough to know he was amped.

My heart hammered as I sped through the city toward the run-down residential area. Duplexes and apartment buildings encroached abandoned storefronts and were shoe-horned between industrial buildings. The dilapidated, deserted buildings were nestled between streets of residential housing. Even knowing the neighborhood, it was difficult to know which were which or what alley led to a courtyard versus a dead end.

Approaching the given address, the commotion outside pointed us to exactly where we needed to go. Two additional squad cars came flying in as I parked. Eric and I exited the car, readying our weapons.

With a series of hand movements, Eric instructed me to fall behind him. The officers behind me began their search on the east side of the looming brick building. As we pushed past the gawkers already forming on the front lawn, I could see that the front door had been kicked in. The frame was splintered around the lock, and chunks of decaying wood hadn't stood a chance from a boot or a stiff shoulder.

Once inside, I swept right and left, the light on top of my service weapon illuminating the cramped space. The room was musty and damp. More than the rain outside, the wetness clung to the air, coating the walls, ripe with mildew. I pressed my tongue to the roof of my mouth to ignore the smell of mold, piss, and dirty laundry.

The only sound was my heartbeat, hammering between my ears as my eyes scanned the rooms. Extensive training ensured my movements were efficient and my senses were keyed into my surroundings. The house appeared empty, but it didn't *feel* empty.

The clawing sense of unease prickled my skin as goose bumps coated my arms. The groan of a single loose floorboard had me whipping my weapon to the right. A shadowed figure ran across the narrow hallway, through the kitchen, and shouldered out the back door.

"Freeze!" I commanded.

"Police!" Eric bellowed at the same time.

I called into my radio. "Suspect fleeing. Dark hoodie, denim pants. Dark sneakers."

Eric burst through the back door. I scanned the room, and instead of following him out, I halted as my eyes landed on a dark, crumpled figure in the corner.

A body.

Instinct took over, and I toed the body with my foot. A pair of wide, frantic eyes stared up at me.

I crouched. "Hey, hey. It's okay. We'll get you out of here. Stay behind me." I pulled the young girl up, and she huddled behind me. Her dark hair was matted and hung in tangled clumps. I moved forward through the house, still unconvinced the place was empty.

When movement through the kitchen caught my attention, the young woman pushed past me, nearly knocking me over, and ran toward the door.

"Stop!"

As I reached for her, the girl glanced back and didn't see the closed patio door. The old glass splintered and crashed around her. She tumbled forward, landing in the shards. I rushed to her. Disoriented, the girl shoved an elbow against my hands, and I turned her over, assessing any injuries. I called into my radio for medical assistance.

Shards of glass pierced her forearm, and deep crimson was rapidly staining the front of her rumpled beige T-shirt. I pulled at the neckline to reveal a deep slash that spread beneath her collarbone and up toward her delicate neck. I pressed my hand into it to try to stop the bleeding, and she called out, crying and fighting against my help.

Pushing onto her feet, she shoved me backward, then scrambled to steady herself. She ran haphazardly into the alley, and I went after her, leaping over garbage and old patio furniture littering the back lawn. The rain came down steadily, obscuring the light mounted to my gun.

I blinked water away and tried to refocus. My body surged forward as I searched the darkness for any signs of movement. The buildings were close together, and it left little room for hiding. In the distance, I could hear the other officers fanning out in different directions, none calling out for assistance.

I took a hesitant step into a dark alley between two brick buildings. It was a long, empty path with nothing but brick doorways to the end. Moving quickly, I pushed forward between the buildings.

Don't do it.

The words whispered through my skull a millisecond too late.

As I passed one of the darkened doorways, a figure surged out, slamming me into the opposite wall. My head rapped against the brick, and white-hot pain screeched between my eyes.

I shook my head and raised my gun. "Stop!"

It was not the same man in the hoodie, but the figure kept running. I chased after him.

"I said 'Stop!'" I yelled again. I was within my rights to shoot, but I knew if I could catch him, I wouldn't have to.

My adrenaline was coursing through my veins. My legs burned as I pushed forward toward where the person had taken off. When I reached the end of the alley, opening into a small courtyard, a hand grabbed my arm and pulled me forward. Off-balance, I struggled and rammed a knee into the ground. A strong, heavy force slammed on top of me, pinning me to the pavement. I watched in horror as my gun slid just out of reach.

"You fucking cunt!" the voice growled in my ear. He yanked my ponytail backward as I gritted my teeth.

"Fuck you!" I spat in his direction.

His reaction was to push my face into the concrete. The uneven surface caused water to surge up my nose and burn into my eyes as the gravel bit at my cheekbones.

"Fuck me? How about fuck you, lady cop." His palm pushed harder and harder into my face and jaw as I struggled to get air around the water filling my mouth and nose.

All the while, I was cataloging.

His voice: noticeable Chicago Italian, scratchy.

His breath: definitely a smoker or tobacco chewer.

His weight: at least two hundred pounds, soft fatty weight, not hard muscle.

Keeping my mind on the suspect and not the fact I was nearly drowning helped focus my thoughts. I coughed and reared my head back just enough to get a gulp of fresh air. The renewed oxygen helped me push and struggle against the knee in my back.

When my knees finally gained purchase, I shoved upward as hard as I could, knocking him unsteady. It was enough to roll and attempt to crawl away. As I turned to face him, a heavy crack radiated across my jaw.

His punch to my face snapped my head back. I moved toward where I last saw my service pistol. In the dim lighting, I felt the ground for the cold bite of the metal against my palm. My fingers curled around the slick, hard barrel as I righted it in my shaking hands. In the predawn darkness, two figures were locked in a stance, both fighting to over-power the other. Another, the young woman from the house, was slumped next to me by an overturned patio table. The sickening thud of punches and grunts filled the air as rain continued to thunder around us and the men continued to fight.

I called for additional backup through the radio on my vest, and I used the brick wall, struggling to push to my feet. As I righted myself, one man reached behind his back, a movement I recognized just as the flash of metal winked from the streetlights. Footsteps thundered behind me.

Officers approaching.

I raised my weapon and pulled the weakening young girl behind me.

Calm.

Ready to defend myself and my fellow officers.

The man raised his arm. I should have shot him. I hesi-tated. The pop of his gun fired twice. Once to my right and again directly at me.

I didn't feel the impact of the bullet, as I'd expected. Instead, the suspect in the hoodie had rushed forward, knocking me back against the wall as his body slammed into me. We both tumbled back to the concrete.

My ears rang from the slam of the brick against my head. My limbs were leaden and my tongue felt thick. Colors and noises swirled in front of me as I tried to focus on staying conscious. I blinked away the raindrops as they pattered into my eyes.

Standard-issue boots lay lifeless in my periphery.

An officer down.

I swallowed thickly, trying to comprehend what the *fuck* had just happened. My head couldn't make sense of it all, and the overwhelming desire to slip under the heavy blanket of darkness was overwhelming.

Flashes of red and blue shone through the alleyway on the street, muddled and swirled by the puddle water that had seeped into my eyes. The body that had slammed us both into the wall, unmoving and still half covering me, sheltered me from the cold. I attempted to shift from under the weight, but he didn't budge. I inched my head up, trying to focus on the face in front of me. Blood covered his clean-shaven face in a mask, and one eye was bruised and angry, completely swollen shut. The only distinguishable part of him was a single, faded scar connecting his upper lip and nostril.

Focus on him. The sirens. The rain. Do not pass out.

I chanted to myself over and over, but the weight on my chest and the pounding in my brain were too much.

Despair crawled inside me and curled around my heart. I should not have gone down the alleyway without backup. In the cold, dark rain, I sent up a silent prayer that this man who had taken a bullet for me and the officer lying still at my side were not dead because of me.

TWO
VAL

"We've got an issue."

I steadied my breath and attempted to look passive as I stared at my superior officer.

Keep your cool. Keep your cool. Keep your cool.

It had been over five months since the shit show at Kilbourn and Maypole that had gotten two men killed—an officer and the man who was stupid enough to throw himself in front of me and take a bullet to the back, doing irreparable damage before exiting his chest. I pored over the report. He'd died as he bled out, pinning me to the ground. That moment ran in an incessant loop in my head. If he hadn't stepped in front of me, my vest would have caught the brunt of the bullet, and while it would have *sucked ass*, I would have survived.

Probably.

"What's the problem, Chief?" My finger scratched at something invisible at the side of my uniform pants in an effort to keep myself from tapping and exposing my nervous energy.

Chief Dunleavy sighed and dropped the thick file

folder on his desk. His head hung while his hands rested on his hips. "You didn't pass your psych."

At that, I shot to my feet. "What?"

He held up one hand. "Relax. I know that wasn't the news you wanted to hear."

My heartbeat thrummed in my neck. I had to keep my emotions in check if I wanted to prove I was ready to be back out in the field. Losing my cool was the exact opposite reaction I needed right now.

"I'm sorry, sir," I said. I smoothed back my tight pony-tail, forced a smile, and sat back down on his old, scratchy chair. "I don't understand."

I did understand.

In fact, it was hard to say that it was all that surprising. Since the incident, I'd been relegated to desk jockey and had to attend weekly sessions with Dr. Brenner to ensure that I was "handling the situation" and mentally stable enough to return to my normal work duties.

The trouble was, I was *fine*. I didn't need to be there. I went to every session, smiled, and attempted to prove just how *fine* I really was. Apparently, the insufferable Dr. Bren-ner, with his greasy smile and nervous tic of staring at my tits, felt differently.

I clenched my jaw and hoped my smile didn't look as forced as it truly was.

Chief Dunleavy flipped through the pages in my file. "Dr. Brenner reported that you still claim there was a young woman at the scene."

Familiar flames of anger burned in my chest. I nodded once. "Yes, sir." I knew that girl was there, scared and in need of my help. I wasn't fucking crazy.

"I have concerns that you recklessly ran after this myste-rious person." He sighed. "The doctor also shared that you are still carrying significant repressed emotions surrounding the shooting and subsequent casualties."

I blinked once, twice. "I can assure you, Chief, I'm fine. While it truly is a tragedy that Officer Bucholz lost his life in the line of duty, I understand that being a police officer is a risk. As did he. I feel as though I have learned a great deal from that incident, and in the long run, it will make me a better officer. More efficient, aware, and proactive."

See? I'm totally fine. Dr. Brenner is an idiot.

Chief looked me over—not in the skeezy way some men looked at me, but rather as if he was trying to decide if I was genuine or completely full of shit. He didn't need to know that I'd practiced that exact speech in front of my bathroom mirror every day for the last five months.

"I believe you, Val. But it's not up to me. That incident got a lot of unwanted attention, and we've got federal bureaucracy to deal with because of it. It's gone up the chain."

"Up the chain? What does that even mean?"

Just as I asked the question, a knock at the door interrupted us. "Ah," Chief said as he looked behind me and waved someone into his office. "There's someone here to discuss it with you."

I turned and immediately recognized the dark suit of a federal agent. His suit was decidedly more expensive than the ill-fitting brown polyester that Chief wore. I rose and stood at attention to show my respect.

"Special Agent Neil Walsh, I'd like to introduce you to Officer Val Rivera."

I reached out to shake his hand with a small nod. "Sir."

The agent was at least two and a half decades older than my own twenty-eight years, best I could guess. His eyes were a warm brown with small crinkles at the edges, and if it weren't for the clean, pressed suit, I would have pegged him as more of a Mister Rogers type rather than a federal agent. There was a softness about him that was friendly and inviting. I'd bet money he used that to his advantage to get people to feel comfortable around him. Even though I recognized that, somehow, it worked.

"Pleasure to meet you, Officer. Please, sit."

I did as I was told and looked between the men.

What the hell was happening? I couldn't possibly be fired, right? There'd be no reason to need a federal agent for that.

Chief cleared his throat. "Here's the thing, Val . . ."

Shit. It wasn't often the chief didn't address me as *Officer* or by my last name, just like everyone else. Small prickles creeped up the backs of my arms, but I willed my hands to remain steady and casual in my lap.

"You're a damn fine officer," Chief continued. "Honestly, she's one of the best." He shifted his attention in the agent's direction, then back to me. "But this psych report isn't helping matters. I can't put you back on patrol if the department shrink doesn't think you can handle it."

"You have an application in with the ATF, isn't that right?" Agent Walsh cut in.

Panic wound itself around my throat and tightened. "Yes, sir." I raised my chin, meeting his gaze. There was a fierceness behind his friendliness after all.

"I reviewed the application. You've passed the ATF special agent exam, assessment test, physical, drug test, polygraph—all of it. Hell"—he flipped through my file as he spoke—"all that's left is the panel interview."

I nodded once. He hadn't asked a question, and I didn't need to give him any reason to think I didn't know I was more than qualified to be a damn fine special agent.

Agent Walsh smiled to himself. "Just so happens that I am on that panel."

A spark of hope bloomed in my chest.

Is this why he's here? Is there some kind of special exception?

My knee bounced twice before I could stop it. I ran my hand over it and said, "I don't know exactly what the psych report says, but I can tell you this. I was meant to be more than a patrol officer. I would be an asset to the ATF. I'm more than capable."

Agent Walsh nodded. "I'm not sure I disagree with you. Your file is extremely impressive. Which is why I'm here. I'd like to offer a solution."

～

"Some fucking solution . . ." I slowed my car as I approached the faded, rusty stop sign. The squeal of my brakes mirrored the ache in my ass from driving for so long.

Four states and twenty hours later, I'd finally arrived on the outskirts of Tipp, Montana. From my vantage point, I could see down the main street, and on the outside, it looked like a typical rural town. Big enough to have its own medical center and a decent variety of restaurants and businesses, but still a far cry from the chaotic charm I'd come to love in Chicago. Considering I'd just spent hours driving through the flats of Montana without seeing so much as a buzzard to peck my eyes out, the cozy town tucked under the base of a looming mountain was an ominous, but welcome, sight.

I eased the car forward, carefully checking street signs, looking for a place to stretch and pee before the last leg of my trip. The familiar *whoop whoop* of a squad car whipped my eyes to the rearview mirror.

I pressed a finger to one eye. "You've got to be fucking kidding me."

I eased my car to the side of the road, lowered the window, and placed my hands on the steering wheel at ten and two.

Relax.

Be confident, not arrogant.

Normally I'd be ready with a smile and the confidence of knowing that I wasn't getting a ticket. But instead of Officer Rivera, temporarily stripped of my badge, I was simply Val Rivera, a woman of color traveling alone in a rural town. An uncomfortable flush of nerves heated my skin.

The stocky officer waddled his way toward my window. "Evening, ma'am."

"Hello." I pressed my lips in a thin line.

"Never seen you around here before."

My head whipped to the side as I eyed him. He rocked back on his heels with a self-satisfied grin. "Just . . . driving through."

"Hmm." We continued our staring match as he sucked his tongue over his teeth. "Might be best you go around town then."

I released a quiet breath and planted on a fresh fake smile. "I'm actually just looking to stretch my legs, and then I'm looking for a place called Laurel Canyon Ranch. Maybe you can help me?"

"You got business up there?"

"Yes, sir." When he waited for me to add more, I simply said, "Personal business."

A sort of disgusted sound escaped his nose. After a beat, he looked at me as though I was no longer a threat and rubbed his palms on his haunches. "You stretch those legs and then take the loop out of town. Keep the mountain to your right and head out that way. Nothing for a few miles, but you'll come up on it."

"Thank you, sir." A deep wave of relief washed over me.

With a nod, he was trudging his way back to his squad car.

So much for a warm welcome.

I tracked the squad car with my eyes and pulled out behind it as he drove down Main Street. If I didn't find somewhere soon, my bladder was going to burst. As the sun sagged behind the jagged edges of the mountain, crisp April air chilled my bones.

I scanned the small shops that dotted the main drag in town—a deli, bakery, cute mom-and-pop-type places that I assumed were part of all small-town life. Only, oddly, most were closed and shuttered despite the early evening hour, as though the lowering sun had pulled a shade down over the entire town.

The harsh neon of a corner bar caught my eye. The Tabula Rasa would have to do. Besides, a quick bite to eat and a stiff drink could help numb the pit in my stomach.

I pulled my car into a parking space and tugged open the marred wooden door. More than a dozen pairs of eyes pinned me in place, and all conversation died at my entrance. The sea of eyes tracked my movements as I walked toward the bathroom. When I finished and headed back toward the bar, I was still being watched. A lone bartender made eye contact, rubbing a glass with a green bar rag.

"Tough crowd." I pulled a wooden stool out and used my palms to tap out a rhythm against the worn oak of the bar. Slowly the din of conversations started behind me, but I continued to feel eyes rake over my back.

"Don't mind them." The bartender was tall and lean. He wore a full white beard, and other than his face, I couldn't see a patch of skin that wasn't covered in tattoos. "Just not used to seeing new faces that often."

"Charming." I smiled at him as though we'd shared some inside joke.

In return, I received a hard stare. "This is our town, darling. Get used to it or hit the fucking road."

I could only blink when he turned his back on me.

"Hey, can I get a menu?" I called. One furtive glance over his shoulder killed all hopes of me getting anything to eat.

I sighed and swiveled in my chair, taking in the patrons that filled the small space. Families eating dinner, a few guys playing darts or pool. A baseball game on the television held the attention of most everyone sitting at the bar. Nothing about the people there seemed cold or dismissive, so their reaction to my presence unnerved me. Everyone looked so *normal*.

Giving up, I stood and tucked the stool under the bar. When I turned, awareness hit me in the chest. Sitting in a darkened corner, the most intense blue eyes pinned me in place. The man sitting alone at the small table was large, almost comically large for the small wooden chair beneath him. His hair hung at the nape of his neck and was thick and dark. The nearly scruffy beard gave serious lumberjack vibes, but the way his eyes held me captive said only one thing: dangerous.

Under the intensity of his stare, I glanced away. I swallowed but looked back and smiled. The dark stranger was still staring, despite the waitress delivering two to-go containers, one large and one small, to his table. I tucked a loose strand of hair behind my ear and turned back toward the bar.

I really need that drink.

I tried again, unsuccessfully, to get the bartender's attention. In fact, he was actively ignoring any attempts I made to signal to him. Tired, drained, and defeated, I slung my purse over my shoulder and headed toward the exit. I gulped the fresh spring air and tried to settle my nerves on the darkening walk toward my car. If this place was going to be my home for the next few months while Agent Walsh worked on my fitness for duty eval, I was going to have to understand it. Get used to its quirks and customs and rules.

Clearly, outsiders were not welcomed with open arms in Tipp. My stomach rumbled, rioting against the twelve hours since I'd last eaten, and I pulled my jacket tighter around my middle. Not two strides from my car, I sensed footsteps on the gravel behind me just before a deep voice called over my shoulder.

"Hey."

My eyebrows popped up when I turned to see the tall stranger from the bar walking toward me. His long legs ate up the distance between us, and *damn* those legs were impressive. Even beneath the denim, his thick muscles were evident. I stopped, staring at the imposing man who'd grabbed my attention.

"Sorry. I didn't mean to frighten you."

I squared my stance slightly. "You didn't." *What an odd thing for him to think.*

"Oh," he said, clearing his throat as I watched his Adam's apple bob. "Good. Well, here." The man shoved a large, white Styrofoam container in my direction.

I raised an eyebrow and eyed the container he was holding up for me. When I didn't reach for it, he added, "Al, the bartender? He's a prick sometimes. Looked like you could use dinner."

I slowly raised my hand to grab the container from him. The warmth from the food inside caused my stomach to groan again, loudly enough for him to hear it. A small laugh escaped him. "Thought so."

"I, uh." I shook my head. "I don't really know what to say. Thank you." I lifted the container slightly in salute.

He waved a hand in dismissal. "It's nothing. This town's just a little weird about strangers. Doesn't mean we shouldn't be polite."

At that, I relaxed and smiled. Something about the way his cool blue eyes softened as they scanned my face caused a pinch in my chest. This man was tall, huge even, with muscles that tested the limits of his long-sleeve cotton shirt. Despite my preference for leaner, smaller men, the most animalistic part of me could appreciate just how well-built this stranger was.

We stood at a standstill, both staring and neither speaking. Finally, I added, "But I really can't accept your dinner. That wouldn't be right."

He stuffed his hands in the front pockets of his jeans, and I couldn't help but appreciate his wide palms as they slid against his trim hips. When he spoke again, my eyes whipped back to his. "Well, don't feel too bad." A boyish grin spread across his face, transforming him from brooding stranger to charming boy next door. That smile was devastating.

Dangerous.

"Tonight was Irma's night to make pie. Apple. I kept that." After a shrug, his cobalt eyes met mine, and a hint of mischief played at their edges. Together we shared a small laugh.

"Well, if there's no pie, I don't want any of it," I teased back, feeling an unexpected blush heat my cheeks. We both laughed again, and I couldn't remember the last time I'd flirted with a man. It felt foreign and unexpected, but also a little exciting. "Actually, I really appreciate this. You made my night."

The man nodded, then turned. "And you," he said over his shoulder as he walked away, "were an unexpected surprise. Welcome to Tipp."

THREE

EVAN

SETTING another chunk of wood on the wide stump, I steadied my stance. My calloused hands gripped the wood handle in front of me. Week after week of consistent work had hardened my palms but smoothed the handle so it fit perfectly in my hands. With an overhead swing, the splitting maul cut through the oak, sending both halves flying to my feet. I grabbed the next piece and did it again.

And again.

And again.

I grunted and split the large pieces of the oak tree I had felled earlier that morning. My arms and back ached in the best way, but the hard labor and repetitive task were the only things that kept my mind truly quiet. I paused just long enough to pull the rich, earthy smell of wood and mountain air to the bottom of my lungs.

It's amazing the things you miss in the city.

"You are *really* leaning into this whole lumberjack thing."

So much for peace and quiet.

I turned to see my little sister, Gemma, stomp up the

hillside toward me. My eyes flicked to her shirtsleeves, and my insides tightened as they always did. I'd seen the scars across her chest and on her forearm only a handful of times. Gemma almost always kept them hidden, but they still haunted me.

I couldn't meet her eyes. "'Sup, Gem."

"Really, Evan? Suspenders?" She ran a hand through her cropped blonde hair as she pinned me with a stare.

I straightened and snapped one suspender under my finger. "What? They keep my ass crack in my pants. Besides, they're cool."

"You are so *old*."

Gemma was only nineteen, a full decade and some change behind me, but some days it felt like thirty years separated us.

I ignored her jab and continued to split the wood logs at my feet.

"This place is so boring," she pouted.

"Did you do your chores?"

I could practically feel annoyance radiate from her as her eyes rolled around in her head. "Of course. I don't want Ma on my ass again."

At that, I smiled. Ma Brown and her husband, Robbie, owned and operated the ranch, and she ran a tight ship. If you were slacking, she called you out on it. If you didn't meet the requirements to be here, you were out. No exceptions.

Instead of helping stack wood, Gemma kicked a few pieces with her toe and sat on a stump to my left. She hummed, filling up the silence with full, warm sounds—something my mother used to do too. I could tell Gemma inherited her voice, a rich and raspy tone that Mom would use only when she was truly happy. I wished I could remember the last time I heard her sing. Pushing the painful memories to the darkest corners of my mind, I swung harder and faster.

Only when I stopped to catch my breath did Gemma speak again. "Did you hear there's a new girl?"

I didn't reply but simply lifted a shoulder. I hadn't heard. I didn't care, and truth be told, I didn't have the luxury of thinking about random women. That was, unless you counted the mysterious woman from the bar last night. For reasons I couldn't quite put my finger on, I was intrigued by her. When she'd stepped into the bar, the frosty welcome she'd received from the town residents hadn't seemed to rattle her. She was all lush curves and delicate features, but she had an edge too.

Strong.

Despite my better judgment, I'd run after her like a lunatic and shoved my dinner in her face. Something about her had made me want to take care of her, though the vibe she'd put out was that she was more than capable without me. I'd gone to bed with her face in my mind and my dick in my hand.

Pushing away the thought, especially with my little sister staring at me, I forced my attention back to splitting wood.

"Ev," Gemma continued, disdain dripping from her words. "Someone *new*. We haven't had someone new here since Christmas. It's literally the most exciting thing to happen since we've gotten here."

"Yeah, well, don't get too close. Not until we know she checks out."

Gemma picked at her sleeve, but nodded. She knew as well as I did that the people who came to Redemption Ranch needed to earn your trust. Sure, there were strict criteria for being invited and working here, but it didn't change the fact that someone came to Redemption for one of two reasons: either you were a criminal, or you were being hunted by one.

WHISTLING INTO THE LODGE, I stomped out my boots before slipping them off on the metal tray in the mudroom. One thing I'd learned *fast* here at the ranch was, no matter where you were, this was Ma's house. That old bird was a tough lady, and she didn't just earn your respect—she demanded it.

I took my time walking through the back door and into the spacious, open kitchen. I swiped an apple from the bowl on the center of the island. I smiled to myself at the wonky, misshapen bowl. I'd tried my hand at wood turning, and though I'd failed pretty spectacularly, Ma had insisted she would use the bowl.

That was the thing with her—even something everyone else saw as trash had value.

I whistled my way to her office and knocked twice on the door.

"Open."

I peered in to see Ma's face scrunched up at her computer, her reading glasses perched at the tip of her nose. She didn't spare a glance in my direction.

"Mornin', Ace."

A warm smile spread across my face at her nickname for me, but I swiped it away with my hand. "Ma."

She pinned me with a stare. "Need something?"

"No, ma'am." I leaned a hip against the chair and took a

bite of my apple. "Just thought I'd stop by and see if there was anything else you needed."

One skeptical eyebrow tipped up, and she returned her attention to the computer.

"I know you're an ass-kiss, but damn you if it isn't charming." She fought the smile that tugged at her lips.

This time I let my smile spread freely. I dug into my pocket and grabbed a small round ball I had happened upon earlier today. "Found this for you." I leaned forward and placed the buckeye seed on the corner of her desk.

"What's this?" Ma picked up the mahogany ball and rolled it around her leathery hands.

"It's a buckeye seed. There aren't a ton of buckeye trees around here, but they're all over back home."

Home. Chicago wasn't home anymore.

I cleared my throat. "I mean, so I've heard. They're supposed to be good luck."

A soft smile played at her lips. "You should keep it."

She tossed the buckeye back to me. I caught it midair but quickly returned it to her desk. "I used up all my luck when you let Gemma and me stay here. Anything leftover goes back to you."

Before she could protest, I pushed off the wall and headed back out the door.

The truth was, it was just short of a *miracle* that Gemma and I had landed at Redemption Ranch. Aptly nicknamed too. Any Google search would only ping on Laurel Canyon Ranch, but locals and those who lived here referred to it only as Redemption Ranch. Those who ended up here were hiding in plain sight in a small Montana town. Managers supervised the daily grind of the ranch while agents worked and protected the guests when necessary.

Hand selected, the guests invited to stay and work on the ranch lived under a very specific set of rules.

New identities.

No connections to your former life. Ever.

Long, grueling work on a cattle ranch.

Provide testimony in federal court.

To save my sister, I'd sold my soul and become a rat. I'd forced Gemma and myself into the Federal Witness Protection Program, but it was the only way to keep her safe from the people who would stop at nothing to end us both.

Including my brother, Parker.

FOUR

VAL

I STARED at the small room tucked in the back corner of the wooden lodge, and a single thought raced through my brain —*This is what prison feels like.*

My stomach curled at the thought of living and working at Laurel Canyon. What the fuck was I supposed to do on a cattle ranch? Groaning, I dragged my suitcase through the threshold and flipped my backpack onto the twin bed. Plopping myself down, the springs squeaked beneath me and poked my ass. Awesome.

Tears pricked at my eyes.

How? How have things gotten so far off track?

Agent Walsh had struck a deal with me: live and work at Laurel Canyon Ranch until my new supervisors, Agents Brown and Brown, completed my fitness for duty investigation. That was it. Simple enough, and it sure as hell beat desk duty. Or so I had thought. I tapped my phone to check the time. Fifteen minutes until my first meeting with the agents, where they would provide more specifics on the ranch and my new assignment.

I scanned the screen. Nine missed calls from my

mother. I chuckled to myself. Such a low number meant she was showing a good amount of restraint.

Thinking of her, I smiled. "Gloria must be busy today."

I made a mental note to call her back before she took it upon herself to track me down. Before I left, I spared her many of the details—it was best for everyone if she thought my time outside of Chicago was training for work and nothing more.

I tried to open Instagram, and when it refused to load, I tried again. And again.

Apparently, the rural location also meant shitty cell service. I stared at the ceiling and felt overwhelmed by the enveloping silence. Aside from the low moos of a distant cow or a farm vehicle crunching the gravel outside the lodge, there was . . . nothing. It unnerved me. I hated the fact that the only sounds I could hear were my own thoughts tumbling through my head.

Sick of sitting with myself, I pulled up from the bed and headed down toward Agent Dorothea Brown's office. The lodge itself was *very* Western, with animal heads on the walls, metal accents, and more wool blankets than anyone had business owning. It had a rustic sort of charm. It was all so very *Montana*.

When I came to the office door, as I lifted my fist to knock, the door swung open. My jaw followed as the enormous, brooding stranger from the bar last night sauntered out of the office. In the daylight, he was even more devastating than I remembered, and a warm flush of desire burned through me. His forearms were sweaty, with flecks of dirt coating them. The muscles bunched and flexed as he shifted sideways to prevent walking into me. Those arresting, mysterious eyes bore into me as recognition and confusion flitted over his features.

"Val Rivera. Come in," the woman in the office ordered.

I tore my gaze from the not-such-a-stranger stranger and stepped into the office. I'd have to find out what the hell was going on and who this delicious man was.

"Please, shut the door and sit." With a flick of her wrist, she dismissed the man, and his features turned dark as he closed the door behind me.

"Uh." I cleared my throat to focus on the task at hand and bury the obvious flash of lust that must have been painted across my features. "Thank you."

As I sat, Agent Brown arranged a stack of papers into a folder and swiveled her chair to face me. "Welcome." Her smile was warm, but the lines on her tanned face showed evidence of strength and hardness beneath it.

"Thank you, ma'am. It's a pleasure to be here at Laurel Canyon." *Lie.*

"'Round here we call it Redemption. Short for Redemption Ranch. Do you know why that is, dear?"

I pressed my lips in a line and shook my head. *Because everything about this place is fucking weird?*

"Agent Walsh told me about you. That you're a hard-working beat cop. He's got his eye on you for the ATF. Is that what you want?"

I had my canned answer at the tip of my tongue. That, yes, I dreamed of being an elite agent for the Bureau of Alcohol, Tobacco, Firearms and Explosives. *Another lie.* Something about the way the woman looked at me—like she could see the bullshit about to pour out of me, stopped me from speaking.

I took a steadying breath and smoothed my palms over my thighs. I lifted my chin and spoke the truth. "I know that I am destined to be more than a police officer. I believe I would be a stellar ATF agent, and Agent Walsh assured me that the ranch is a means to that end."

Her eyebrow crept up her forehead once again as she took me in and considered my answers. Panic licked at the base of my skull. I should have just lied to her. Told her that I had always dreamed of becoming an ATF agent so that she could sign off on the paperwork.

"You surprise me," she said. "Most people in your position would have fed me some bullshit answer and kissed my ass." She smiled, and it warmed her whole face. "I think Agent Walsh may have been on to something with you. Walk with me."

Agent Brown rose and walked out the office door without waiting for me. I jumped up and quickly got into step with her as we walked through the main lodge.

"Here at the main lodge, there's four rooms, like the one that you're in. A kitchen"—her arms spread across toward the space—"living space, and rec rooms. The main lodge is for all of us to share and build our community. The rest of the property we have is roughly two thousand acres."

She stopped and turned toward me. "This is a real, backbreaking, dust-on-your-nuts cattle ranch. We have chores and deadlines and protocols."

My eyes flicked above her head and landed on a discreet security camera—one of many I had documented on my way to and from her office.

She noticed my glance and said, "I see you've also noticed that we aren't *just* a cattle ranch. Very good." Agent Brown continued walking.

"What does that mean?" I asked.

"Here at Redemption, we have agents, like my husband and me and a few others, to round out our security team.

There are also people working here who are federally protected."

"Like WITSEC?"

"Similar idea. *Very* different approaches. The current model for a witness under federal protection is to hole them up in a remote hotel, hoping they stay protected, until they're ready to testify, which could take years. Nothing is ever fast at the federal level. Then they're given a new life and dropped off. Many struggle to find housing or work. Here, we provide both."

"I see." I didn't have a fucking clue what she was talking about, but my brain was whizzing in a thousand different directions. I worried the bottom of my lip with my teeth. "But I'm not an agent *or* a criminal."

"You, my dear, are somewhat of a mystery. An in-between. Agent Walsh called in a favor to find you a place here. It's the safest place in the country and it's temporary. While you're here, I will be assessing your fitness for duty."

"But why grant him the favor if I don't fit in?"

If she was stunned by my boldness in asking, she didn't let it show. "I owe Agent Walsh the life of my husband."

Agent Brown pushed open the back door to the lodge and the midmorning sunlight blinded me. "Treat this as your home, for now." Her eyes were kind as she tipped her head. "But it's also the home of many others. Some of the cabins on the property are occupied and considered private residences. The barns, stables, and the other outbuildings are fair game for exploring."

"That's it? Just . . . explore?"

She only smirked. "Welcome to Montana, Ms. Rivera. You'll get a list of chores in the morning." Her tone turned dark and foreboding. "If you leak the identity of any agents or witnesses living and working at the ranch or generally cannot be trusted, you're gone and will face federal charges of obstruction of justice. No exceptions. No second chances."

The harshness in her tone iced my veins. She wasn't fucking around. My voice felt tight. "Yes, ma'am."

With a hearty laugh, she smacked me hard on the back and smiled. "Ah. You can call me Ma Brown. Evan started that some months ago, and it's stuck." She shrugged, any evidence of her previously stern demeanor gone. "I kind of like it. Now go off and explore. Your duties officially start tomorrow."

Without another goodbye, the lodge door was closed behind me. The gravel crunched under my canvas sneakers as I walked the driveway to get my bearings. Laurel Cany— no. Redemption Ranch. It was a bustling, dynamic cattle ranch. Even knowing there was more to it, it was difficult to see anything other than the farm operations. Trucks and farm vehicles were hard at work, and as each passed me, the driver would offer a wave or a tip of the hat. The general friendliness was significantly improved from the towns-people of last night. The sounds of cattle caught my attention as I walked up to a wired fence. Hundreds of cattle spread across the valley and dotted the grassland.

I turned in a slow circle to scan the expansive property that surrounded me. Several buildings dotted the pastures ahead: a large red barn with peeling paint, a stable, small stone buildings with cedar shake roofs that I assumed were the cabins. When I turned my back to the pasture, the lodge was enormous, but the wood and earth tones blended perfectly with the landscape around it. To the left, a path of gravel wound through a copse of trees and around a small lake. The dock jutted out into the water and reminded me of skipping rocks with my grandfather. Beside the lodge was a large, neat garden. The smell of nature and hay and animals hung in the air.

A bubble of laughter rose in my chest. A city girl from Chicago. A cop. Expected to work and live on a cattle ranch in Montana. A ranch full of criminals. The sheer absurdity of it had laughter ripping from my midsection and tears streaming down my face. I swiped the tears and tilted my face to the warming sun. I wasn't afraid of a challenge. Hard work didn't scare me.

No.

The only thing that caused a ripple of fear to dance through me was the unexpected encounter with *him*. I had a thousand questions. Was he an agent? A witness? A worker here?

I closed my eyes as the sun warmed my face and dried my tear-stained cheeks. Sunny warmth spread through me. I could do this. A few months, tops, and I would be back in my beloved Chicago. Hopefully, I'd even be starting my new life in the ATF.

Just a few months and nothing more.

FIVE

EVAN

ADMITTEDLY, seeing the woman from the Rasa standing outside Ma's door was a shock to my system. For more than a few seconds, I'd thought I'd actually lost my mind. Ma's gravelly voice had ripped me back to reality, and instead of saying hello, I'd panicked.

Just as well. Her reason for being at Redemption couldn't be a good one. Everyone here knew that. I just couldn't shake the feeling of unease. All afternoon something had dogged me, and I couldn't quite place it. After my responsibilities were done, I'd checked on Gemma's chores and had had to finish those too. I rubbed my aching shoulder. I really needed to talk to her about getting her shit done on her own. While deep down I knew I was only enabling her by doing the unfinished chores myself, I also couldn't afford for us to get kicked off the ranch. Not when it was her life on the line.

Being at Redemption was the only way to keep her safe.

Gemma's chores had taken almost as long as my own because I was so distracted by thoughts of our new guest. I'd spent the better part of the evening walking around like a stalker, just hoping for a glimpse of her shiny black hair or the slope of her toned shoulders. After tossing and turning for most of the night, I gave up hope that I was going to get any sleep at all.

Four a.m. came quick, and I dressed in my standard tan field pants, white T-shirt, suspenders, and boots. I didn't mind the early-morning hours. The quiet had become something I craved. I brewed a cup of strong black coffee, filled my travel mug, and headed out to the main barn. It was easier to hammer out the chores and care for the animals before the rest of the crew showed up for work.

A dim light illuminated the inside of the barn, and my heartbeat ticked upward. No one was ever awake at this hour, and a wave of unease roiled in my stomach. Less than a year ago I would have been reaching for a gun, and my hand twitched.

You are no longer that man.

I closed my eyes and breathed through the panic that heated my veins. I softened my steps as I approached the barn and hugged the outside wall. It could be anyone—a ranch hand who got an early start or someone who'd left the light on by mistake. As I listened around the buzzing in my ears, faint grunts and sighs floated on the night air.

Maybe one of the heifers is laboring.

A smile cracked my face wide open when I peered into the barn to see it wasn't a heifer but our newest ranch guest grunting and muscling her way around the bales of hay. Hair in a tangled mess and slipping out of her loose ponytail, she grabbed the twine wrapped around the bale and hefted it up.

"Argh!" When the bale didn't move, she kicked it. "Fuck!" She glanced at her hands and wiped them on her jeans. Bits and pieces of hay floated around her and stuck into the tops of her sneakers. She really needed to buy some work boots. The woman bent down, and I had a full, uninterrupted view of her perfect ass. A scrap of black lace peeked out over the waist of her jeans, and I had to tear my eyes away. That skimpy thong was definitely not functional ranch underwear.

Another grunt and swing of her arms and the bales barely moved from one pile to the next.

"Need a hand?"

Her head whipped up, and her gorgeous caramel eyes pinned me in place.

"It's you."

"And you." A smile twitched at my mouth. "Let me help with that."

She said a tight "No, thank you," but her eyes most definitely said *Fuck you*. A surprising and unfamiliar bubble of humor tingled in my chest. As I walked closer, I slipped a pair of leather gloves out of my back pocket and held them up for her. "Here."

Through the strands of hair stuck to her forehead, she glanced between the gloves and my face. Clearly, she did not want to have any help. "Go on," I continued. "You're gonna tear your hands up like that, and then you'll be useless around here. I don't want to have to do your chores and mine."

She scoffed and swiped the gloves from my hands. They were comically large on her, but at least it would keep the delicate skin on her hands from tearing open. I'd also learned that the hard way my first week on the ranch.

"Well, I see your charms are limited to strange women and dark parking lots." She turned her back to me and continued to ineffectively move hay. I watched, allowing her to work in silence. I grabbed a rake to muck out the stalls to keep myself from moving her aside and taking care of the bales myself. When she'd gone silent, I risked a peek at her and saw her studying a small piece of paper. She looked around and then raised her arms, letting them fall down and slap the outside of her thighs.

I stifled a groan at the way her muscles jigged slightly and caused the flash of an image of how those thighs might quake if I were between them. I set my rake down and stalked toward her.

"What is it? Show me." My voice rattled out harsher than I'd intended. I nodded toward the paper.

She looked at me and seemed to be debating whether I was worth the time and energy. "My chore list. I don't have a clue what half of this shit even is."

I laughed. "Yeah, I hear that. I felt the same way. Why don't you let me take a look at it."

Her eyes flicked up and down my body before she handed me the small slip of paper. "I'm Val. New here."

Val.

Her name bounced around my head and settled in deep. I studied her short chore list, and she took the opportunity to smooth her hair back, resecuring it tightly. With her dark strands pulled tight and away from her face, familiarity bloomed.

And then it hit me. *Chicago.*

I cleared my throat and delivered my well-practiced introduction. "My name is Evan Walker."

Her eyes narrowed.

Damn. I fucked that up.

I still hadn't gotten used to my new name, and although I'd always been Evan Marino, Walker was who I needed to be. Despite the clunky, overly formal introduction, she didn't question me.

"I take it you're not from here." Her eyes still raked up and down my body. An unexpected urge to spill everything —tell her that we'd met before, kind of—clawed at my throat.

A strangled "No, ma'am" was all I could muster. While I couldn't bring myself to lie to her, I needed to get out of that barn. To talk to Ma about why the hell a police officer, let alone the one I'd taken a bullet for, was standing in front of me at the ranch. It was too close. Too risky for Gemma for us all to be in the same location.

I needed answers. Now.

I turned on my heels and stomped toward the exit.

"Hey!" she called after me. "Where are you going? I thought you said you'd help!"

"I'm going to find Ma." I didn't bother to turn as I moved across the barn. "I need to find out why the fuck you're in Montana."

DESPITE THE EARLY HOUR, Ma was already in the kitchen arranging grab-and-go breakfast for anyone who might wander in looking for food. Humming to herself, she all but ignored my heavy footsteps and glare as I planted my hands on my hips. "What the hell, Ma?"

"Oh, Ace. Good morning."

"Why is she here?" I demanded.

"Oh, I see you've finally realized who our new guest is. Less than a day. I'm impressed. That means Agent Walsh owes me twenty dollars. He bet it would take at least a week, but I knew you're too sharp."

"Is this a joke to you?" Anger rose and flared in my chest.

Ma's eyes whipped to mine, and before she could speak, Val burst into the kitchen. "What is going on around here?"

Ma tipped her head. "My office."

My jaw ticced but I followed her order. Val stomped behind me. After closing the door to her office, Ma leaned against her desk to face Val and me.

"I'm sure you're both surprised."

"I don't even know what's going on." Val gestured toward me. "What's your problem?"

"Val," Ma began, "Evan has just discovered that you share a very important connection."

Val looked between the two of us.

Ma added, "Evan is also from Chicago. He is the man who stepped in front of a bullet for you."

Val shook her head in disbelief and raised her palms. "No. That's not possible. Both men died that night." She steadied herself and seemed to be processing the information Ma had slung at me. "Wait, is Officer Bucholz alive?"

Ma's voice dipped lower. "Unfortunately, no. You did lose a fellow officer that day. However, as you can see, Evan is very much alive."

Val rubbed her temples as the weight of the information settled in. "The girl. There was a girl there. Tell me she was real."

"Gemma." My voice was rocky over my sister's name.

A deep sigh whooshed out of her. "I knew it. I knew I wasn't crazy."

"Ma, why is she here? Is she testifying? She's a *cop* who was there that night. She puts us all in danger." Anger dripped from my words, and Val winced beside me.

"You know as well as I do that everyone is well protected here, if the need should arise. The reasons for Ms. Rivera working on the ranch are a federal matter. I may like you, Evan, but don't forget I am a federal agent, and you are working for me."

Respect bolted my mouth shut, but untethered rage whipped through me. Rather than lash out, I stormed from the cramped office. Burying myself in work, I refused to think about the reasons I'd stepped in front of Val that night or how her showing up in my life knotted my insides.

SIX
VAL

THE HOT STRANGER had saved my life.

I still couldn't believe it. I knew his name was bullshit as soon as he'd spoken it. Stuffy, too formal, and obviously a canned answer. If he had a chance of pulling off a new identity, *Evan Walker* was going to have to work on that.

Despite my suspicions, I *never* would have guessed that the man at Redemption Ranch was the same man who had taken a bullet to the back—who had stepped in front of a gun—*for me*. It didn't make any sense. Why would he do that? I had a thousand more questions for every limited answer Agent Brown gave. I sat for more than an hour going through the same information over and over again.

She didn't have all the information, but what she could tell me was that Evan and his family were part of a well-connected branch of a crime syndicate in Chicago.

"It still doesn't all make sense." A dull throb formed behind my eyeballs. "Why was he there? Why did he step in front of that gun? He didn't even *know* me."

"Evan is exacting. I'm certain he had his reasons. None of which he has ever shared with me."

The way he'd croaked out the name *Gemma* told me there was definitely more to that story.

Gemma.

I was so relieved that she was real. I had scoured the filed police reports, and not a single one mentioned a young woman being there. A dozen police officers had been questioned, and not one mentioned seeing her with me. More than once I'd worried that maybe I was losing my mind or had invented her completely, but I knew in my heart she was there and was the central reason that it had all gone south that night.

"Evan is providing testimony that has the potential to dismantle a very powerful entity in the city of Chicago. Nothing that's discussed here can leave this ranch."

I nodded. "Why did Agent Walsh suggest I come here?"

Ma's features softened. "Redemption Ranch is the only place of its kind. He knows that it lives within my very soul. He wouldn't have sent you here without a reason."

"So blind faith? I'm supposed to move forward with the blind faith that I'll pass whatever kind of test this is in order to get my life back? That's ridiculous."

"Many people who've walked through these gates have found themselves. I have a feeling you'll be one of them. But remember this—when someone is accepted to be here, their past is left behind them. Can you do that?"

AGENT BROWN's question looped on repeat in my head. Could I leave Evan's past in the past? Could I leave my own?

I knew the answer was no when I'd spent forty minutes wandering around the ranch, looking for him. Finally, a cattle roper had taken pity on me. He spoke broken English, but after a series of hand gestures—big shoulders, grumpy face—he'd pointed up a path toward the edge of the pine forest.

"Up that path? In the woods?"

His single nod sent me on my way.

Out of breath and feeling the breeze cool my damp skin, I trudged up the dirt path. At the top of a small hill, hidden from the main path, an all-terrain side-by-side vehicle was parked. With his back to me, Evan placed a large chunk of wood on top of the widest stump I'd ever seen. With quick, efficient strokes, he lifted an axe above his head. In a single swing, the wood split in half and went flying. Without stopping, he grabbed another piece with one hand and centered it on the stump.

Thwack. The echo of his axe matched the pounding in my chest.

With his back to me, I could truly appreciate how spectacularly built he was. His back was broad, and sculpted muscles were evident, even through the white cotton of his shirt. Suspenders—*Who knew those were so freaking hot?*—trailed down his back in a V to narrow hips and the best ass I'd ever seen on a man. It wasn't flat, but rather muscled and round, and his work pants hugged his delicious curves. A brief thought of grabbing his ass and pulling his hips into me sent a sizzle of desire straight between my legs. I shifted quietly as I stared at him.

"I know you're there."

I was ripped from my inappropriate thoughts by the sound of his deep, penetrating voice.

I cleared my throat and took another step toward the path. "Sorry. I don't mean to bug you."

Evan cast a glance in my direction but kept splitting

wood. I stood like an idiot, staring at his muscles and then looking around while I searched for my voice on the forest floor. He didn't look anything like the man who'd slumped across me in that darkened courtyard. Granted, his hair was longer, the thick strands teasing the bottoms of his earlobes, and he sported short scruff now. Plus, at the time, his face had been swollen and bloodied. My mind raced to piece together the events of that night and fit them with the man standing before me.

At a total loss and giving up for the moment, I needed to move. I thought better when I moved. I stepped forward and began stacking the pieces of wood Evan had split. A small pile had been started, so I mirrored the stack. Evan paused, looking at what I was doing, but besides one small *hmmph*, he didn't speak another word. After a torturous few minutes of not ogling him while I stacked wood, he finally took a break. Leaning the ax against the stump, he bent to grab his water bottle.

My eyes tracked his movements, and I watched as he brought the bottle to his full lips. The column of his throat was sinful, and my mouth went bone-dry as he chugged the water. It immediately felt twenty degrees hotter. The spring air did little to cool my tacky skin and quiet the hum that formed between my legs. Crisp pine air floated between us and carried his deeply warm and manly scent—laundry and wood and *good-smelling man* assaulted my senses.

Evan didn't seem to care that I was eye-fucking him. Rather, he seemed amused. "Did you need something?" Humor danced in his eyes.

I pulled my ponytail loose, letting my dark hair tumble down before I raked my hands through it. "I don't understand any of this." I paced between the stack of wood and the ATV. "How are you here? *Why* are you here? What does it mean? Who *are* you?" The questions stacked on top of each other.

Evan stepped in my path. His large, rough hands wrapped around my biceps, and I swallowed my words. I could feel my face flush at his closeness. His piercing blue eyes peered down at me under his dark brows, and the sounds of the forest faded away.

"There's a lot I don't know." His voice was low and rough. His eyes flicked to my lips, and I swiped my tongue along the bottom.

I felt breathless, but I had to know the one question that I couldn't let go unanswered. "Why? Why did you step in front of the gun?"

His hands squeezed my arms gently. I could feel my body sway toward him as though an invisible tether pulled me closer. "You saved my sister's life when I couldn't."

As soon as he spoke, Evan sidestepped and went back to chopping wood and ignoring me.

Did he feel the spark between us when he touched me? Have I lost my damn mind? This man is a stranger. A criminal. He is everything that you stand against.

Disgusted with myself and how easily I was charmed by him, I fled.

SEVEN

EVAN

I NEVER SHOULD HAVE TOUCHED her. Val's unyielding stream of questions tumbled out of her, and deep in my soul I knew I couldn't lie to her. Fuck if I knew why. Hiding the truth to get what I needed had never been an issue before, but there was something about Val Rivera that prevented me from lying to her. When she'd asked *why* I stepped in front of the gun and took a bullet for her, the truth was simple.

If it weren't for Val, Gemma would be dead.

A week had passed since the afternoon in the forest when I'd touched Val and nearly pulled her into me. She was a dichotomy of muscle and softness, vulnerability and strength. I'd never met anyone quite like her, and it bugged the shit out of me.

It had always been easy for me to be singularly focused. Whether it was on a job in Chicago or here at the ranch, I was steadfast and reliable. I did what needed to be done. Now I thought of Val constantly, and it was messing with my head. Had she figured out the chore list? Did she know to stay away from Ray when he was having a bad day? Had she finally gotten some decent work boots?

After seven days of only glimpses of her at breakfast or dinner as she'd grabbed a plate and scurried to her room, I was losing my mind. Though she was invited, she'd declined to go to our weekly group dinner on Sunday. Her presence gnawed at me. There was just something about her that I needed to figure out. On the following Saturday, I was in town for dinner—a burger and a beer—when I finally saw her strolling into the town's only workout facility.

A split-second change of plans and I was running back to my truck to grab the gym bag stashed there. The small town had a surprisingly top-notch workout facility, with everything from weights, mats, and a variety of classes. Looked like I was joining a yoga class. Only a few minutes late, I grabbed a towel from the stack by the door and unceremoniously unrolled it next to her. She spared me a disinterested glance, but I still noticed the way her heartbeat hammered at the base of her neck. She might look at me like I was something she'd stepped in, but her body reacted to me, and that was like a fucking drug.

"What are you doing?" she whisper-yelled.

I made a show of bending and stretching and swinging my arms. There were about a dozen people in the workout class tonight, and my big ass was definitely out of place, but I didn't care. "I'm working out." I shot her a side glance and did my best to hide the smirk that pulled at my lips. "Obviously."

I was rewarded with an eye roll, and I inched closer, just to piss her off and get a whiff of her shampoo. It was bright and citrusy, and I did my best to commit it to memory. I took in her tight leggings and the strip of bare skin between her waist and the hem of her cropped tee. The words *Namaste on the Couch* stretched across her chest, and I smirked at its silliness but glanced away.

The instructor took us through a series of simple bends and stretches. Brute strength had always been my go-to, and I was much more comfortable lifting weights than contorting myself into those positions.

Val's limber body ebbed and flowed with each movement throughout the warm-up. I struggled to reach my toes, and more than one uncivilized grunt escaped me. Once our muscles were warm and loose, the class fell into a quiet rhythm.

A time or two I caught Val's eyes tracing along the tattoos that roped up my forearms and disappeared into my shirtsleeves. I bit my cheek to hide the pleasure that her interest and approval tugged out of me. From the corner of my eye, I could see Val's strong, muscular frame bend and stretch. Her endless legs met the most perfect ass I'd ever seen. She was all power wrapped up in a gorgeous package. Focusing on our instructor while keeping my dick in check was one of the most difficult things I'd ever done. Val did her best to ignore my presence. As the class wound down, I watched her fiddle with the seam of the towel, anxious to get away.

Just as I was about to get her attention and ask her to grab a beer with me in town, the instructor broke in.

"Our last sequence tonight will be some deep partner stretching. Please pair up." Though her voice was calm and soothing, my heartbeat ratcheted higher. Val intentionally didn't look my way, and when a young guy with floppy blond hair glanced at her with his eyebrows up and face full of hope, I threw a murderous glare in his direction. He caught my stare over Val's shoulder and quickly turned to find someone else.

"Looks like it's you and me."

Val turned with a tight smile.

The instructor's low voice flowed throughout the gym space. "Okay, I need one person lying on his or her back. Palms down. Deep breaths."

I motioned for Val to lie on the ground. Her eyes never left mine as I stood, looming over her while she took her position.

"The other partner, please kneel to the side. Partners in Savasana, I want you to lie still and breathe. Eyes closed."

Val did not do as instructed. Her eyes stayed pinned to mine. "You know this is called the corpse pose."

A low rumble akin to a laugh moved through my chest. "I did not."

As the instructor moved around the small space, she paused by us. "Eyes closed. Breathe."

Val looked at me again, warily. I nodded. "You heard the lady. Dead body." After a beat, I added, "It's all right. You're safe with me."

I didn't miss the sharp intake of breath at my words, but Val simply closed her eyes and lifted her chin.

"Do you feel zen yet?"

She peeked at me through one slitted eye, a suppressed laugh teasing the corners of her mouth as it twitched. "So fucking zen."

She closed her eyes, and after a few moments, her breathing evened out and her shoulders relaxed.

"Now," the instructor continued, "partners kneeling in Vajrasana, I want you to slowly move toward your partner's feet. We will begin a gentle stretch of the legs and pelvis."

At the word *pelvis*, one of Val's eyes whipped open. I

shrugged and kneeled at her feet. My large frame loomed over her, and even with her curves, I realized how slight she was in comparison. One lean forward and the entirety of my body could cover hers.

I ached to know what it would feel like to sprawl across her and feel her strong, pliant body beneath mine.

"From Savasana, lift one leg and rest your ankle on your partner's shoulder. Keep the leg straight and feel the stretch run along the hamstring."

Val carefully lifted her leg and placed it on my shoulder. My fingers grazed her slim ankle, and I could feel her pulse hammering beneath the thin skin there. Our eyes locked.

"Now, kneeling partners, gently tilt forward to deepen the stretch. Be mindful of your partner's cues. They will tell you when to stop."

I continued to stare at Val's perfect face. She nodded, and I slowly leaned forward. There was little resistance with her leg. Apparently, she was much more flexible than I'd realized, and I couldn't help but think of all kinds of interesting things we could do in this position. Though the room wasn't hot, a small bead of sweat escaped her hairline.

"Breathe." The instructor stepped closer to us and used hand motions to pace our breathing in and out. "Now lean back and allow your partner to switch legs."

Val changed legs, placing her right one against my shoulder, and I gently leaned forward.

"Is this far enough?" My hand stayed planted on her ankle, and I leaned far forward, stretching her leg.

"Deeper." The husk in her voice sent a bolt of lightning straight down my spine, and it settled between my thighs. I gently moved forward, deepening the stretch so I was almost pressed against her heat. One more inch and Val would not only see but feel exactly how much she affected me. I was certain rubbing up on my hard-on in the middle of a public yoga class was not the relaxing time Val had envisioned.

Because I was a glutton for punishment, I risked placing my free hand on her thigh, just above her knee. A flicker of something passed through her gorgeous caramel eyes, and when I lightened the weight of my hand, she only nodded, allowing it to stay planted on her thigh. My palm twitched as I gently rubbed the muscle as she stretched.

The class faded away, and it was only she and I in that room. Desire coursed through my body, but I also felt a strange connection to her—like something in my chest was tethered to hers. I'd never felt anything like it, and an aching twinge passed through me. Val's eyes were locked on mine.

Does she feel this too?

Before I could say anything, the teacher cut in and instructed us to switch positions. Val let out a hearty sigh and swiped the loose hairs that had escaped her ponytail. She took one last look at me, gathering her towel. "I'm sorry. I have to go."

I stared, mouth agape, as she hurried out of the studio and into the darkness.

THE NEXT NIGHT I still couldn't get Val out of my head. No amount of extra chores or an additional grueling workout helped to clear my thoughts of her. There was something about that woman that sucked me in and wouldn't let me go.

It was what forced my feet to trudge the path to her room in the lodge on Sunday evening. I paused for a moment. It was quiet, but a faint humming traveled through the thin wooden door. I lifted my hand to knock.

She didn't answer right away, but when I knocked again, the door cracked open and one dark eye peeked out at me.

"It's you."

I nodded. "It's me."

Val's smoky eyes raked down my front at a pace that said she was more than comfortable appreciating the male form. A swell of pride filled my chest at her assessment.

When she didn't close the door in my face, but also didn't speak, I cleared my throat. "Tonight is Sunday supper. Family dinner."

She scoffed. "*Family* dinner?"

"Yeah, well, it's all the family we've got right now. Ma doesn't cook worth shit, but Robbie is decent. Those of us who stay here sit around and enjoy each other's company on Sundays. You should come."

"I may be staying here, but I'm not anyone's family." I sensed a hint of sadness in her tone, and my jaw clenched.

"Come." The word came out harsher than I'd intended, and her eyes whipped to mine. I cleared my throat. "Please."

With a huff, she moved away from the door, not opening it, but also not slamming it in my face. I used the opportunity to push the door open, and I was immediately enveloped in her scent. Val's room was tiny—a bed, one dresser, and one nightstand. I heard her move around the small attached bathroom as I took in her space. Clean and organized, there was nothing out of place, but also nothing personal. If she'd packed up her bag and left, there'd be no sign she'd ever lived here at all.

"Settling in, I see," I teased.

Her eyes followed mine around the empty room. "Yeah, well . . . some of us aren't staying." Val pulled a sweater out of the top dresser drawer and sailed toward the door.

I happily followed, my eyes flicking down to the curve of her ass only once. We walked in silence down the hall. Val tapped a rhythm against her thigh with her thumb.

I placed my hand in front of her, stopping us both. "Why are you nervous?"

Her pretty face twisted. "I'm not."

My fingers caressed beneath her chin as I tilted her head up to examine her face. My voice skated over gravel as the intensity of her eyes bored into me. "Bullshit."

Val puffed out her chest in fake bravado, causing her breasts to push against me. I stepped forward, reveling in the feel of her pressed between me and the wall in the darkened corner of the hallway.

"I will never lie to you. Don't lie to me."

The sweet, peppermint fragrance of her breath hung between us, and I wanted nothing more than to devour her right there. I brushed my fingers against her temple and dragged them down the slender column of her neck. Her pulse jumped.

"I'm a cop. In a house full of criminals. I doubt I'm someone they'll welcome with open arms."

"When you're with me, you don't have to worry. I'll take care of you."

At my words, her face hardened, and Val planted her palms against my chest and shoved me away. As she sailed down the hallway, she shot a glare over her shoulder. "I don't need anyone taking care of me. I can take care of myself."

Goddamn, that woman is infuriating.

I pressed my forehead against the wall and let her walk

alone toward the dining room. After gathering my resolve, I steadied my pulse and walked toward the laughter in the lodge. Only steps behind Val, the conversation died when she made her entrance.

Wary glances were thrown her way, and it pissed me off that she was partially right about them. Every single one of them was tight-lipped and cold. Val's shoulders squared, and as she turned to leave, I stepped up beside her. Unable to get around me, she rolled her eyes.

"Well, there you two are!" Ma cut in just before Val could do something crazy like knee me in the balls just to get around. "Val, grab a plate. It's family style around here, so take what you like, pass what you don't."

Val smiled, but it didn't reach her eyes. "Thank you, Mrs. Brown."

"Oh, stop with that. Call me Ma, just like everyone else. Mrs. Brown is my husband Robbie's mother, and between you and me, she's a real bitch."

That got a chuckle out of Val, and I could breathe again, knowing the tension was leaving her shoulders. I grabbed my plate and found a seat. Val sat across the table and a few seats over. "Gem." I nodded at my sister, who playfully stuck her tongue out at me before plopping into the seat next to me.

Conversation was slow and easy, mostly about life on the ranch and the work we needed to get done. Val stayed quiet, not contributing to the conversation in any way, but no one engaged with her either. Several times I saw her staring at Gemma.

Gemma noticed too. "What the fuck is she looking at?"

"Watch it with that mouth."

"Whatever. She's creeping me out."

"She's allowed to."

She stared at me with disgust. I continued, "That's *Officer Rivera*. As in, saved-your-ass Officer Rivera. Treat her with a little respect."

"Oh shit . . ."

"Yeah. Oh shit."

Gemma toyed with the inside of her lip and looked nineteen again. "Should I go talk to her? Thank her or something? She looks so different."

"I'm sure she would say the same thing about you." I tugged on the ends of her newly blonde hair. I thought about her question. "Give her some time. She needs to settle in before you adopt her and trick her into playing Barbie makeover."

"I do love a good makeover. But she's pretty enough." Gemma's eyebrow raised. "Don't you think?"

I gave her only the satisfaction of a grunt before moving the conversation in a safer direction.

"Hey, Ev—" Scotty, an agent assigned to the ranch, cut in with a whisper. "He's on the move. Asking a lot of questions. As far as we know, your position hasn't been compromised."

Darkness crawled over my shoulders at the mention of my brother. My jaw ground together so hard that it ached.

The thick, raspy sound of Ma's voice silenced my response. "No business at family dinner. Take that shit outside."

"Yes, ma'am." I nodded at Scott. That conversation was far from over.

Dinner passed, and the tensions in the room seemed to fade slightly. A time or two Val laughed at the conversation around her, and the tinkling sound brought a lightness to my chest that I hadn't felt in a long fucking time. Maybe ever. It was the prettiest sound I could imagine.

EIGHT
VAL

I SCANNED the room over the rim of my glass. The fizzy liquid mirrored my jittery nerves as I watched the rest of my housemates. To the untrained eye, it looked as though family and friends had come together for a casual Sunday meal.

For me, however, the differences among people were astounding. Clear as day, six people were *guests* at the ranch. Criminals. I was fascinated by accents as a kid, when I realized not everyone spoke in the same manner as my parents. Because of that fascination, I could easily pick out three Midwest, one New York or vaguely East Coast, and a Southern drawl—maybe Texas.

The others in the room were clearly federal agents, though they had varying degrees of comfort with the rest of the group. Half the dinner guests were in WITSEC, either criminals themselves or so deeply ingrained in that lifestyle they were now testifying against said criminals. Looks of unease and mistrust were understandable. I wasn't a federal agent assigned to protect them, and I definitely was not on their side of the law either. Rather than be welcomed into either group, I was quietly banished to the outskirts.

Not that it mattered. I needed only to bide my time until I proved to Agent Walsh that I wasn't a basket case and a risk. Then I could finally be welcomed into the ATF. They would be my family. Not some mismatched, ragtag group of misfits posing as cattle ranchers.

I could feel Evan's eyes on me even before I caught them. I wanted to hate it. I wanted his gaze to make my skin crawl.

My body wasn't getting that memo, because instead of disgust, it was pure desire. Heat licked at my skin just beneath my sweater. In this light, Evan's eyes were dark and rich, and in the hallway, I'd discovered they were blue but with beautiful flecks of navy and gray. What was more unnerving was that his stare held more than appreciation. It was protective. His body stiffened if anyone moved too quickly in my direction or when I tensed at the clattering of a fork. A deep, burning part of me wanted to melt into him and be devoured by the warmth and strength of his muscles. Our night at the yoga class had been intense, and I'd replayed it over and over in my mind.

I may pride myself on mental toughness, but I was still a woman, and it had been a long, *long* time since my body had reacted to a man.

And what a fucking beast of a man Evan Walker was.

After that class, I had imagined what it would have been like if we hadn't stopped. If the class wasn't really there and we were alone, moving and stretching and sweating with each other in the privacy of the gym. He was careful not to touch me, but *oh, how I'd wanted him to*. If his cock matched the rest of him, being intimate with him would take some time to adjust, especially since it had been over a year since I'd been with a man. I craved that delicious fullness, and my lower belly clenched at the mere thought of Evan settling between the cradle of my hips.

My face felt hot, and when I looked up, Evan wore a curious smile. When he smirked at me like that, it was easy to forget who he was.

What he was.

A criminal—only the worst of the worst who had turned on their friends ended up in the Witness Protection Program.

Then again, he could've been a witness to a crime. I let the thought tumble through my mind. No. I knew better than that. The way Evan carried himself, moved with power and dominated any space he took up. That alone told me that he had seen, and more likely had done, horrific things in his lifetime.

Who are you, Evan Walker, and why can't I leave well enough alone?

I survived Sunday dinner. I was rather content being ignored, and the ability to watch from the sidelines was preferable. I tried so hard not to stare at Gemma. She'd caught me once or twice, and I had to force myself to stop creeping her out.

A major part of me was relieved that I hadn't made her up. She had been there that night. From Agent Brown's report, I learned Evan had broken into the house that night in an attempt to get Gemma from the men who'd taken her, but he was ambushed. Evan and at least one other man had fought, leaving Gemma behind in the house.

The V in Gemma's T-shirt barely hid the bright-red,

angry scar that raked across her chest and disappeared behind the fabric. With her arms exposed, I could see that one forearm was littered with marks from when she'd fallen into the glass. My stomach curled at the thought of her carrying the reminders of what she'd survived around with her every day.

By midday Monday, I was folding my freshly washed T-shirt when a soft knock sounded at the door to my room. When I cracked the door open and peeked, it was as if I'd manifested her myself. Gemma stood in the hallway, a bright-as-sunshine smile on her face.

"Hi! I'm Gemma."

I raked a hand through my long hair and smiled. "Hello. I'm Val."

A quiet laugh bubbled out of her. "Oh, I know who you are. I was at dinner, but we didn't get the chance to talk—I didn't know who you were then."

"Oh, um. It's okay. Can I help you with something?"

Gemma fiddled with the hem of her shirt. "I was hoping you were done with your chores. I have to run into town, and Evan says I'm not allowed to go without someone else." She rolled her eyes at her brother's rule. "I think he forgets that I'm not a kid, but . . ."

I stared into the light-blue eyes in front of me. She looked nothing like Evan except for those eyes—it was a wonder they were even related. She was slight and pale, and her face was lit up with hope. My eyes flicked down to her collarbone, and a pang of sadness pierced my gut. I may have helped her in the house that night, but Gemma had survived something pretty gruesome, and she was standing in front of me like a new puppy.

I couldn't kick the puppy.

"Yeah, I just finished. I can run into town with you."

"Great!" Gemma moved forward, gently pushing past me into my room. She made no secret of looking around at my things. "This room is boring."

I laughed. "I know," I said, then shrugged. "It's temporary."

"Ugh! I know it. This place is just so . . . *brown*."

Her obvious disgust mirrored my own. Gemma was funny. I was so intrigued, and suddenly I was looking forward to a trip to town with her. I wanted to know more about her. "Do I need anything before we go?"

"Nope! I've got the truck and my list—I just need a few things in town."

I locked my room tightly, double-checking the latch was set as I pushed on the door. In front of the main lodge, an older Ford truck was haphazardly parked at an angle and taking up two spaces.

Gemma rounded the hood and tapped it twice. "Hop in!"

For the next fifteen minutes, I bounced around the cab of that old truck and maintained a death grip on the bar above my head. Letting Gemma drive was a huge mistake, but as she took turns too quickly, sped down the open highways, and talked nonstop, there was nothing I could do but laugh along with her.

When we pulled into town, Gemma slowed—barely—and found an open parking space. I let out my breath and tried to rearrange the wild mess of my hair. "Where to?"

Gemma pointed out the windshield. "There's a funky little shop down that way. They've got the best products. I can't stand the generic crap they have at the ranch—it dries out my skin. Then I wanted to walk through town and maybe get a hot chocolate at the café. Is that okay?"

"Lead the way."

I was surprisingly comfortable with Gemma, though it was hard not to be. She waved and smiled at everyone, and they seemed genuinely pleased to see her. In the daylight, this town was amazingly charming and friendly. I glanced at the sign hanging outside the shop—REBELLIOUS ROSE— and smiled at the ornate floral design around a white skull. Once in the shop, a man around my age walked up to us, recognition for Gemma evident on his face.

"Hey, beautiful!"

Gemma turned and wrapped him in a hug. "Johnny! *Please* tell me you got the new lotions in."

"I can do you one better," he said. "The lotions *and* your purple shampoo came in."

Gemma squealed—actually squealed—with delight. Johnny must have caught my wince at the piercing sound and laughed. "Who do we have here?"

"Oh! Johnny Porter, this is Val Rivera. She's a new guest at the ranch." She leaned in slightly, and her voice lowered at the end, laced with meaning. Awareness bloomed on his face as he held out a hand for me to shake.

"Well, Miss Val." He patted the top of my hand with his. "Welcome to Tipp. Looks like you're one of us now."

Gemma grinned between us.

"Thank you?"

At my uncertainty, Johnny and Gemma laughed. "Well," he continued, "let's hook her up. What do you say, Gem?"

Gemma clasped her hands under her chin. "Yes!"

Twenty minutes and an obscene amount of money later, I was sufficiently swindled. Gemma and Johnny had revamped my nonexistent self-care routine from head to toe. From moisturizing shampoo and conditioner to fresh razors, bath salts, and polishing body scrub. I had no idea why I needed any of this if I was eyeballs deep in cow shit all day, but I had to admit that a hot bubble bath would feel pretty glorious after a grueling day in the field.

Loaded down with products, we stashed the bags in the truck before heading toward the café. People in town smiled as we passed and offered quiet *hello*s.

"This place is a lot different than the first night I came."

Gemma nodded. "Oh, I'm sure."

"What Johnny said . . . do the people here *know*?"

She shrugged as I held the door to the café open. "Some know more than others, but everyone's kind of wary of new faces. Until you get settled in, you're definitely on the outside of the circle."

"And once they know you're on the ranch, you're magically *inside* the circle?"

"For the most part. We haven't been here all that long, but I know that part of it is that the local cops are pretty useless. Mostly old men who don't know what the hell they're doing, and if they do know, they pretend it isn't happening. Also, the small-town vibe, maybe? They stand by each other, and when you live or work at the ranch, you're 'welcomed into the fold'—at least that's how Ma explained it."

I looked around the quaint café. "Fascinating."

"It really is. But sometimes I think it's nice to have a fresh start and forget about what's been done to you."

I stared at her back as she walked up to the counter to order, and the weight of her words hung in the air. Did I want a fresh start? I wasn't sure how I felt about not having to be anyone other than who I decided to be. Here, I was a worker on the ranch. I wasn't a female officer battling against archaic ideas about women in law enforcement. I wasn't a woman clawing my way up the ladder or a daughter desperately trying to not disappoint her parents.

But if I wasn't those things . . . who the hell was I?

NINE
VAL

I FELT LIGHTER after my shopping trip with Gemma. We visited a few more shops, all with similar greetings. Everyone welcomed me with open arms, and often their greetings were laced with quiet knowing and acceptance. It was quite possibly the strangest, but most comforting, shopping trip I'd ever had.

I didn't have the guts to ask Gemma about her scars or push her for details about what had happened to her the night I found her in that house. On the outside, Gemma was happy and carefree, but if you looked closely enough, it was a veil that hid pain and suffering just below the surface. We were having fun, and I didn't want to dredge up old wounds just to satisfy my own curiosities.

My days on the ranch were passing quickly. Each day was filled with chores that brought aching muscles and new blisters. I had always been fit, but the work on the ranch was grueling, messy, and demanding. I had never been so bone-tired in all my life. The work was hard, so I didn't have much time to dwell on anything other than getting through the day. My thoughts often wandered to Evan, and I would find small excuses to explore the grounds or take a walk down the path where he had chopped wood or linger in the common area of the lodge in hopes of getting a hit of his woodsy, masculine smell.

Unfortunately for my libido, Evan was practically a ghost around the ranch in the days since family dinner. Whether he was just busy or actively avoiding me was a mystery.

By Friday night, I was feeling stifled by the four walls of my room, and a little bit brave. I decided to wander out of my room and toward the kitchen. I had put Gemma's lotions and potions to good use, and after a long soak in the tub, I was energized. I poked around a few cabinets, looking to scrounge up something a little stronger than the Diet Coke I had pulled from the fridge.

On my tiptoes, I stretched to reach the cabinet above the fridge, hoping they kept the booze in the same spot my parents did.

"You aren't going to find any alcohol, if that's what you're hunting for."

Evan's deep voice warmed my skin, and the tiny hairs on my arms stood up. I turned just in time to see his eyes flick up from my ass, and a wave of satisfied pleasure tingled my middle.

"Well, that's a travesty," I joked.

Evan's easy smile, the one that crinkled the sides of his sapphire eyes, was back. "Ma doesn't keep it in the main house. I'm headed to town for a bite to eat and a beer." He thumbed toward the door. "Come with me."

The stern warmth in his tone bordered on an order, and I fought a smile. "Oh, I don't know about that. Big Al might not like to see me back at his bar."

"Fuck that guy. He'll be fine once he realizes you're one

of us." Evan moved toward the back door and held it open for me. "Besides, you're with me."

My body warmed at the thought of being *with* a man like Evan. He commanded respect, and his sheer size would be protection enough. I could hold my own, but knowing a man like him could come to my defenses held a certain allure.

"All right, big guy. Let's do this." I swept past him and out the door, but paused when a low rumble escaped him. "Are you okay?"

When I met his eyes, they darkened and my pulse skittered. "You smell nice."

I clenched my jaw to keep my cool. I'd owe Johnny a thank-you later.

Sitting in the cab of Evan's truck was a mistake. I was surrounded by the warm, comforting smell of him. Wood and leather and a freshness that was only him assaulted me. My panties were drenched even before I caught sight of the way his forearms flexed and moved as he shifted gears. There was something innately sexy about a man who drove stick shift.

Evan kept the conversation light, asking about what I had been up to the past week and how I was settling in. I was honest, and we had a small laugh over grumpy Ray. I retold a joke that one of the farmhands told me, and his laugh was quick and comforting. Everything about that man drew me in.

I knew it was wrong—to not rein in my obvious desire for someone who was a hardened criminal—but I couldn't seem to help it.

At the bar, Al softened immediately when he saw me arrive with Evan. Not everyone seemed to know him, but those who recognized Evan waved, nodded, or walked over to our small table to greet him.

A mother and her four wild children stopped to say hello on their way out. They all knew Evan, and the young boys took turns hanging on his forearm while he hoisted them higher and higher. I noted that I wasn't the only woman in the bar who appreciated how impressive those muscles were.

"We'll get you one day, Mr. Evan!"

Evan grinned at the youngest, gap-toothed boy. "I know you will. You keep growing and listen to your Mama, and one day you'll be bigger than me, I'm sure of it."

The young boys' eyes all went wide as the mom made them say goodbye and collectively scooted them out the door.

"What, are you the mayor of this town or something?" Our eyes met, and affection danced over his features.

"If you would have told me a year ago that I would be living in a small ranching town in Montana, I wouldn't have believed you. If you would have told me that I would not only live there but actually enjoy it? I would have called you a fucking liar."

I shook my head in disbelief. I was dying to know his story. Ma Brown's report left me with more questions than answers. How did a man come from a Mafia family in Chicago and find his place on a ranch in Montana? Did he miss any part of his old life?

"You know I can see you're racking your brain with questions, right?"

I glanced down and tucked a strand of hair behind my ear, embarrassed he could read me so easily. "You're just a mystery, that's all."

Evan leaned his large frame in my direction. We were

so close I could feel his breath dance across the skin of my neck, and I resisted a shiver. "I told you before. I will never lie to you. You can ask me anything."

The moment felt significant. I leaned back and smiled a tight smile before gathering my resolve to ask him the questions I had burning in my gut. As I took a deep breath, the waitress interrupted the moment by bringing a basket of bite-size bar food and our drinks.

I pushed my feelings aside. I could figure out the best way to get to the bottom of who Evan Walker really was. This was one of the rare nights I left the ranch, and I didn't want to spoil it. Instead, I settled into my chair and watched people as they danced and played pool or darts. My eyes caught on a lone man with his back to the wall, scanning the crowd.

I tipped my chin toward him. "One of ours?"

Evan sipped his beer and nodded. "They're always around."

The man ignored us, and I tried to shake the eerie feeling of being watched. When a pool table opened up, I stood and knocked the back of my hand against Evan's bicep. "Come on. Let's play."

I started racking the pool balls into the triangle as Evan grabbed two cues leaning against the wall. "Do you know how to play?"

Evan threw me a blank stare.

I raised my hands. "Okay. I hear you. We've got a pool shark over here. But I have to warn you. I'm pretty good."

I smiled at Evan and felt lighter than I had in days. Around him, it was easy to forget the circumstances we were in. I didn't feel like a police officer at the end of her rope. I felt like a woman, laughing and having a great night out with a man. Compounded by the fact the man looked like *that*, the situation had me doing everything in my power to shove away any warning bells blaring about our pasts and our current circumstances.

After one turn, I knew I was in trouble. Evan wasn't just okay at playing pool—he was phenomenal. Despite his large frame, he moved gracefully around the table. After sinking several balls in a row, I decided to not-so-subtly remove my chunky sweater, leaving on nothing but a thin white tank top. It didn't go without notice, and he botched his next shot.

As I rounded him, I flashed a cocky smile. He leaned in close, his masculine scent enveloping me and his voice barely above a whisper. "Cheater."

I feigned shock but laughed and leaned a hip against the table as I assessed my shot. I sank a few balls easily, but the last ricochet put the cue ball behind the only two balls Evan still had on the table. I bent to adjust, but the angle I needed was awkward, and I wasn't happy with how everything was lined up. "Shit," I whispered to myself as I tried to readjust. I hated losing and was not about to give him the satisfaction of beating me so easily.

Warmth covered my back as Evan moved in behind me. His chest ran every inch down my back, and I stiffened at the contact. He bent lower, placing his mouth next to the shell of my ear. "Need a little help?"

I resisted the urge to scissor my legs as desire crawled through me. When I nodded, Evan's arms wrapped around me and followed me as I bent at the waist. His hips pressed into my ass, and my hip bones pushed against the smooth wood of the pool table. Together we lined up the shot, but I couldn't focus on anything but the warmth of his chest and the low throb between my legs.

"I think if you come at it from this angle, you can sink it into the corner pocket."

I tilted my head to look at him, my eyes dropping to his full lips.

Take me. Push me up on this pool table right here and take me.

My rogue thoughts were on my tongue when he brushed the tip of his nose down mine. I wanted to puddle at his feet. Evan moved away, standing back behind me. I swallowed thickly and tried to adjust and make the shot.

From the corner of the bar, I heard a man say, "Think she'll let me show her how to make the next shot?" The comment earned a few laughs and high fives from his idiot friends. To spite them, I made the shot and straightened.

In a heartbeat, Evan was in the man's face. "Disrespect her again. I fucking dare you."

The man wilted in Evan's presence as I wrapped my hand around his biceps. Tension radiated through him like a lid rattling on a pressure pot. "Come on, let's go, Ev."

"Sorry, man. We were just joking around."

I tugged on his arm. "Time to go."

Evan let me lead him away, but anger was still coursing through him. I pulled a few dollars from my purse and left a tip, along with our drinks, on the table. Once outside, the spring air cooled my lungs.

Evan took long strides toward the truck, and I scrambled to keep up with him. He yanked the passenger-side door open and practically shoved me inside. He rounded the hood in seconds and climbed in the cab. Instead of starting the car, he gripped the steering wheel with both hands.

He wasn't looking at me, rather just staring out the windshield.

I tested the waters. "So . . . I guess not everyone's so friendly in Tipp."

"They aren't from here." His voice was strained. "I didn't like the way he spoke about you."

"It's fine." I didn't have the words to explain that, while I didn't need him jumping to my rescue from some mouthy drunks, coming from him it was fucking hot. I'd have to unpack that later and figure out what that meant about me, but for now it was easier to move on and ignore it.

I tried to speak again, but Evan cut in. "Let's go home."

TEN

EVAN

I wanted to rip that guy's head from his shoulders. The fact he thought he could disrespect Val like that burned acid through my veins. Younger me wouldn't have thought twice about beating the shit out of him just because I didn't like the way he looked at my girl.

My girl.

The thought was there before I had time to stop it. But Val wasn't my girl. She was a cop and someone on the ranch who knew I was never the good guy I was pretending to be. I may have skirted the law more often than not, but with her resources as a cop, she could easily look up the muddied life of Evan Marino.

I let the hot spray of the shower pound over my shoulders and run down my back. All I'd wanted tonight was to take her out and try to lighten her mood. I could tell she felt stifled by life on the ranch and the weight of the secrets we all kept.

Instead, I'd nearly hiked her ass up on the pool table and driven into her. A low groan escaped me at the thought, and my cock thickened. Lately, fantasies of Val interrupted my daily work and absolutely consumed my nights. All week I had tried to keep my distance, to let my initial attraction fade into the background, but it wasn't working.

I ignored my aching hard-on. Jacking off in the shower would only make me want her more. I knew that for a fact because I'd tried it a few nights ago and was even more amped up than before. There was no getting Val out of my system. Clearly, she was here to stay, and the fantasy and my hand just wouldn't do.

No.

I needed more of her.

I'd always been good at torturing myself, so instead of going to bed, I toweled off and slipped on a pair of jeans and a T-shirt. Val had left her chunky sweater in my truck, and I nodded to myself at the reasonable excuse for knocking on her door so late.

The ride to the lodge was short and dark. Others had mentioned that the vastness of the ranch could be overwhelming, but to me it represented everything I was grasping at and desperately trying to keep hold of: *freedom*.

The gravel crunched beneath my tires, and when I swung around the hood of the truck, I nodded a silent acknowledgment to the agent posted outside the entrance. Staying at the lodge wasn't ideal—the rooms were small and communal living could take some getting used to, but I liked knowing Val was guarded around the clock.

She was a cop and I was sure she could hold her own, but the murky pasts of the people who lived at Redemption meant danger was never far from our doorstep. My boots were heavy on the wood floors of the lodge, and after a few strides, Scotty came into view.

"Evan." He nodded in greeting. He was dressed casually in jeans and a flannel, but his posture was rigid, alert. Scotty was on night duty tonight.

"Agent Dunn." I shook his hand.

His easy smile split his face. "Get out of here with that shit."

I laughed. Scott was a good guy, and we'd become friends. In addition to working on the ranch, he was, in fact, an agent, and I loved giving him shit about it.

"What brings you 'round tonight?" His eyes caught on the feminine sweater I clutched. "Sniffing around the new gal?"

I tightened my grip on the sweater. While we were expected to lead "normal lives," I was keenly aware that everyone here was being watched. Judged. Sex made people stupid, and the federal government didn't want their cases blown because people couldn't keep it in their pants. "No," I lied.

He lifted one eyebrow. "Hmm." After eyeing me a beat longer, Scotty decided to let it go. "Well, I'm glad I ran into you. There's news."

My skin prickled. Scott had been assigned to the ranch around the same time Gemma and I had arrived. He'd been a marshal for some time and had connections all over the country. Those connections helped keep tabs on my brother and his movements. If Parker discovered that Gemma and I were alive, it would be only a matter of time before he sent his men to hunt us down.

"He knows." The gravity of his words settled in on my shoulders.

Fuck. Parker knows.

He knew that Gemma was alive. That I didn't die in that courtyard as reported.

"How?" I ground out the word.

"How the hell do any of these guys get their dirt? They're parasites—eyes and ears everywhere. Somehow he found out that you are very much alive. Though it doesn't seem like he knows where you are. *Yet.*"

My nostrils flared as Scott droned on about the details he knew. Heat crept up my neck. My thoughts flashed back to finding Gemma in the basement of that house, broken. Her chest and neck carved into, covered in blood and piss that weren't even hers. Parker had had his own sister kidnapped, and it had taken me six grueling days to find where his men had taken her.

The names and faces of the four men I killed as I dragged her from that basement didn't haunt me. I felt no remorse for doing what had to be done to save my little sister. Had it not been for the fifth who'd gotten me with a baseball bat to the ribs, we would have gotten out and disappeared.

Instead, the cops had shown up, the man had fled, and I had hunted him down. Twisting and turning through the alleyways, doubling back and searching, I'd reveled in the hunt. When I'd come up on him beating the shit out of a female police officer and Gemma cowering behind her back, I'd panicked. That piece of shit had shot an approaching cop and raised his weapon toward her.

Val.

At the time, I didn't know who she was or that she was funny and stunningly beautiful and strong. All I knew was that she had protected Gemma, and when the gun was turned on her, I did what I had to do. When the bullet tore through me, it all went black.

I'd take that bullet again in a heartbeat, though now it might be for slightly different reasons. Val had a way of crawling under my skin, and whenever she was in the room, it felt like my chest was cracking open.

"Just don't do anything stupid." Scotty's words snapped me back to the present, and I nodded. Somehow Parker knew that Gemma and I were alive. Gemma had uncovered his secrets, and to him that was all it took to turn on his own blood.

"Thanks, man." I shook his hand again. "If you could keep this between us, I'd appreciate it, but I understand if you can't."

"Just looking out for you, man. Long as this shit isn't dropped at my doorstep, I figure it's no one's business but yours. I'll have my guy keep digging. But if this gets bad or he makes a move . . . I'll have to tell Ma about Parker."

"'Course. I understand."

Scotty turned and made his rounds through the darkened lodge.

Gemma was in danger. It was only a matter of time until Parker sussed out what had happened to us. We should probably leave the ranch. Run. It would be the only way to stay one step ahead of his unending reach.

The soft yarn of Val's sweater burned beneath my fingertips as I clutched it tighter. If I left and Val was still here, she'd be as good as dead too.

I couldn't win.

Defeated, I trudged back to my truck and headed back to my cabin. Val's sweater lay in a gentle heap in the passenger seat, her soft scent filling the cab of my truck. I could have left it in the lodge for her to find in the morning, but for some reason I didn't have the heart to leave it.

ELEVEN
VAL

I POPPED a Sour Patch Kid in my mouth and let the sour burn in my jaw as I lay back on my tiny bed. I had grabbed the candy from the gas station in town on my shopping trip last week with Gemma.

Thank god for small miracles.

When my fingers hit the sandy sugar at the bottom, I peeked down at the extra-large bag and frowned. I really needed a more reliable mode of transportation. The unpaved, bumpy roads were brutal on my poor car, and grumpy Ray was working on whatever was wrong with it. Who knew how long it would be out of commission, and I was stranded unless I wanted to rely on Gemma's erratic, and potentially deadly, driving to get me to town. My thoughts immediately flicked to Evan.

I could ask him for a ride into town. I'd be rewarded with a hit of his cologne and feel the heat radiate off him in the cab of his truck. For a brief moment, I closed my eyes and let my imagination wander.

Where Evan was concerned, it was easy to do. He took up not only the physical space in a room but all the empty corners of my mind as well. Heaven help me if I stumbled upon him during chores—the roped muscles of his forearms bunching and rippling as he split wood or hammered boards. Earlier in the week I'd walked into the barn to see him petting a baby cow, and my ovaries had exploded.

A low, needy breath rattled through me as I closed my eyes.

I wondered what it would be like to be consumed by a man his size. To feel the weight of him pressing into me as he flexed his hips. To feel his rough, scarred hands roam over my skin and hear the low rumble of his voice in my ear as he groaned in pleasure.

Despite my better judgment, I wanted him. More than I had ever wanted a man, I wanted to feel what it was like to be Evan's woman. There were times I could tell he wanted me too. His eyes would flick down to my lips, his shoulders twitch as though all it would take was one decision to push forward and consume me.

Only he didn't.

Evan kept a respectable distance.

I grunted in frustration as I rolled over in my bed. I knew it was for the best, but as vast as the ranch was, it still felt tiny compared to my old life, and I couldn't escape him. If he wasn't everywhere, people would talk about him. Sing his praises.

I needed to hate him or at the very least hold a mild disdain—not this low, achy need that settled between my legs. I needed to focus on getting home and earning my promotion.

A sharp knock at my door was a welcome distraction.

I pulled it open without bothering to check who it was— I'd learned that it was either an agent checking in on me or a worker on the ranch. No new faces had much access to the lodge.

Gemma's bright white smile and sparkling blue eyes greeted me.

"Hi, Val! Are you done with your work? Do you want to go explore? I was thinking of hiking the ridge."

Her sweet, innocent face beamed up at me. I had the hardest time telling her no, and I actually looked forward to hanging out with her. She never made me feel like I had anything to prove. Our easy friendship had become a comfort.

I smiled back at her. "It was slow for a Tuesday. I could go for a hike."

After gathering my things, we drove up the hills toward the buttes that lined the edge of the ranch.

Gemma slammed the brakes, and I braced myself as she threw the truck violently into park. "There's a trailhead just up here that will wind up the butte and back around. Sound okay?"

The looming butte shadowed the valley, but the prospect of tackling it ran a zip of excitement through me. "Let's do it."

The path crept at a slow enough incline to allow Gemma and me to get in a good workout, but it didn't leave us so breathless that we couldn't talk. Conversation ebbed and flowed, and the view was breathtaking. Just when we thought the path would turn back, another winding trail hooked around. Up and up we followed it, my thighs burning as we climbed. Trees were dwarfed by the massive earth that climbed out of the valley. I focused on moving forward as my heart pounded.

As the afternoon sun rose higher, sweat began to trickle

down my back. I huffed a breath and planted my hands on my hips. "I need a minute."

Gemma paused, also out of breath, and stretched beside me. "Gorgeous, right?"

There were no words to describe how insignificant nature can make you feel. Growing up in the outskirts of a major city, I had never seen anything like it. We hadn't seen a single other soul, and the land stretched out for miles and miles. "This is . . . wow."

Tears pricked at the corners of my eyes. The burn of emotion was surprising but not unwelcome. The expanse of Montana had a way of being both humbling and comforting. It reminded me of the old Westerns my father would watch, and I loved knowing something could remain steadfast for so long. Have permanence.

"All that time I spent moving from one shithole to another and I never knew places like this even existed." Sadness had settled into Gemma's voice as she looked out onto the scenery. She hooked one hand under her long-sleeve shirt and pulled it from her body to tie it around her waist. Underneath, she wore only a tank top, making her red, angry scars clearly visible.

My eyes tracked down her jagged, disfigured skin, and I tried to look away. When my eyes met hers, shame heated my cheeks. "I'm sorry."

Gemma brushed her fingertips over the scar. Her voice was quiet. "I'm not embarrassed in front of you. You saved me."

I scanned her face. Curiosity held my tongue, hoping she'd tell me more about what had happened to her. Any trace of her had been scrubbed from the police record. I knew nothing of the horrors she'd experienced that had caused her so much pain.

Gemma started walking up the path, and I walked in step with her. "Evan's my half brother, did you know that?"

I shook my head. "No, he didn't mention it."

She smiled. "He wouldn't. He once told me that he thought the term 'half brother' was *total bullshit*."

"Sounds like him," I agreed.

"That's why he's so much older than me and we look nothing alike. We have the same mom."

"Mmm." I stayed quiet, urging her to continue.

"She was a piece of shit though. She lost Evan and his brother to the state because of child neglect. I came along later but probably should have been taken from her too. I was fifteen when she died of an overdose."

"I'm sorry."

"Don't be. I'd been in and out of wherever she was staying for a while by that point, avoiding the strange men she attached herself to. I couldn't stand to be around the people she shacked up with. I guess because I saw what that lifestyle did to her. When Evan found out she was dead, he came around asking questions and found me. He gave me a job, helped me find a place to stay. Our brother, Parker, can be scary as shit, but Evan always looked out for me."

"Evan loves you."

Gemma's voice was thick with emotion. "Yeah. He came back for me." I paused and looked at her. She held her hand across her scarred collarbone. "After a job, I accidentally walked in on one of Parker's meetings. Heard things I shouldn't and saw the faces of everyone in the room. Bad men. They made sure to *remind* me what they were capable of if I talked to anyone. I tried to go to Evan, but I was taken before I had the chance."

"Jesus." My hand flew to my mouth.

"If it weren't for Evan finding me, and then you coming

into the house and grabbing me, I'd probably be dead. Even after Evan dragged me from the basement, I was stuck. I couldn't move."

"You were abducted. You were in shock."

I watched Gemma stuff down her emotions and flash a perky, fake smile. "Wow. Am I a total bummer or what?" Her laughter bubbled, and she tried to brush off the weight of our conversation.

I placed a hand gently on her arm and squeezed. "Thank you for trusting me."

Gemma wrapped me in a tight hug and continued down the path without another word.

I was still reeling from my earlier conversation with Gemma. Before knowing her, I'd felt sorry for myself because I had unsupportive parents. In reality, they were afraid for me, but there was always love. How pathetic was feeling sorry for myself in comparison to the nightmare Gemma and Evan had lived? It was no wonder he'd done what he'd had to do to survive.

A helpless sorrow for the two of them burrowed deep into my bones. Children should never have to experience what they had. It was unfair.

My heart ached for both of them.

Anger toward the adults responsible for caring for their children soured my mood. I needed to get out of there, away from the polite, surface-level conversations at the lodge. Away from the curious-yet-untrusting glances of everyone who worked there. Away from the sympathetic nods of the people of Tipp who eagerly wanted to give me some kind of second chance I wasn't even sure I needed or deserved.

From under my bed, I pulled out my backpack and felt for the unopened bottle of bourbon I had purchased earlier in the week. After pulling on a sweater, I tightened the backpack and headed down to the kitchen. Always well stocked, I tucked a small baguette into the backpack along with sliced cheese, a hand towel, and a small container of blueberries.

An evening picnic with the cows was just what I needed.

"Going somewhere?" Agent Brown's voice startled me, and a small yip escaped.

I straightened my shoulders. "I thought I was free to go anywhere I pleased."

Her smile softened. "Of course you are, dear. This is your home. I was simply going to ask if you needed to borrow one of the work trucks while Ray takes a look at your car."

Shame burned from my toes to my nose. I cleared my throat. "That would be helpful. Thank you, Agen—I mean, Ma."

She smiled again. "There's a board with spare keys just inside my office. The blue key ring is for the Chevy in the garage. It's all yours."

I watched her move down the hallway until she turned a corner, out of sight. I quickly found the key and the sunburnt Silverado. A thrill of exhilaration ran through me at the small taste of freedom.

The drive to the outer pasture took only a few minutes, and I drove slowly to enjoy the splash of pinks and oranges that rioted against the indigo buttes silhouetted during sunset. The Chicago skyline was nothing compared to a sunset in Big Sky Country.

I pulled the truck against the wire fence that penned in

the cows. Their low moos rang out, acknowledging my presence.

"Yeah, yeah. I hear you."

I found a thick wood post and had bent to crawl under the wire when a hint of panic raced through me.

Are there bulls in here?

Realizing I wouldn't know the difference between a bull and a cow, as well as the fact I wasn't planning on venturing into the pasture, I nestled myself against the post.

I leaned my head back, closing my eyes and taking in the sounds and smells of nightfall in Montana. The air was pine and smoke. I pulled it deep into my lungs and held it there.

Stress melted from my shoulders, inch by inch. I watched the cows laze in the pasture. Their long horns and rakish, floppy hair delighted me for reasons I couldn't pin down. Their expressive eyes and easy nature were a reprieve from the watchful stares of their human counterparts. On the days when I was feeling extra sorry for myself, I found imagining the dramas of life on a cattle farm amusing.

Lost in thoughts of cattle romances, the soft sound of boots through the tall grass had my ears pricking and my head whipping around.

As I pinned the silhouette with a stare, my fight-or-flight response on edge, my jaw dropped. Evan sauntered toward me, his hands deep in his back pockets, emphasizing the expanse of his broad chest. A small smile tugged at his lips as he came into view. His head hung low, and when he got close enough, he peeked at me through his long, dark lashes.

My body tightened in response.

Holy fuck this guy is hot.

I cleared my throat. "How did you know I was out here?"

"You passed my place on the way over. I was out on the porch when you drove by."

I took my time looking him up and down, hoping the gesture helped me look indifferent rather than appreciative of how the T-shirt beneath his flannel molded to his body.

"Can I join you?" he asked, gesturing to the space beside me.

I nodded and scooted my butt to the left, leaving my back partially rested against the thick fence post. Evan moved between the wires to sit beside me. He propped his forearms on his knees and looked out onto the pasture.

"I always thought the Highland cattle looked more human than cows."

I peeked at him and fought the smile that tugged at my lips. "It's the hair. They just seem so *emo*." I was rewarded with a deep rumble of Evan's laughter. The tension in my back dissolved further, and I nestled my shoulders along the thick fencepost.

Once I rifled through my backpack, I smoothed the tea towel out and placed the food between us. When I pulled the bottle of bourbon from the pack, Evan quirked one eyebrow.

I smiled. "Secret stash."

He bumped his shoulder into mine. "I won't tell if you share." Instead of moving back into his space, he left his shoulder lightly touching mine, and my brain swam with endorphins. I wanted to feel his heat, to let it curl around me and pull me closer.

I uncapped the bottle and took a healthy sip. The buttery, caramel flavor crept over my tongue as the burn of the alcohol warmed my belly. My eyes never left Evan, and his eyes never left my mouth. I sucked the excess liquid off my lower lip and passed him the bottle. Evan shook his head before taking a sip.

"Mmm. This is good." Surprise was laced in his voice.

"I had a friend who was really into old fashioneds. I learned how to find a decent bourbon."

I finished putting the rest of the food on the towel and tore off a hunk of bread to hand to Evan. When he took it, I could appreciate, up close, how wide and rugged his hands were. Long, thick fingers gave way to a massive palm. I noticed his right hand was streaked with old, crepe-paper scars, the knuckles uneven and bumpy.

I gestured toward it. "Broken hand?"

Evan looked down as he flexed his hand. "A few times." One finger tracked down the large bumps on the back of his hand. "One time needed plates and screws."

"Looks painful." I tried to read his impassive face.

"It was." I hated the grim line that deepened the furrow in his brow as he rubbed his hand.

I held my hand toward his face, fingers spread. "I'm pretty tough, too, you know. Do you see this one here?" I pointed between my pinky and ring finger. He squinted and held my hand in his, the contact shooting rioting ripples low in my belly. "Well, that scar is from a minor disagreement with a kitchen knife."

His chuckle danced over my skin, the sound deep and warm. I didn't want him to let go of my hand, but when he released it, I could still feel the tingle of his fingers on mine. Evan shook his head as he took a bite of bread.

"Okay, fine. Well, this one here . . ." I bent to trace a finger up the long scar that ran from my left ankle eight or so inches up my leg. "When I was sixteen, I snuck out to go sledding with friends and ended up breaking my leg in three places. Needless to say, I did not get away with it."

A small laugh escaped his nose. "Yeah, I guess not."

The soft buzz of cicadas filled the late spring air around us. I nestled back into his strong shoulder as I looked out onto the pasture before turning back to him.

"What about this one?" I flicked my thumb over the faint scar that ran above his lip into his nose. It was the only physical evidence that Evan was the same man who'd been in the courtyard that night. Something pulled at my chest, squeezing it tight. "Another fight?"

Evan's thumb found the scar on his lip, and he swiped over it but didn't speak.

I bumped my shoulder into him. "I almost forgot that brooding silences were a part of your charm."

His head turned to me, and a soft smile played on his lips. "Not a fight. I was born with a cleft lip."

I stared in stunned silence at the faint white scar that interrupted the scruff of his mustache.

"It caused plenty of fights though." When I scrunched my eyebrows, he continued, "Kids are assholes. Teased me about it a lot. It's where I learned to fight."

Sadness and silence blanketed me. Evan had lived a very different life than I had.

Finally, he broke the silence. "You're a good girl. You're not supposed to have scars and broken bones from things you wish you couldn't remember."

I glanced at him, but his eyes were hard, cast out across the pasture in the fading light of evening.

I saw the opening so I took it. "So you . . . were like a Mob guy?" My voice felt tiny and quiet compared to the roar of questions threatening to spill from inside me. Dredging up the past was a dangerous game.

"My name is Evan Walker, and I grew up in Montana. I work at Laurel Canyon Ranch."

I tried not to roll my eyes. "First of all, everyone's going to know that's total bullshit if you don't fix that Chicago *A* sound. It gives you away. And second of all, you said you'd never lie to me."

Evan's eyes searched my face as he leaned back against the post and stretched his long legs. He sighed. "I was born Evan Marino. When I was eight years old, the county took my older brother, Parker, and me away from our mother after we showed up to school bruised, dirty, and hungry a few too many times. We were shuffled from place to place, no one wanting to keep two brat-ass kids who didn't listen. When Parker was sixteen and I was thirteen, we ran. Parker met Michael, who was a numbers runner for the Mob. He got a job collecting bet receipts, and we survived."

I took in the information he threw at me. A sad story of children without someone to love them, take care of them. My heart broke for them as I imagined those lost little boys.

Evan picked at the bread, tossing crumbs of it out into the grass as he spoke. "Parker and Michael started running other errands for some connected guys in the city—it was good money. Over time he worked his way up. Parker's always been a smooth talker. He could get anyone to trust him. I followed along. Kept my mouth fucking shut. As I grew up, I used my size and strength to do the jobs I was given and keep a roof over my head."

"Sounds scary."

He shrugged one hard, muscular shoulder. Lost in thought, he kept rambling. Hidden secrets spilled from him. "We had this thing. A lot of times you couldn't talk openly, especially when people were around. You couldn't trust anyone. 'No bullshit.' It's how we knew that the words we spoke to each other were true." He laughed a sad, quiet laugh. "Turns out it was all bullshit, I guess."

I propped my elbow on my knee and leaned my head on my hand so I could study his expression. Evan didn't look at me but rather let his gaze trace over the mountains on the horizon as he picked at the grass and threw the pieces into the wind. Was it sadness? Remorse? Then it hit me.

Loneliness.

This man had never known kindness and love. "It sounds like a scared boy who did what he needed to do to survive."

His dark eyes met mine. "In the beginning, maybe. But somewhere in there, I began to enjoy the work I did. I had a purpose, a family. And I didn't give a fuck who I hurt in the process."

"And then came Gemma."

"Yeah, then came Gemma." Evan looked down at his hands as she scrubbed them together. "When we found out about her, Parker wanted nothing to do with her. She looks so much like Mom, and I think that was too much for him. She was the last connection we had to her, and I couldn't just walk away. It was actually nice having her around. Then again, I never thought Parker would be capable of doing what he did to his own blood. That's when I realized that my brother was gone. He let his darkness consume him. If I didn't help her, I knew I'd end up the same way."

"But you didn't. You are not your brother." His forearm flexed when I placed my hand across it. My heart hammered in my ears.

"There's darkness in me, Val."

"Maybe some. But I can see the light."

Before I knew what was happening, Evan's hands were in my hair, and we were tumbling into the soft grass. His long, hard body covered mine. His mouth crashed down, rough and demanding. The air whooshed out of my lungs and came out as a needy, breathless moan.

Desire took over all rational thought. Bourbon still flavored his kiss, and I wound my legs around his waist as his hips pressed into me. Evan's hands were locked in my hair, gently pulling until my mouth opened and his tongue delved into me.

My nails raked down his back as my hips bucked, begging for more pressure. A throaty moan rumbled through him, and warmth pooled between my legs. I was soaked through, and he had only kissed me.

But damn. That man could kiss. His lips moved down the column of my neck, sucking and nipping with his teeth. Desire swept through me. Darkness was a blanket that protected me from caring we were in the middle of a pasture and anyone walking or driving by would see us.

The stubble of his cheek tickled my palm and sent tiny sparks racing up my arm as my fingertips explored the planes of his face.

Evan kissed the hollow beneath my collarbone, his tongue dipping and tasting my skin before he rested his forehead against my neck. "Goddamn it. You smell so fucking good."

"Don't stop." My voice was breathless and needy as my hands traveled down the hard lines of his chest and abdomen.

"If I don't stop kissing you now, I'm going to tear you apart."

I palmed the hard length of his cock through his jeans. Jesus Christ that thing was going to take some getting used to. The girth of it had a scared giddiness skittering below my skin and settling as an empty clench where I wanted to be filled.

His approving grunt was all the permission I needed as I continued to lick and kiss up his neck, my teeth scraping against his warm flesh. His masculine smell—clean air and fresh pine—soaked into me. I didn't care who could see us, I wanted Evan to unleash everything he had into me.

He pinned my wrists to stop my hands as I tried to stroke his cock again.

"Val, we can't." His breath was coming fast and quick. His gentle hands squeezed my wrists as desire darkened his expression. His eyes traced over me, our faces mere inches apart. "You are so fucking beautiful."

My hair was fanned out beneath me, and my heart beat wildly against my ribs. Evan's hard cock was still seated between my legs, teasing my clit, and I ached to feel more of him. To be stretched by him. Connected to him. I tried to move, to grind myself against him, but Evan moved one hand from my wrist to my hip and squeezed.

I brushed back the hair that tumbled on his forehead with my free hand and studied his face. "Evan, this feels so good."

I parted my knees farther apart and quirked an eyebrow, tempting him.

Evan lifted, refusing to let his body make contact with mine. "Careful. You don't know what you're asking."

"I know exactly what I want. Do you?" Our breath mingled in the air, and I wanted his warmth seeping back into me.

"A man like me always wants what he can't have. But you, baby girl, are the most dangerous thing on this ranch."

His soft touch moved from the side of my face, down the column of my neck, and stopped at the base. My body arched toward the warmth of his hand. Evan ran his nose along the side of mine before whispering a kiss at the corner of my mouth. His eyes finally met mine before he closed them and rested his forehead against mine. "We can't do this."

Despite the protest that gurgled in my throat, Evan pushed off me, leaving my body cool and achy in his absence. He sat back on his heels and raked a hand through his hair. I propped up on my elbows and tried to read the warring expressions that danced across his face.

Hating the sadness that was creeping over his expression, I grabbed a piece of bread beside me and hurled it in his direction. He swatted at it and glared at me, though humor tugged at the hard line of his mouth.

"All right, cowboy. If you won't make out with me, the least you can do is walk me to the truck."

Evan helped me to my feet, his hands careful not to linger or brush the skin that peeked over my jeans at the hip. We gathered the remnants of our sad little picnic, and I stuffed it all back into my bag. Disappointment was dulled by the newfound affection I had for this complex, intriguing man. There were so many layers to him that much of the fun was peeling one back to reveal what lay just below it.

Tonight I had learned Evan Walker was a criminal who didn't want to break the rules.

TWELVE
EVAN

Kissing Val in the pasture had been a mistake. If I thought getting her out of my head was difficult *before* I knew what it felt like to have her pinned beneath me, I was a fucking idiot. Thank god she'd taken my rejection in stride. It truly wasn't a rejection at all—I wanted her, more than I cared to admit—rather my rational brain overrode my dick for once, and it was the right move.

Above all else, the rules at Redemption Ranch were clear. I could have no ties to my former life. Val was off-limits.

Days later I was still thinking about kissing Val under the stars in the pasture. It was easy to forget myself—to forget that a man like me didn't deserve to kiss a woman like her. I'd chosen my path, just as she had chosen hers, and in no way did those paths meet at a happy ending. Yet here we were. Thrust together and working on the same ranch, day in and day out.

Sure, I'd swapped a few chores that strategically put me closer to where she'd be spending her days. I was a man, after all, and I enjoyed the view. Plus, it allowed me to jump in and help Val out when she was still learning the basics of animal care.

It was strange to feel helpful. While Val didn't *need* my help, any time I offered a suggestion, she listened with rapt attention and simply nodded and tried again. Though her stubborn streak was a mile wide, she wasn't too proud to try things a different way.

Today I was going to have a little fun with her.

"What the hell is that thing?" Val looked up and down the three-foot-long glove.

"It's a glove." I smirked and continued gathering our supplies.

"Why is it so long?"

"Gotta go all the way up." I was intentionally leaving out key details. The ranch was moving toward utilizing artificial insemination rather than natural breeding to manage the herds. While Val wouldn't have to do much but watch, it was too easy to mess with her. I'd spent some free time working under one of our suppliers, Don. He supplied the training many of us needed to learn how to take advantage of high-quality genetics from top-notch bulls. Artificial insemination was looking like a key factor in keeping the herd productive and keeping our costs down, and it was tricky business—from how to properly inseminate, handling the semen, to overall reproductive management.

Don walked into the barn and nodded in greeting. "We got company today?"

I smiled. "Val's just here to learn a few things. An extra set of hands in case things get sticky." I stifled a laugh at the way her eyes slitted and her nostrils flared.

She followed as Don and I walked toward the alley where the first cow was secured and waiting for us. On the small table, Don arranged everything we needed, and I started cleaning the cow's backside.

"Today's Friday. It's your day," Don said as he nodded toward the glove.

"Yes, sir." I started rolling the long glove up my arm to my armpit. I placed one gentle hand on the cow's rump and began guiding the other into the cow's rectum.

I locked eyes with Val as hers went wide as saucers. "What are you? Oh my—oh my god!"

Don and I shared a laugh as she looked on in horror. Don talked me through feeling for and tilting the cow's cervix into the correct position. He then guided me through inserting the tube of frozen bull semen and depositing it correctly. Unceremoniously I removed my arm from the cow's ass, then the tube, and deposited it along with the glove in the trash.

All in all, it was done in less than a few minutes, and besides an initial moo, the cow was none the wiser.

I flashed a cocky grin at a shocked Val, and Don shuffled away to get the next cow lined up.

"What the hell just happened?"

"We're making babies today." I winked, and Val turned an adorable shade of pink.

"You could have at least bought her a drink first. Jesus." Val laughed and flipped her hand through the dark strands of her silken hair. She moved closer to the cow and gently stroked one side. "You all right, girl? Do you need a cigarette?"

"Hey, I think I left her more than satisfied."

"Yeah. You're a real Casanova." Val's eyes sparkled over the back of the cow, and the dull ache was back beneath my ribs. I rubbed it absently and went about cleaning up for the next round.

After a few more cows, Don, Val, and I worked in a steady rhythm. Val lined up the supplies, watched the thermometers, and swept away messes while we worked quickly to keep the cows as comfortable as possible.

I turned to Val. "Last one. You want to give it a shot?"

She chewed her lower lip, and despite the musk of animals that hung in the air, I wanted nothing more than to capture that lip between my teeth. "Will you help me?"

A slow smile spread across my face. I loved that she was fearless. "Of course. Step up here."

I helped Val roll the long glove up her toned arm and lingered just a fraction of a second as my hands wrapped around her rib cage. I could feel the hammer of her heartbeat beneath her work shirt at our closeness. I settled her warm body between me and the heifer.

"I have a stupid question." Val chewed her lip.

"Shoot."

"Are cows built different? Like, why the butt?"

I couldn't help but laugh. It was a reasonable question, but she was delightfully nervous in asking.

Don jumped in to say, "Anatomy is pretty much the same. It's just for easier access. To get everything lined up just right."

Val nodded, soaking in the new information.

I lowered my lips to her ear. "Are you ready?"

Her lips were set in a determined line, and with a firm nod, she stood. Don lubed up her arm, and she positioned it at the cow's entrance.

Don talked her through the process of locating and tilting the cervix through the cow's inner walls. He did the job of inserting the tube and dispatching it correctly to ensure it was placed properly. In less than a minute, it was finished.

"Make sure you hold the top of the glove before you pull out," Don instructed.

I flashed Val a cheesy grin. "Congratulations! You're a father."

"Hopefully," Don added.

Val dissolved in a fit of laughter. "This is so nuts. How is this my life?"

I steered her shoulders toward the sink at the back wall. "Pretty wild, isn't it? I've found it's messy, it smells, and I'm dog-tired at the end of the night. But . . . I've never done anything like this. I feel accomplished most days. That's a new one for me."

We lathered our hands with industrial soap, and she watched me as I spoke. Something passed over her face, an expression of wonder or curiosity—something I couldn't quite name, but then it was gone. Instead, she focused her energy on scrubbing the dirt and muck from her hands.

"Ugh. This is never coming off."

"Here." I pumped another squirt of soap and grabbed her hand. "Let me try." I rubbed and soaped her hands, enjoying the feel of her petite, soft hands in mine. As they slipped together, our fingers intertwined, and I pressed my thumb into the pressure points of her hands.

"Mmm." A throaty sound vibrated out of her and sent shock waves straight to my cock.

"Feels good, right?" I continued to massage her palms and stroke her fingers as I worked. Val shifted toward me. The warm water ran over our hands as I rinsed hers, but she didn't pull away. I took the opportunity to breathe in her soft, feminine smell. Such a contrast to the dirt and sweat of the ranch, I could lose myself in it entirely.

"You about done in there?" Don's voice cut through the air. "These girls are ready to go back to pasture."

I swallowed thickly. "Yeah. I'm on it."

Val's eyes tracked down to our interlaced fingers, my wide palm nearly enveloping hers. Our eyes met, and for a fraction of a second, I almost kissed her again. Everything inside me screamed to taste her one more time.

Instead, I grabbed her a towel and stalked out into the afternoon sun.

"THERE's a matter to discuss as a family." Ma's voice cut above the chatter at Sunday dinner, and everyone got quiet. "As you know, with summertime just around the corner, the town's farmers market will be in full swing. It's important to me for everyone here to be a part of this community. They're good people. They protect their own and they don't ask questions. One of the big draws for the county market is the opportunity to purchase fresh beef. We'll have our stand, as we always do. I'll post the sign up. Volunteers first, but if I have to assign you a shift, I'll do it."

Murmurs of "Yes, ma'am" simmered through the dining room. "All right then, join hands. Let's pray. I'm famished."

Everyone gathered around, linking hands and bowing their heads. I felt Val's warm palm slip into mine before I saw it. She wore a shy smile as her dark eyes looked into mine. I could get lost in her eyes and never want to be found. Gemma was on her other side and whispered something that caught her attention. I cleared my throat and bowed my head while Robbie said a nondenominational prayer before dinner.

When it was over, Val didn't immediately release my hand, and I gave it a light squeeze before dropping it.

In the few weeks that Val had settled onto the ranch,

she had found her groove. She laughed across the table, joked, and playfully teased. Val was no longer an outsider. Her hard work and grit had earned her the respect of everyone at the ranch. She may be a city girl through and through, but she wasn't afraid to put in the hard work and get a little dirty. Pride swelled in my chest, and I found an odd comfort in knowing she was getting her footing here. Finding her place.

Even if it was temporary.

A firm hand on my shoulder dragged my attention away from Val. "Got a minute?" The serious tone in Scotty's voice immediately put me on edge.

I glanced at Ma, who hadn't missed the interaction. "Let's go for a walk."

As we walked out the back and into the warm evening air, the buzz of cicadas mirrored the swarming thoughts in my head.

"What is it?" I asked.

"It's not good. They definitely know you're alive. My source also said that the organization is distributing pictures of you and Gemma and . . ." Scott dragged a hand across the stubble at his jaw.

"And what?" I urged.

"Val."

My stomach swooped low at the mention of her name. My heartbeat clawed up my throat as panic raced through me. "Val? What's she got to do with anything?"

He only raised an eyebrow, as we both knew Val was connected to the whole thing. She was there that night and not only saw Gemma and I, but the other men as well.

"When she was in Chicago, they could keep an eye on her. Someone got nervous when she disappeared."

"Do they know where we are?" Protective rage

simmered just below the surface, vying to be unleashed. I flexed my fist, wishing I could drive it through something.

"No." His hand clamped on my shoulder. "But you may want to consider requesting a transfer. I don't feel good about you all being here together."

"Gemma and I stay together. There's no other option."

He nodded. "You've been here a while. You're doing everything right. But maybe we talk with Ma and see if it's really smart to have Val here too. She's a liability."

I was sickened at the thought of Val leaving the ranch. I knew my time with her was already limited, but the thought of cutting it shorter was unbearable. And her being transferred to god knew where without any sort of protection? Over my dead fucking body.

"No. She's safer here. We're surrounded by nothing but mountains and valleys. There are federal agents here. Plus, I can hold my own."

At that, Scott laughed. "I know you can. Just be smart. Don't do anything to force Ma's hand."

Scotty shook my hand and looked me in the eye. I knew he meant sleeping with Val. All connections to my previous life were supposed to be severed—that included her. I had already determined that we should just be friends, but with every touch and smile, it was getting harder and harder to see why I shouldn't risk everything to be with her.

I stared out into the open valley beyond the main house.

Why couldn't things be different?

Why couldn't I have been born Evan Walker, cattle rancher, and met Val Rivera? Then nothing would stand in the way of learning everything about her—every secret, every curve.

I let out an exhausted sigh and moped my way back into the house. Dinner was winding down, and dishes were being cleared. I caught sight of Val pouring a few cups of coffee, and she tipped one toward me in salute.

The tension in my shoulders dissolved as I took in her happy, radiant face.

Gemma walked passed, placed her hand on my arm, and whispered, "I think you liiiiike her . . ."

"Shut it, Gem."

Her gentle laugh echoed down the hall as she left out the back door.

Val smiled up at me, holding two steaming paper cups. "Feeling up for a walk?"

My guts twisted and rearranged. There wasn't much I wouldn't do to feel the warmth of her smile. "'Course."

I led the way out the back door and around the house. We headed down a winding path toward a pond at the back of the main house. The trees stood tall above the path, towering over us and slanting early evening light across the planes of Val's beautiful face.

She talked about her day, and we laughed. After making a loop around the lake, she walked to the end of the dock and swung her legs beneath her like a kid. We barely fit at the end of the dock, but I settled in close to her.

We watched the sun shrink down over the tops of the pines. Her even breathing blanketed me with calm. I turned my head to find her, eyes closed and face tipped toward the fading light. Everything about her was perfection. Strength wrapped in softness.

I was looking at the plush pink of her mouth when she caught me.

"What are you thinking about?"

My voice was thick. His eyes flicked across her face and back to her mouth. "The same thing I've been thinking about since the pasture."

Val sucked in a breath, and I wanted nothing more than to gather her in my arms. My cock strained painfully against the zipper in my jeans. "You said that was a bad idea."

"It is a bad idea. We're not supposed to have connections to our old life for good reason. Ma would do anything to protect this place. That's why she has rules."

"The rules are stupid." Val's voice had gotten quiet, breathy.

"You're a cop. You're supposed to live and die by rules."

Val chuckled softly and leaned back on her arms, pushing her perfect breasts torturously into my view. "So we're going to be, what? Friends?"

I ground my teeth together, hating the idea. I sighed in resignation and held out my hand. "So, Valerie Rivera. My new best friend."

She slipped her hand in mine and laughed as she took in our hands. "Valor."

I paused to consider her. "No shit?"

"In Spanish, it means courage, value, or worth." She shrugged as if that name didn't suit her perfectly. "Also, my mom was really into Robin Hood. Knights and medieval romances and all that. She could have picked something sweet and feminine, like Marian or Guinevere. But no. I got Valor."

My thumb stroked the back of her rich, tan skin as she rolled her eyes and smiled. I looked at her, willing her to see the affection I held there. "I think it's perfect."

THIRTEEN
EVAN

Midweek, I pulled open the door to the gym and was hit with the familiar smell of rubber mats and cleaner mixed with a hint of sweat. Low music thumped in the background. The back windows were open, pulling a crosswind through the space, and the low whoosh of cars on the street was all but drowned out by the heavy clank of weights. As I signed in at the desk, I noticed a few guys squaring off and grappling on the mats, a few others hammering out push-ups. Several other people I didn't know, townspeople with a paid membership to the gym, I guessed, worked out on the machines, lifted weights, or stretched casually off to the side.

I was headed toward the back by the weights when the swish of a jet-black ponytail caught my eye. With her back to me, Val was squared up with Scotty, circling him. She was dressed in a tight tank top that left very little to the imagination and a pair of tiny black shorts that made her already long legs seem miles longer. Scotty wore an Army T-shirt and athletic shorts. Both were barefoot and circling each other. Val grinned at him, a glint of intensity in her eyes.

Her training was apparent, even to me. She kept her eyes on her opponent, her shoulders squared and her center of gravity low. Her hands were up, and she kept a healthy distance from Scott's long reach. The brawler in me knew a trained stance when I saw one, and she had it.

Like cat and mouse, they circled, neither willing to give in to the other. She faked, but he didn't take the bait, and a sly smile played at her lips. Scott moved quickly, dropping low to shoot toward her. He wrapped his arms around her waist, but she reacted just as quickly. Val sprawled, leaning her body weight into him and never allowing him to gain control.

Fuck. She was good.

Unable to gain control, he lifted and they locked up at the arms. With several inches on her, she struggled to break free of his grasp. He left his ribs open, which any street fighter would have easily taken advantage of, but rather than shout out instructions, I continued to watch.

In a flash, Val broke free and went in for a leg. Surging forward, she pushed them both to the ground. When he twisted, it looked like she'd be done for, but somehow she used Scott's momentum against him to regain control.

She was fast too.

Her legs were locked around his waist, feet locked. He outmuscled her by at least forty pounds, but her agility combined with speed kept him tangled with her. My heartbeat ratcheted higher at seeing her in a vulnerable position, but I stayed rooted to the ground. She shifted her weight, twisting her torso to gain better access to his arm. The muscles in her thighs rippled as she struggled against his attempts to break her hold.

A timer buzzed from the corner of the mat, and they both relaxed, collapsed. Val rolled off him and smacked the mat beside her. "Ah! I almost had you that time!"

Scott laughed, and when they stood together, exchanging a few quiet words, the sour taste of jealousy filled my mouth. As he spoke, she focused on the words and nodded. Scott bumped her on the arm, and she turned toward me just in time to catch me standing in the middle of the gym, staring.

When our eyes met, hers lit up, and a wide smile split her face. She was flushed, and a thin sheen of sweat coated her skin. Her black hair rioted against her half-loose pony-tail as she trotted toward me.

Goddamn, she was a beautiful, sweaty mess.

"Hey, *buddy*. I didn't know you were working out today."

"Very funny. I wasn't planning on it, but Marcus asked me to swap a shift with him, so I had a little time."

"Unfortunately, it's not yoga today," she teased.

"No yoga for me today. I just came to lift weights. You looked good out there."

"Thanks." She was still a little breathless, and I fought to keep my mind out of the gutter. "I'm actually waiting on Gemma. Want me to help you warm up?"

When her eyebrow lifted and she smiled, I wasn't sure if she was talking about lifting weights anymore. I still needed to maintain my distance if we had any chance of keeping our relationship strictly platonic. "I'm good."

"Aw. You're not afraid of getting beat up by a *girl*, are you?"

She was testing me, and I knew it. Something about that sly little smile made me unable to help myself.

"Hardly. It has nothing to do with you being a girl. You fight like someone who's trained. I fight dirty."

She stepped an inch closer, the heat from her skin seeping into me. "Is that so?"

My back tensed, every muscle on fire. It took every ounce of restraint I had to hold myself back. I wanted to wipe that cocky grin from her face—throw her over my shoulder and drag her somewhere private, rip those tiny shorts down her legs, squeeze my hard cock in my hand, and spread her open until both of us couldn't see straight.

It was torture to see my need reflected in her eyes. She wanted it just as badly as I did.

But we couldn't. Not just because we were in the middle of the gym, with prying eyes all around us, but because it was the stupidest thing we could do. One word of us hooking up and we'd both be kicked out, left to fend for ourselves without any federal protection.

I couldn't do that to Gemma, and I couldn't do that to Val. Not with my brother Parker's army of rats sniffing around.

But, fuck, Val was hard to resist.

"A warm-up." I pinned her with a stare. "Between friends."

She caught her lower lip between her teeth to hide her smile. "Of course." She slapped my back and skipped away toward an empty mat. "Let's go, big guy."

My restraint and sense of self-preservation were unraveling fast. A warm-up. Between friends. Friends could grapple and work out together, right? It didn't need to be weird.

Only with any other friend I wouldn't be thinking about rolling around the mat with them and touching every inch of silken skin. I wanted to do the right thing, but my willpower was threadbare. I was reaching my limit. A quick warm-up and I'd go to the back, lift weights, and be on my way.

Easy enough.

When we reached the center of the mat, she suppressed a grin. I slipped off my socks and shoes as she fixed her ponytail. Waiting for me, she widened her stance, bent her knees, and bounced lightly—her tits keeping time with my heartbeat.

Fuck.

With a smirk, she tipped her head to come get her.

She was strong and fast—I could give her that. But where her training kept her sharp, my experience in street fights allowed me to see things others couldn't. A drop of the shoulder, one foot crossing the other—it was all an opportunity to attack.

We moved together and shifted. If I overpowered her, I'd let her up, and we'd square off again. If she had me tangled up in those long legs of hers, I could shift and move until we broke apart and went at it again.

Pure brawn helped me some, but there were times my muscles were more of a hindrance. I was far less flexible and lithe than Val, and she used that to her advantage. Her legs wrapped around my torso and her arm at my throat, she leaned in to whisper, "You're holding back."

My hips bucked forward, knocking her off-balance as I rolled. I should have been able to pin her down, but she was fast. I surged forward and shoved her onto her back. I sank my weight between her legs as she wrapped them around me and locked her feet. I gripped her wrists and pinned them above her head. Val didn't push or struggle against me, but held my eyes with her own.

Every reason I couldn't have her surged through my mind. None of them mattered when she was right there, pinned beneath me on the ground. My cock thickened between us, and I knew she could feel it. Ever so slightly, she moved her hips—just an inch, just enough to let me know she understood exactly what I was thinking. I pushed harder against her, her lips dropping open on an exhale. My nose inches from her. I was a breath away from taking her mouth.

She laughed.

The sound ripped me from the fantasy, reminding me of where we were. I pushed off her, jumping to my feet to create some distance. Val felt good, too good, and I was high off her smell alone.

"Looks like you got me this time." Val cocked a hand on her hip and smirked.

"Yeah," I said, shaking my head to try to ground myself. "Thanks for the warm-up." I turned and stalked toward the weights without looking back at her.

Fuck. Being friends with Val was going to kill me.

I spent the next hour in a grueling workout, pushing every intrusive thought of Val out of my mind. If she popped up, I punished myself with another set. My guard was down when I was around her, and that was dangerous. I was calm. Comfortable, too comfortable. But despite my best efforts, thoughts of Val filtered in above the noise.

I knew I should leave well enough alone, but the feeling of ease I had whenever Val was around was like a drug. I had to be careful. While I couldn't deny that Val and I were connected in some way, the pain of my past and all the shit it brought with it wouldn't go away simply because Val made me feel good.

There were so many ways this could go wrong. So many

ways I could fuck everything up for the people I cared about. But my efforts to keep Val at a friendly distance were slowly turning into the slowest form of torture.

FOURTEEN

VAL

"What crawled up his ass?" Gemma stepped up beside me as we both stared at the expanse of Evan's back.

Thank god she wasn't on time. Ever. Five minutes earlier and she would have caught me dry humping her brother on the mat.

I pulled a calming breath to the bottom of my lungs and shrugged, not giving voice to the warm simmer of desire that simply watching Evan move caused beneath my skin.

"Ready to do some work today?" I assessed Gemma as she turned toward me. She wore workout leggings and a tight, long-sleeved workout top that covered her from neck to wrist. Her socks were tucked into her shoes and haphazardly thrown at the edge of the mat.

"I think so." Gemma played with the hem of her sleeve, her eyes not meeting mine. "Evan has shown me how to punch and stuff."

"Evan might be able to show you a few things, but he's all brawn. He's got the muscle to back it up. As a woman, there are a few things that you can do, despite your smaller size." My heart broke for her as she toyed with her lip, and a nervous bounce shook her leg. I gently touched her arm. "You don't ever have to feel powerless again."

Her stark cobalt eyes, the one characteristic she shared with Evan, met mine. A determined line formed at her lip, and she nodded once.

Atta girl.

"That's the fighting spirit you need. Hold on to that." I squared her shoulders to mine and stood in front of her. "Okay. We'll start simple. How to get away if someone grabs you."

Gemma's eyes darted around. Despite her brave exterior, panic licked at her. "Take a breath, Gem. We'll start with me first. Go across and grab my wrist."

Gemma relaxed, being able to emulate the attacker rather than the victim. She reached across and grabbed me.

I went through the movements slowly. Showing her how to move quickly and assertively to break the hold.

"It's all in the momentum. Little movements can give you power. Step forward here, then shoot your arm down as you twist your wrist." After a few times in slow motion, I instructed her to grab my wrist as tightly as she could. Despite her grip, I could use my movements to break free quickly.

Gemma's eyes widened in surprise, and I grinned. "See? It's pretty cool, right? Let's try it on you now."

We went several rounds with Gemma practicing the basic movement. Each time she moved more confidently and aggressively. I tightened my grip fractionally each time until I was confident she would be effective.

"Okay. Now I'm going to grab you. Hard. And you won't know which wrist I'm going to grab. Just trust the movement. Break free and then you run."

She nodded once. I walked around her slowly until I

shot forward, grabbing her wrist as tightly as I could manage. Without hesitation, Gemma stepped forward and broke free by doing exactly what I'd taught her.

"Yes! That's perfect."

Gemma beamed.

For the next hour, we practiced simple movements and ways to move her body so that she could escape if she were ever grabbed again. I explained the physics behind the movements and why they're effective, despite the attacker being bigger or stronger. Gemma ate the lesson up. She asked thoughtful questions and soaked in the knowledge.

Never having sisters, a gentle, affectionate warmth spread through me. I loved being able to teach her, empower her.

"You're ready for the next level. I'm going to show you my favorite one—for next time. What to do if you *can't* break free. Okay . . . grab my wrist again." A smile danced across her features. Gemma was much more confident in the short time we'd been working together. "So if you grab my wrist and I can't break it, I drop down here." I patted my thighs and showed her a simple martial arts horse stance, my legs wide and knees bent. "I've lowered my center of gravity so the attacker can't pull me around very easily. I'm in control."

Gemma mirrored my movements as I explained them.

"Now take your free hand and wrap it around your fist. With a pull back and a jerk up, I'm going to pop my elbow up and out. If he's close enough, that elbow will pop him in the jaw, but the simple force of the motion will break his grip. Then what?"

"Then you run."

"You got it." I stood and patted her on the shoulder.

"We'll practice this one more next time, but you did great today."

I walked Gemma toward our shoes. "Thank you for this, Val."

Gemma wrapped me in a hug and squeezed the breath out of my lungs. Over her shoulder, I didn't miss the heated stare of Evan as he toweled off the weight bench. I couldn't tell if it was annoyance or anger or something else that darkened his features.

All I knew was it was fucking hot.

BEING *friends* with Evan was just about killing me. Between the smoldering hot looks he shot my way and the small, gentle touches that lingered for hours, I was about to combust. And the warm-up in the gym? That was a mistake.

Instead, we'd taken to doing our morning chores together, and by the time sunset rolled around, I was a needy ball of energy, coiled and ready to ignite.

A critical part of being in WITSEC was severing all connection to your former life. Being friends was probably a gray area, but having sex with me would definitely be against the rules and likely enough to get Evan kicked off the ranch. That, or put him and Gemma in serious danger if anyone cared to connect me to him. It also wouldn't bode well for my hope of a promotion. I was going to have to figure out something else to burn off this unrelenting sexual tension.

Something battery powered.

I snort-laughed to myself at the thought. What would I do? I couldn't very well get Gemma, Evan's nineteen-year-old sister, to go with me to town to pick up a vibrator. I highly doubted Bob's Hardware carried what I was looking for. Plus, if I wasn't with Evan, Gemma and I were attached at the hip, and she'd definitely know something was up if I went to town without her.

Although I tapped my lip at the prospect, I'm sure Johnny could pull me a solid and get a discreet package sent to his store for me. My cheeks flamed at knowing I would have to ask him to find me a vibrator because two-day shipping wasn't a thing in this tiny town.

I watched Evan muck the stall next to mine. His breaths were even and steady compared to my huffing and puffing. The man really was a *beast*. The reality was, I already knew a battery-operated toy would be a second-rate replacement for the real thing. Likely, I'd just end up disappointed and eighty bucks in the hole.

We hadn't really talked about what being *just friends* meant, but aside from wanting to climb him like a fucking tree, he was great company. We joked and laughed. Worked and got things done. Took quiet drives around the ranch while Evan pointed out what he'd learned about cattle ranching during his stay here. Even quiet moments weren't uncomfortable.

The dull ache in my chest pinched and grew when he looked at me in a way that said he, too, wished there could be more between us. Over the past few weeks, I knew a few things to be true.

One, Evan was a criminal and I was a cop.

Two, I was leaving as soon as I was cleared by Agent Walsh.

And three—most important—nothing more could come between us without burning both our lives to the ground. It was the wrong time for either of us to start anything serious.

Not that I suspected Evan wanted anything serious.

Maybe I'd been used to being single for so long, or that my line of work kept me at a certain distance from men, but it was hard for me to imagine a man like Evan being interested in me. His attraction both surprised and delighted me. But I did know that he couldn't afford to get kicked off the ranch—not with him preparing to testify against his brother and the ranch providing protection for Gemma.

Even if I did catch him staring at my ass again. "See something you like?" I asked.

Evan grunted in response as he looked away and continued to muck the stall. "You working or just standing around?"

I propped my arm on the top of the manure fork. "Taking a breather." He glanced at me and I winked. Evan shook his head, and the rhythm of his shoveling got quicker.

So Evan and I couldn't be open with any kind of sexual relationship, that much was clear. It also made zero sense to get emotionally involved with someone. The good news was that I could definitely work with *no strings attached*. Maybe there was a way to meet our needs without anyone finding out. An excited ripple danced through me.

Despite the knowledge that these things rarely worked in the long run, Evan and I weren't here for the long run. He didn't talk about what would happen after he testified, and I planned to be back in Chicago as soon as I could. Stealing moments with him was a sacrifice I was more than willing to make. As long as we both agreed to keep it casual and we were extra careful not to get caught, everything would be fine.

Probably.

Another hard truth was that it could never work out between us, given his criminal past and my duty as a civil servant. As much as the thought of waking up to Evan

Walker every morning made tingles race down my spine, I couldn't live my life knowing—or worse, not knowing—all the horrible things he'd done. Plus, if his true identity was ever revealed, we'd live our lives constantly looking over our shoulders.

I saw the way he looked at Gemma. Evan's regrets were painful, her scars a reminder to the world that he hadn't been able to save her from that pain. Gemma deserved a new life. Something deep and quiet inside me whispered that Evan deserved one too. A life where he wasn't constantly reminded of his past. He could truly become Evan Walker and let Evan Marino die and fade into a distant memory. My lasting presence would serve only as a constant reminder of his sister's pain and the night that forced us together at the ranch.

But it didn't have to be that way. I could keep it casual. Light. Use Evan to fill a need, ease the loneliness in both of us, and warm his bed for as long as it felt mutually satisfying.

I glanced around the large barn. No cameras were inside that I could see. The security cameras around the ranch were strategically placed to watch for *outsiders*. I knew there could be plenty of ways to go unnoticed, and outside of the lodge, the outbuildings and cabins were not as closely monitored.

Once the idea took root, a springy ball of excitement bubbled through me. Evan and I couldn't do anything publicly, but what no one knew . . .

"Hey, Ev."

"Mmm." His grumpy mood only enhanced the thrill.

I glanced around, making sure that we were alone, then waited until he paused and looked up. As soon as his eyes met mine, I lifted my shirt and bra, flashing him a millisecond glance of my breasts. A giggle shot out of me as his eyes went wide with shock.

In a heartbeat, Evan dropped his shovel and stalked toward me. The clang of the metal on the concrete floor echoed through the barn. I squealed in delight and took off like a shot toward the back of the building. As I rounded a stall, Evan's strong arms captured me around the waist, hoisting my feet from the ground as his other hand pushed open the door to an office.

I struggled and squirmed as I laughed, but then his mouth was on me, hot and needy. Desire snaked up my back, and warmth spread through my limbs. My pussy clenched in anticipation, his arms tightened around me, and his tongue licked and sucked at the base of my neck.

"Playing games, baby girl?" Evan's voice was pure velvet over gravel. A breathy groan was all that I could muster. "If you don't stop making noises like that, I'm going to lose my fucking mind."

He swiveled and leaned against the empty desk, my legs straddling him. Heat pulsed through me, and a warm trickle soaked my jeans where his muscular thigh pressed between my legs.

I arched my back to get closer. "Just teasing you. Thought I'd show you what you were missing out on."

Evan shoved his hand up my T-shirt and palmed my breast, squeezing and stroking my nipple. "I know exactly what I've been missing." His jeans rubbed mine and created a delicious friction. I needed more.

Ground rules first.

"I've been thinking about us." I raked my nails through his hair, and I kissed my favorite spot on his jawline.

Evan squeezed my ass and chuckled—a deep, rumbling sound. "Me too."

"We can't get caught."

"I know." His head moved back to look me in the eyes. His blue eyes were fierce. Desire raging war against common sense.

I moved my hips against his erection. "But I want this. I *need* this." He gripped my hip as I rubbed against him, and he groaned in pleasured agreement. "I don't know how I can be here with you without this."

"Neither do I." Evan captured my lips with his. The kiss was searing and intense. Unspoken truths passed between us, and I knew his desire was as fierce and needy as my own.

Relief flushed through me as Evan sat back farther on the desk, gripping my hips and pressing my clit against his hard-on. I linked my fingers behind his head. "If we're together, no one can know. Nothing serious. Temporary— until either of us leaves."

Something on his face faltered, but his eyes moved to my lips as I licked them. He nodded once. "Just between us."

My cheeks flushed with heat as our agreement electri- fied the air. I tamped down the fluttering in my rib cage as he looked at me under hooded eyes. "If we're going to do this," he continued, "we need to be smart about it."

I nodded.

"During the day, it's business as usual. Chores. Sunday supper. Just friends."

"I can do that," I assured with a nod and the tiniest movement of my hips.

"Nights are mine." Evan paused as his eyes drank me in. His wide palm delicately wrapped around the column of my throat. My pulse hammered beneath it. "You," he whis- pered as his head bent forward to nip my ear, "are mine."

The dam broke free on a cry, and I arched back farther into him. If Evan wasn't inside me soon, I was going to die. I surged forward, pushing his back flush against the desk. Rather than give in to me, Evan gripped my ass and sat up, then stood, settling my feet on solid ground.

"Smart." Evan's thumb brushed the furrow from my brow as a frustrated grumble escaped my throat. He left me to straighten myself as he peeked out the office door to make sure we were still alone and no one had come into the barn. I pulled my wild hair into a low side ponytail to tame the strands and readjusted my bra and T-shirt. I was hot and sticky under my tee, but no amount of fussing was going to fix that.

"We're good," he said, and swung the door wide, staying to the side and allowing me to exit before him.

I growled in his direction as I passed him. "Don't make me regret this."

He smirked and rewarded me with a swift smack on the ass when I walked by. Affections warred with my heightened desire as I found my way back to finish the morning chores.

I had better be right about this.

FIFTEEN
EVAN

THE SECONDS on the clock advanced torturously slow, each tick deafening in my ears. I'd thought of nothing but her all day. It had taken every ounce of willpower I had to keep from driving my cock into Val on that office desk. Once she'd given me the green light, I was barely contained. But I meant what I'd said: we needed to be smart if sneaking around was going to work. I ignored the gnawing thought of having to sneak around with Val. Something in my gut knew she was worth so much more than that, but the selfish part of me was willing to take any time I could with her.

Trouble was, Val was like one of those flowers you'd sometimes see in the city. The ones that can grow between cracks in the concrete or through a brick wall—burrowing under your skin and setting down roots before you even realized it had happened. But the alternative was impossible. The pull I felt toward her was something even I wasn't strong enough to fight forever. And maybe she was right. Maybe we could fuck each other out of our systems and still come out on the other side of it when we were through.

The other side of it being Val returning to her life in

Chicago and me living a lie in Montana. It would have to be enough, despite the roar of protest I suppressed any time it tried to surface.

My excitement built as I thought about where I could take Val. She was eager and willing, and with two thousand acres at our disposal, I was sure I could find more than a few places to be alone with her. As I hoisted the leather saddle onto the saddle rack and began the process of cleaning and oiling it, I looked around.

The tack room was attached to an outbuilding by the riding arena in the south forty acres just beyond the main pasture.

Secluded.

My eyes roamed to the large island in the center and over the boot shelves and tack-cleaning racks. I paused on the leather straps that hung from hooks.

Oh fuck, yes.

I hurried my movements, needing to finish as quickly as possible and find a way to let Val in on exactly what I had planned for us.

I FELT LIGHTER than I had in days, a low hum of anticipation rolling through me. Walking into the lodge, I glanced at the clock. I had purposely arrived a few minutes early for Sunday supper, hoping to catch Val and arrange for us to meet in the tack room tonight. As I rounded the corner, Ma walked out of her office and intercepted me.

"Hi, Ace. What brings you around so early?"

I glanced past her shoulder but kept my breathing steady. "Just finished up early. Thought I'd see if you needed any help before dinner."

Her sharp green eyes squinted. "Isn't that sweet." Ma looped her arm through mine and guided me toward the large dining room that opened to the kitchen. There, Ma's husband, Robbie, was cooking at the stove. "Tonight was Robbie's night to cook."

He turned and picked the spoon up in salute. "Spaghetti."

I smiled, relieved. "It smells delicious."

Ma leaned closer to whisper in my ear. "I didn't just marry him because he's good with a gun."

A strange warmth spread through my chest. I hadn't grown up in a household with a mother and father who loved each other—far from it. The life I'd known was strange men and favors and money exchanged. It was a comfort knowing that there were couples like Ma and Robbie who'd been together forever and still loved each other. It was too late for me to expect anything like that, but maybe there was hope for Gemma.

Ma slid a large bowl toward me. "Mix up the salad, and we should be all set."

"Yes, ma'am." I smiled at her and winked, which earned me an affectionate swat with her dish towel. In her presence, it was easy to forget about my shitty childhood. For a little while, at least, I could pretend that this was a normal Sunday dinner with a real family.

Just as I was adding cheese and fluffing the salad, my eyes found Val. Her arm was looped in Gemma's, their heads bowed as though they were sharing secrets. Both were smiling, and my mind went blank as I took her in.

Val had traded her dusty boots and dirty jeans for a dress that skimmed the tops of her knees. Her toned, bronze legs were on full display as my eyes traveled the length of them. I blinked and attempted to breathe normally.

"'Bout done with that?" Ma's voice cut through the fog in my brain as she grabbed the salad bowl.

I cleared my throat and tried to ease the tightness in my voice. "Uh, yeah. It's all set."

"Hey, bro! You look good." Gemma's cheery smile caused a pinch in my chest. I looked between the two women.

I smoothed a hand down my chest, thankful I'd decided to take the extra five minutes after my shower to throw on a nice shirt before heading to the lodge. "Thanks. You both look . . ." The words were clogged in my throat. "Wow."

Val's skin blushed the most gorgeous shade of pink, and I had to remind myself to play it cool. Keep my distance and not let on to the raging emotions that were swirling through me. Her eyes flicked with a hint of amusement and pure satisfaction at my reaction to her outfit.

As more people filtered in, I focused my attention on helping Ma set out plates and silverware. The large island was perfect for staging the dinnerware so everyone could grab a plate and find a seat around the huge farmhouse-style dining table.

I busied myself with helping Robbie and stalled to get my reaction to Val under control. When I finally made my plate and walked into the dining room, the only chair left was next to Val. Equal parts relief and nerves skittered through me. The pull to her was undeniable, but I also had to make sure that no one else sensed it. Under Ma's watchful eye, I had to appear aloof. *Normal.*

Trouble was, I couldn't stop the flood of memories of Val and me together in the office. Her strong body pressed against me. Every time I looked in her direction, I remembered the softness of her lips against mine. I was certain the entire room could see me unraveling at the seams.

"Numbers are good. It's been a big help in consistency as we move forward with AI." Don's rough voice broke through my thoughts. He was making small talk about our efforts with artificial insemination, pregnant heifers, and the calves we could expect in the late winter and early spring of next year. "The conception rate is slowly creeping up. We're just under forty percent. The naturally bred herds are a lot more variable. Some are expected to give birth any time now. We'll see what the numbers show in another six months."

Six months.

The thought of where I might be in six months was overwhelming. Would I still be at the ranch? Would I have been called to testify? Would Val be back in Chicago? Anger swelled in my gut and dinner soured on my tongue. For years I'd spent my life living one day at a time, one paycheck at a time. I hadn't given a fuck where I ended up, so long as I had a roof over my head and food in my stomach.

Now I had Gemma to think about.

And Val. I already knew the day I watched her leave the ranch would be brutal.

As Don continued talking, I sneaked a look in her direction. She was engaged in the conversations around the table, but when her eyes flicked to mine, she must have sensed my unease. Without missing a beat, her arm dropped from the table, and her gentle hand rested for the briefest moment on my thigh. One quick squeeze and her hand was gone. But I felt calmer. More in the moment. Focused.

I could smell the clean citrus of Val's hair, and I let it soak into my brain.

Goddamn, she smells good.

I couldn't wait for this dinner to be over. To whisper in her ear and tell her all the things I'd imagined doing to her.

Val's warm laughter floated in the air. When she shifted her weight and crossed her legs, the flash of her tanned thighs was nearly my undoing.

Tonight's dinner included the agents on duty, a few daily staff, and us. It was a real motley crew that made absolutely no sense being together, but that was just how Ma liked it. She was a beacon for lost souls.

Gemma teased Scotty and challenged him to a rematch in gin rummy—he'd taught her how to play after we first got here and she'd had trouble sleeping. Their easy banter was a comfort. It was good that Gemma was settling in and making friends, though sometimes his gaze lingered a fraction of a second longer than I appreciated.

When dinner was finally over, I hurried to clear my plate. "Let me help you with that." I gathered Ma's plate with my own and started rinsing and stacking the dishes.

"It's beautiful out tonight. I'm starting a fire out back if you want to shoot the shit." Robbie rubbed his wide palms against his jeans before slinging an arm across Ma's shoulders.

"I'd like that." I gestured toward the dishes. "Gotta earn my keep first."

Ma leaned in and gave my forearm a rare but affectionate squeeze. "You really are a gem. We'll all be out back when you're finished."

I nodded and filled the sink with warm water as the rest of the family stacked dishes beside me.

"You coming, Val?" Gemma asked as she started toward the back door.

"Of course," she answered. "I'm going to grab a sweater first. Meet you out there."

Alone in the dimly lit kitchen, Val leaned against the large island across from the sink. Over my shoulder, I scanned her body. "You need a sweater because you forgot to put on half your clothes."

She smiled her knockout smile and kicked my foot with hers. "Stop with that overprotective bullshit. You know I wore this dress for you." Fire danced in her eyes as her hand skimmed her hips, and my blood warmed.

I glanced around, sure that no one else was nearby as I dried my hands. I spun on her, pressing my hips against her as she arched backward against the kitchen island. My lips grazed the shell of her ear. "You don't have to wear anything special for me. I don't plan on keeping you in it for long."

The soft moan in her throat had my cock straining against my zipper. "Damn, I want to kiss you."

Her soft breath floated over my skin. "Then kiss me already."

There was no fucking way I could make it all the way to the tack room across the farm before feeling her surround me. I grasped her wrists in my hands and swiveled, tucking us into the slanting shadows of the kitchen. "Come with me."

SIXTEEN
VAL

Evan led me down the long corridor and pulled me toward the laundry room at the back of the lodge. A warm early-summer breeze floated through the open window as the dying light filtered between the gauzy curtains. I had only a second to notice how clean the space was before he was hauling me against his large frame.

All I could think about was the fire blazing between my thighs as Evan held me against him. He lifted me as if I weighed nothing and set me on top of the cool metal of the dryer. My skirt pooled at my hips as my legs straddled his waist. His full, soft lips teased the skin at my jaw as his scruff tickled my neck.

Our mouths opened, his tongue curling against mine, my hands threading into his thick hair. His mouth moved down, blazing a trail of hot kisses along my neck. A moan rose from my throat as my eyes opened to look through the small window and see people gathering around a fire in the distance. We could get caught at any moment, and the risk of that sent a new, hot fire burning down my spine.

Evan's mouth explored every bare inch of my neck and

shoulders. His hands moved up my thighs and settled on my hips, and his thick fingers dug into my flesh. My clit buzzed with need.

I wanted more.

My nipples tingled for his touch as his hands roamed higher, circling my rib cage. The only sound was our soft moans melting together in the darkness. Sparks of electricity coursed through my body, warming every inch of me, and I was consumed by the fresh, woodsy scent of him.

Evan's mouth returned to mine, not as frantic as I felt, but demanding and in control. He deepened the kiss as I arched into him. His body was firm and tight, and I wanted every inch of him surrounding me. He rocked me against the dryer, the swell in his jeans pressing torturously against my clit. I was so fucking close.

I needed to feel him inside me.

"Evan." My voice was a hoarse whisper I barely recognized. Evan's hand dipped to my hip again, exploring the soft skin there, before running a long stroke of his fingertip along the edge of my panties.

"Fuck, you're soaked." His voice was laced with barely contained lust.

I tipped my hips forward. "Feel it. Feel how wet you make me."

Deftly, he slid one finger inside me, and my inner muscles clenched around him. "Mmm. Val." He slipped a second inside me, and energy flooded my system. I palmed his cock through his jeans as he slowly pumped his fingers in and out of me, lighting every inch of me on fire.

I made quick work of unbuttoning his jeans and sliding his zipper down. When his cock was free, my hand gripped it tightly. "Holy shit, you're huge."

My eyes met his, and a cocky smile teased the corner of

his full lips. "It'll fit." My core tightened at his promise. "But we can warm you up first." Then Evan slipped a third finger inside me.

Dangerously full, I stifled a moan as I bit his shoulder. "Yes."

"Shh. Careful now."

"Now, Evan. I need you inside me."

He slipped his fingers from me to reach into his pocket, grab a condom, and roll it down his length. The sight of him had my arousal running down my thigh as he lined the head of his cock up with my entrance. As he pushed inside me, I realized that three thick fingers were still not enough to prepare me for how full his cock made me.

Evan moaned and gripped my ass as he surged in, down to the hilt. As deep as I could take him, he paused, and I reveled in the fullness. I stifled a trembling moan into his skin. The cold metal against my ass and his masculine scent had me reeling.

His voice was rough. "You're perfect. You feel so fucking perfect."

His mouth found mine, and I caressed the side of his face as he pumped in and out of me. Overcome with a strange swirl of emotions, I tried to swallow it all down. The base of his cock dragged along my clit, sending me careening closer and closer to my orgasm. I gripped his waist with my thighs, holding on as he moved. His cock stretched and massaged me as I clenched around every hard inch of him.

"Tell me you feel that too." The gravel in his voice sent tingles racing down my spine.

I couldn't give words to the out-of-control thoughts that ran through my head. Instead, I gave in to my body's demands. When I leaned back, Evan's hand found my breasts and tweaked a nipple. As my orgasm exploded around his thick cock, his hand moved higher, wrapping around my mouth to quiet the high-pitched whimpers that came from me. Fueled by his touch, I gently bit down on his thumb as I rode the waves of my orgasm. He bucked me hard against the dryer as I cried out.

Evan thrust long and deep before pulling me close and burning his face in my hair. The sexiest guttural moan escaped him as he pumped his hot cum inside me. I stayed wrapped around him for several moments, trying to catch my breath. Tiny spasms of my orgasm were still fluttering around him as his ragged breathing kept time with my own.

He moved away slowly, dragging his thick cock out of me, and I couldn't stop a whimper. "That sound is so fucking hot." His hands threaded into the hair at my temples. His eyes searched mine, seeking something, before he pressed more hot kisses against my neck and jaw.

I pressed my face against the scruff at his neck and inhaled his scent. "I thought you said we needed to be safe," I teased.

Evan's blue eyes were darkened with desire. "Nothing about you is safe."

A satisfied smile spread across my lips, and a bubble of excited laughter threatened to escape. I bit down on my lip to keep it contained.

"Let's get you cleaned up, baby girl." Evan ran a gentle hand down my thigh before slipping all the way out of me and reaching for a clean towel. I'd moved to hop down from the dryer when his hand steadied me. "Let me."

Moving toward the white farmhouse-style sink, he soaked the washcloth in warm water. I spread my knees apart and allowed him to clean me. It was single-handedly the most erotic thing a man had ever done for me. I studied his face as he looked at me with a reverence I had never known.

Who is this man?

I fluffed his hair as he moved to clean himself and tuck his impressive cock back into his jeans. I could definitely get used to this—Evan was a beast in bed, just as I'd expected, and if we could keep it a secret, my time at the ranch would be much more enjoyable. Evan was just so . . .

Dangerous.

I pushed the thought away and instead focused on the warm, tingly glow of the best orgasm I'd ever had. Evan pulled me from the dryer but didn't let me go. Instead, he held every inch of his body against mine as he tipped my chin up.

"You're amazing."

I felt a blush bloom under my cheeks.

Keep it light. Fun.

"You're not so bad yourself."

When he brushed across my brow with his thumb, I closed my eyes and allowed myself one tiny moment of bliss.

No secrets.

No lies.

No witness protection or police duty.

Just Evan and I wrapped in each other's arms until his voice brought me back to reality. "You should get out there before someone comes looking for us."

I swallowed past the hurt that rose unexpectedly. With a nod, I left the laundry room and hurried to grab a sweater from my room. I wrapped it tightly around my middle and tried not to feel the hurt of leaving him when everything inside me wanted to stay.

I knew Evan was right. Because that was all we could ever have.

Secrets.

SEVENTEEN
EVAN

THE BUZZ and commotion of the Cedar County Farmers Market used to make my skin crawl. Once mid-May rolled around, Tipp was a hub that drew in local crafters, vendors, and farms from several counties over. At the Cedar County Farmers Market, you could find everything from a bouquet of flowers to your next puppy, and the sea of unfamiliar faces always put me on edge. It took months before I stopped constantly scanning the crowd for a face from my past, though I still caught myself doing it once or twice.

Laurel Canyon Ranch, as we were officially known, had a sizable booth. We used it to strengthen our presence in the county, form friendships, and sell beef. Today it was even better because I had been able to swap shifts with Ray and spend the entire day with Val. I was packing the cooler we'd brought on a trailer and couldn't help but watch her dazzle everyone as she set up pamphlets and said hello to the strangers who walked by. When one man stopped to ask beef questions she had little to no idea how to answer, it took only one flick of his eyes down her front for me to step in.

"All the beef is grass fed, grain finished, registered High-land beef." As my voice cut in, the man stood back and gave me a once-over.

"It's kind of pricey. Don't you think?"

"I think you get what you pay for." My arms crossed over my chest as I fought the defensive tone in my voice.

"Hormones?"

"No hormones, no steroids, no subtherapeutic antibiotics."

The man nodded, considering the information I gave him. "All right, what's your ordering process?"

"You can order in quarters, halves, or wholes. A standard quarter will have a hanging weight of around one hundred fifty to two hundred pounds. You pay for processing and pick up directly from Cedar Processing."

I glanced at Val and caught her wide eyes staring at me, and I fought the twitch of a smile at the corner of my mouth.

Who knew that impressing Val, no matter how small, would give me the thrill it did?

I took the man's order down and tucked the form into the binder before returning to set up the rest of the booth.

Val walked up behind me. "Well, I'll be damned." Humor laced her voice, and I turned to see the full radiance of her smile directed at me.

"What?" I shrugged and tried to appear unaffected by her approval.

"Nothing . . . just . . . you'd never know. You know?"

I looked at her in question.

"You know, Evan *Walker*." She gestured to all of me.

I smiled and winked at her. "I'm Evan Walker. Born and raised in Montana."

She shook her head and laughed before returning to the other side of the booth with a muttered *Mm-hmm*.

The town buzzed with energy. The smells of kettle-cooked popcorn, flowers, and pine-laced mountain air wafted through the county fairgrounds. A sea of familiar faces from town stopped by the booth to say hello or place an order.

On a sunny early-summer day, with the mountain breeze at my back, it was easy to forget my shitty childhood or the horrible things I had done in my former life. I wanted nothing more than to leave that behind.

Start fresh.

I knew I didn't truly deserve it, but somewhere along the line, Tipp, Montana, had come to feel more like any home I'd ever had. Its residents accepted everyone who filtered in—as soon as they proved worthy. I only hoped I could do that acceptance justice.

Val's eyes were wild as she scanned the booths and took in the true magic of a locally run, large-scale farmers market. I could tell she was itching to explore.

"Hey, Scotty." He turned away from his conversation. "Can you cover for a while? We're gonna grab a bite to eat."

"Bring me back one of the good sandwiches from Mrs. Roberts if she's got 'em."

I nodded and turned toward Val. "Hey, come with me."

Her eyes were questioning, scanning the crowd as I pulled her away from the booth.

"Relax." I lowered my voice to whisper in her ear. "We're taking a break."

She exhaled. "Oh. Sounds good. I've got no clue how to answer any of the questions I'm getting anyway. What about Scott?" She moved her eyes toward him.

"We have an agreement. We'll be fine for a few minutes anyway."

She nodded, and as we wound through the crowd, Val's excitement built. "This is incredible. I've never seen anything like it." She paused in front of a booth and toyed with her lip. I wanted to pull her close and suck that lip in a kiss, but instead, I chose to share her excitement.

"Well, go on. We've got plenty of time. Stop anywhere you want to."

Like a kid on Christmas, Val squeezed her hands together and barely contained an actual squeal. She paused at nearly every booth to run her delicate fingers over the items for sale. Honey, paintings, fresh produce. Dozens of stalls had fresh baked bread, artisan cheeses, and crafts.

"Can't get this in the city, huh?"

Val shook her head. "Not even close. I thought the farmers market in the city was nice, but this is unbelievable. It reminds me a little of the Mercado de San Cosme outside of Mexico City. And this is all homemade. Someone made or grew or built these things, you know? Just incredible!"

Her enthusiasm was infectious. I itched to touch her and ran my palm down her forearm, capturing her hand in mine.

Val paused and glanced down at our linked hands. Her gorgeous, deep-brown eyes met mine. I leaned to breathe in her citrus shampoo and whisper in her ear. "We're safe in the crowd. I have to touch you."

She pumped my hand once and gripped my forearm with her opposite hand to pull me closer. Together we walked, linked and looking like any other couple we saw wandering through the crowded market. Warmth radiated up my arm at her touch.

We laughed and talked about the different booths, and

we stopped at each of them that caught her eye. I didn't give a shit about any of it, but because of the simple fact it made her as happy as it did, I would forever be willing to look at someone's crocheted scarves. Toward the end of the row, something caught Val's eye, and she pulled away to go into the booth.

Handmade jewelry hung from small displays. Some were simple metal pieces and others had gemstones or rocks with bits of wire spiraled around them.

"Aren't these pretty?" Val held up a necklace and smiled.

I shrugged, not knowing much about women's jewelry.

"Look, this is a geode." Val picked up a small necklace that from the outside looked like it had a simple gray rock hanging from the chain. But on the other side, it was a tiny cavern of glittering, colored crystals. She placed it in my palm so I could look more closely.

"It is pretty," I conceded.

Val continued to scan and touch every piece in the booth. Over her shoulder, she said, "It reminds me of you. Craggy on the outside, but on the inside is something special." A small smirk played at her lips as she absentmindedly moved on to other pieces, but I was rooted to the ground. I stared down at the pretty gemstone, not truly believing her words.

Had anyone else ever thought I was good on the inside?

A war of emotions tumbled violently in my chest. I didn't deserve her affection, or her thinking I was special. She had only the vaguest idea of the man I was before ending up in Montana. The thought of her knowing the real me, the scary and darkest parts of me that still lingered at the edges, made my gut pitch and lurch.

She needs to know.

I replaced the necklace and followed Val out of the booth and toward the horses that were penned at the end of the row. Workers milled about, walking or training the horses as people gathered to either watch or assess a specific horse they were interested in buying.

I ran a hand down Val's back, settling it at the small of her waist. She leaned on the gate, resting her chin on her hand, and looked out over the small arena and watched the horses trot and eat the hay that children fed through the bars.

"I told you I would never lie to you."

Val tipped her head sideways, resting her cheek on her hand and looking at me. "Then don't."

Her simple statement held so much weight. She made me want to crack open and reveal all my secrets.

My sins.

I still didn't know if that drive to open up was to draw her closer or push her away.

I settled next to her, resting my forearms along the metal fence. "I did a lot of very bad things for a very long time."

"I figured."

"There's still a chance I have to serve time." Her eyes ripped from the horses to look at me. I stared out over the gate with my boot propped on the metal bar, but continued on. "It's not that I shouldn't have to pay for what I've done. I've come to expect it. In a way, I even welcome it."

"You really think you'll have to serve time in prison?"

"I don't really know. Joining witness protection doesn't always erase the past. Part of my plea deal was that I could be free to care for Gemma. All it takes is one prosecutor or federal judge to change their mind and I go away for a long time."

"And you're not afraid?"

A grim line formed in my brow. "I'm not." I'd become a snitch, and it was like trading away my very soul.

She studied my profile. "You think you deserve it."

"I know I do."

"There are other ways to relieve you of the burdens you carry." Her voice rose, laced with what almost sounded like anger.

"Kind of ironic, coming from a cop, don't you think?" I finally mustered the courage to look at her. Her brow was furrowed, and her eyes danced with fire.

She rolled those gorgeous eyes at me. "If you would have asked me that a month ago, I think my answer would have been very different." She rolled her lips together. "So," she said, her voice going quiet, "you were in the Mafia."

I looked around. No one was even remotely paying attention to us. We were protected by the anonymity of the crowd. "Connected. My brother, Parker, was much deeper in the organization, but we're not family. Just hired muscle."

"Muscle?"

"I was a *Reminder*. When someone was behind on payments or owed one of the guys something . . ."

"You reminded them payment was due. By hurting them?"

"An enforcer. When I had to be. Sometimes, just a visit was enough; other times it wasn't."

The weight of the truth lightened with an exhale. With Val there was no pretending. There was a strange comfort in her knowing who I was before I became Evan Walker. I could exist in my new life without having to lie about my past. We didn't need to keep up the facade of my new identity when it was just the two of us.

She sighed and stretched her arms, bending at the waist

and bowing her head between her arms. "Ugh . . . that is so illegal."

A sad chuckle escaped me. "Yep."

"Have you ever been to jail?"

The muscle in my jaw flexed. "Once or twice."

She stretched back up and looked at me. I searched but couldn't find judgment in her eyes. "So you're a Mafia cowboy?"

"Former Mafia. Guess I'm just a cowboy now."

Her eyes scanned down my back and paused on my ass. "Well, you do wear your jeans tight like a cowboy. And I'm not mad at that." Her hand found my back pocket, and she leaned into me.

The air smelled of animal and grass and fresh air, but I couldn't help but let the scent of her fill my lungs as I held my breath to savor it there. I didn't deserve for her to understand me or my past, but I had learned a long time ago to take my chances when I got them.

"We should head back. Get Scotty his sandwich before someone comes looking for us."

"Only if we can go past the nuns' booth again. I need that cheese in my life."

I mussed her hair as she bounced on her toes and looked up at me. "Deal."

As we wound back through the crowd toward the Laurel Canyon Ranch booth, I let myself imagine a life here with Val. It could be full of laughter and farmers markets and nuns who make cheese and no more agents who follow us or secrets.

The lie was easy to hold on to. My life was riddled with unforgivable sins, and Val's acceptance eased a bit of the ache that took up permanent residence in my chest.

A flash of dark hair pulled me from my thoughts. For a

split second, recognition hit me as a man walked through the crowd. Panic crept up my spine as I tried to locate him again.

It was like seeing a ghost—clear as day one second but gone the next.

I tried to shake the feeling, find the place of warm comfort I felt with Val, but my mind wouldn't let it go. The singular thought dogged me the rest of the afternoon.

Parker.

EIGHTEEN
VAL

EVER SINCE OUR hookup in the laundry room, my body had been a coiled spring, ready to explode. I craved his touch. The tender familiarity that we shared at the farmers market was surprising, but not unwelcome. Being there, walking around and enjoying the day together, was freeing.

Back at Redemption, acting like there was nothing more between us than friendship was significantly harder.

Every glimpse I caught of Evan roping cattle or bending to rake out stalls had my body thrumming with desire. It had been two days, and besides the occasional hot look he'd shoot me across the barn, we hadn't had a single opportunity to sneak away.

Gemma was also proving to be a pesky little cockblock.

I'd learned that they stayed together in one of the larger cottages, and that meant his space was off-limits. If we wanted to hook up again, we'd have to get creative. Much of my day was spent fantasizing about all the places I'd let Evan push me up against a wall and take me.

Spoiler: pretty much everywhere.

I missed his hands—the way his wide palms claimed me

and stroked fire down every inch of my skin. I could tell he was frustrated too. He was grumpier than usual, and a time or two he snapped at a worker for no reason, only to exhale deeply and walk over to apologize.

That was one of the things I'd grown to appreciate about that complicated and brooding man. If he was quick to temper, he was just as quick to apologize and try to make it right. It didn't matter if it was Gemma he snapped at or a ranch hand—he treated everyone with the same respect. Having grown up in a home where my parents never apologized but rather swept things under the rug and pretended as though they'd never happened, I was shaken to my core.

How could someone so selfless and kind get caught up in the criminal lifestyle he'd led?

It was a struggle to remind myself of who Evan truly was—at least, who he *had* been—and to make sure I wasn't viewing him only through my extremely horny rose-colored glasses.

As if I'd conjured him straight from my thoughts, I smelled his delicious man smell before I sensed Evan behind me. As I stood in the corner of the barn, finishing up my chore list, his front pressed into my back. His breath hot on my ear.

"Tonight."

A thrill ran through me.

God, yes.

I could only nod.

One large hand squeezed my hip before he slid something into the back pocket of my jeans and stomped away, his heavy boots softly echoing through the large barn. I stood for a moment, my eyes closed and already missing the heat of his body pressed against me.

I glanced around, making sure none of the other

workers saw us and appeared suspicious. He'd slipped a small piece of brown paper into my pocket. I unfolded it to find his small, blocky handwriting.

I can't think of anything but you.

Tack Room, 10 p.m.

Simple and to the point—my heart tumbled at his words. He seemed just as affected by whatever this was between us. I glanced at the clock. It was going to be a long seven hours.

"What are you looking for exactly?" Gemma flipped through the clothing rack in Johnny's boutique.

Something your brother can rip off me.

"Um . . . I'm not really sure. Just something that makes me feel more *me*." It wasn't a total lie, but I added for good measure, "All the work clothes just make me feel kind of gross sometimes."

"I hear you. I wouldn't have been caught dead in this outfit." Gemma gestured to herself in work boots, jeans, and an oversize flannel, and we shared a laugh.

I flipped through a few more tops but wandered closer to the small table with delicate bras and underwear laid out.

"Special occasion?" Johnny's upbeat, playful voice startled me, and a fresh blush heated my cheeks. I moved away from the table and scanned a new rack.

"Me? No. Definitely not."

He quirked one eyebrow, clearly not believing my bullshit. "That's too bad. My aunt Trina lives over in Chikalu Falls, and she's an absolute *genius* when it comes to women's undergarments. She sent over a few items last week to see if they'd be a hit here in Tipp." Johnny moved toward the table again and rearranged a few delicate, silky pieces. "She has a knack for picking the perfect set to have any man eating out of the palm of your hand."

"There'd actually have to be guys around here worth feeding first," Gemma chimed in as she walked up.

I bit my lip, trying to reel in the bubble of nervous laughter that threatened to escape. Johnny pinned me with a stare. "That's too bad. You know, it never hurts to have a set or two, just in case." He shrugged. "And there's nothing wrong with having sexy underwear that's just for you."

Gemma was enticed by his words as she looked over the small display. Deep down, I yearned for something lacy or silky. Something that would surprise and, hopefully, delight Evan.

"Maybe something fun just for me would be nice." I did my best to sound as casual as possible.

"Mm-hmm," he agreed.

The options were limited but a sexy step up from anything I'd worn before. I found the few lacy thongs I'd packed too scratchy for the grueling, sweaty work on the ranch, so I'd all but abandoned them for the more functional underwear I wore when I was on duty. Beige was decidedly *un*sexy.

I let my fingers roam over the silky fabrics, and one deep orchid purple set caught my eye. It wasn't overly intricate, but the smooth fabric was thin and luxurious. The matching balconette bra had a thin feminine lace. I imagined how hot it would be to feel Evan's mouth on my nipple as he toyed with it through the delicate fabric. My nipples tightened in anticipation.

"This one." I had to clear my throat, thick with desire.

Johnny winked. "Perfect choice."

"I'm getting some too. I like the black lace. So hot."

I nodded in encouragement. Gemma may be younger, but she was a woman in her own right and deserved to feel sexy too.

With my new lingerie tucked away in tissue, I found a simple black wrap dress that complemented my curves. I really had nowhere to wear it, but I meant what I had said—work boots and flannel shirts were fine, but sometimes I just wanted to hold on to the last, fading bits of *me*. This dress was something I would have chosen for a night out in Chicago or a dinner date.

Something small and sharp twinged in my chest. There was excitement sneaking around with Evan, but given our current situation, we could never go out on a proper date. It would always be lies and secrets. The truth was too risky.

As Gemma continued to browse, I went to the register.

Johnny's voice was low enough so only I could hear. His eyes flicked in Gemma's direction. "Are these for a certain tall, dark, and stunning man?"

Panic flickered through me, but there was something deep and trusting about Johnny. "Please don't say anything," I pleaded. "Not even to Gemma. I could lose my job and they could be in danger if anyone uncovers his connection to *before*. Besides, his future is here and mine isn't."

He straightened, rang up my items, and squeezed my hand as he handed the small bag to me. "Your secret is safe with me."

Relief flooded through me.

When we finished walking through town, we grabbed a bite to eat at the local coffee shop and café, Brewed Awakening. I looked at the coffee shop's sign with the happy little mug with hearts for eyes and chuckled at the pun. Warm, smiling faces greeted us both, and I was reminded of the small-town charm I'd only ever read about or seen in Hall-mark movies. In the late-afternoon summer sunlight, the entire town felt enchanted.

Safe.

It was a feeling I couldn't quite place, but it felt alto-gether glowy.

Later, Gemma drove recklessly down the open roads, reminding me that I should offer to drive next time. She then dropped me off at the lodge before bouncing down the dirt path toward her and Evan's cabin.

Four hours to go.

NINETEEN

EVAN

When the door to the tack room creaked open, my heart jumped into my throat. Slim fingers wrapped around the thick wooden door as Val peeked in.

I crossed my arms over my chest, leaned against the island table, and smiled.

Her dark eyes went wide, taking in the interior of the tack room. I'd forgone the harsh overhead lighting and instead brought two small lanterns. The dim, warm lighting soaked Val's tawny skin as she stepped inside. She was glowing and my chest swelled. Her dress was a simple black that wrapped around her small waist and flowed out around her hips. My eyes traveled down her tight little body and stopped when I came to the canvas sneakers. She wiggled her toes and my eyes met hers.

"Apparently, heels really aren't great on a ranch."

I moved toward her, capturing her elbow and dragging my hand down her arm. I gave her hand a gentle squeeze before brushing my lips against the back of her knuckles. "You're perfect."

Her lashes lowered as she tried to hide the blush that

stained her cheeks. My fingers felt her pulse point beneath the thin skin of her wrist—her heart hammered wildly out of control.

I used my other hand to brush a strand of hair from her face as she closed her eyes and leaned into my touch.

"You are stunning. But why are you nervous?"

Her eyes fluttered open. "I'm not nervous," she lied.

I smirked. In the weeks Val had been at the ranch, I'd been studying her. Learning her quirks and tells and the masks she sometimes wore.

Her throat bobbed as she swallowed, and I followed that path with delicate, featherlight kisses. The ache in my cock intensified the slower I went. It was a delicious torture for both of us.

"Evan," she breathed.

"Mmm." The rumble from my throat had Val's hands tangling in my hair, pulling me closer. She arched slightly, urging me to go faster, give her more.

I took a step back. "I have something for us."

Her breathing was uneven as she looked at me. I know she figured coming here was just to fuck, and her look of surprise was worth it.

Next to the large island, two stools were pulled up, facing each other. A bottle of wine and two paper cups, along with a stack of playing cards, were on the table. I gestured toward one seat.

"Evan. What is this?"

I couldn't hide my smile at the confusion and awe laced in her voice. "A date."

She sat, crossing her gorgeous, toned legs and resting her chin on her hand. "You are full of surprises."

A wink was my only response.

You've got no idea what I have in store for you, baby girl.

I poured two glasses of wine. "Red okay?"

She took her glass and sipped. "More than okay. It's my favorite."

I took a tentative sip and tried not to make a face.

"You don't like it?"

I shook my head, surprised by the dry, complex flavors that exploded on my tongue. "No. I'm just a little surprised. Wine isn't really my thing. Really, the only wine I've had was the table wine at some Italian restaurants, but this isn't half bad."

She nodded. "All wine is definitely not the same. You made a great choice." Val clinked her paper cup with mine, and her coppery brown eyes sparkled in the dim light of the lanterns.

I grabbed the stack of playing cards and started shuffling. "How about a game?"

Her eyes danced with excitement. "Yes! I love cards. What's your game? Texas Hold'em?" She tapped a finger against her plump lower lip, and I paused. "No," she continued. "I bet you're a blackjack kind of guy."

I smiled. "You got me. But how about we up the stakes?"

Val sipped. "What do you have in mind?"

I traced a finger up her arm. The goose bumps that erupted under my touch only spurred my desire for this woman. "Truth-or-dare blackjack. If I win the hand, you pick. Truth or dare."

"You forgot I was a cop who worked the midnight shift. I had *plenty* of boring nights to get good at cards. You're on."

I dealt the hand and watched as Val eyed me carefully.

A jack and three for her. "Hit."

I flipped a card, revealing the king of spades, and she shot me a playful glare. "Bust. Okay, truth or dare?"

Val's pert mouth twisted as she considered her options. "Truth."

"What's your favorite color?"

Her brows drew downward. "That's it? Of all the truths, that's the thing you want to know about me?"

I leaned in close to her, breathing in her bright scent and running my nose along her jawline. My hand gripped her thigh and squeezed. "I want to know everything about you. But I gotta start with the basics."

A shiver ran down her as I nipped at her jaw.

When I leaned back, releasing her, she sighed. "Green, you tease."

My laugh was hearty and genuine. It was so easy to allow myself to be open with her. I lived my life being guarded and careful. It was the smart choice, but there was something about Val that pulled me in and wanted to share every corner of my soul with her.

We spent the next few rounds with simple truths—my childhood pet (I never had a pet, and she looked genuinely heartbroken at the thought), how difficult her first years as a Latina police officer were, and her first boyfriend's name (Derrick—he sounded like a douche). Val upped the stakes when she finally dared me to take off my shirt.

I happily took my time unbuttoning and peeling it off. For a moment, her eyes held on the scar on my chest. Something passed over her features, but she seemed to hide it, and I didn't miss the way Val licked her lips as I tossed the shirt aside. When I won the next hand and she chose a dare, I couldn't resist. "I dare you to not move."

Her eyebrow tipped up. I grabbed her hips and positioned her in front of me. My fingertips started at her shoulders and made a torturously slow descent to her hips. There I found the tie to her dress and pulled. She sucked in a breath as the cool air hit her skin. I allowed the black fabric to drape open, revealing a matching bra-and-panty set in a deep plum.

"Holy fuck." I sucked in a breath.

Her chest heaved as my eyes roamed over the perfect curves of her breasts. Just under the dark fabric, I could see her nipples, tight as diamonds beneath the lace.

Leaning forward, I nipped one firm peak with my teeth and felt the weight of her in my other hand. Her moan sent hot liquid pooling in my middle as my cock strained against the zipper of my jeans.

I took my time torturing us both. Heat rolled off her in waves as I kissed and teased and sucked at her over the lacy bra. Her hands shot to my hair, threading around the back and pulling just enough for the pain to stack and build upon my growing pleasure. She was a wildcat and I needed more.

With her hands tangled in my hair, I looked up at her, heat intensifying my glare. "You moved. I win."

Desire darkened her eyes, and she looked down at me under her lowered lashes. "What's my punishment?"

My cock twitched at her words. "You want to be punished for breaking the rules, baby girl?"

Val sucked her lower lip into her mouth, and I had to stifle a moan. She was so fucking hot. I hitched her hips up and sat her atop the island table. With her dress still draped open and pooling at her sides, I reveled in her beauty.

"You are so fucking gorgeous. Just look at you."

Her eyes glanced down, then met mine again as she opened her knees a bit wider. Glancing around, I spotted the thin leather strap of a horse rein hanging on a wrought iron hook beside us. Slipping it from the hook, I let the smooth, worn leather glide through my palm.

I carefully laid her back and positioned Val's arms above her head. "Seems like you need a little help staying still."

She flashed me a wicked smile as I anchored her to the table. After I tied her hands with the cord of leather, I trailed my hands down her skin. Heat radiated from my fingertips up my arm. I tucked the stool underneath me as I settled between her open legs. Wrapping my hands around her thighs, I gently squeezed. "Don't. Move," I warned.

Val arched her back and nodded.

Starting at her knee, I peppered her toned thighs with open-mouthed kisses, licking and sucking as I drew closer to her center. The smell of leather and sex hung in the air, and the anticipation of touching her, tasting her, was almost too much to bear.

"Talk to me. Tell me what you want." I rubbed my nose along the slit in her underwear, loving the damp spot that gathered at her opening.

"Yes. That."

I licked again at the edge of the purple thong, not giving in to what she wanted. "No, baby. You can do better than that. Tell me you want me to eat your pussy."

"Jesus, Evan. Yes."

I planted one hand on the table beside her and leaned over her. Layering kisses over her ribs, I nipped at the thin skin. "Say it."

"I want you to eat my pussy. Fucking devour it."

A growl tore free from my throat at the desperation in her voice. Without removing them, I pulled the fabric to one side and ran the flat of my tongue up her seam. The taste of her slick arousal crashed over my tongue, and I nearly came. I licked and swirled around her clit, using every moan and arch of her back to learn what she liked—what she needed to get closer and closer to the edge.

Her inner walls pulsed around my tongue as I groaned into her. Tasting her, touching her, was better than I could have ever imagined. Using my thumb, I teased her clit and watched her teeter on the line between ecstasy and bliss. I slipped one finger into her heat and had to palm my raging cock. I needed to make her come before I slipped deep inside her. Still circling her bundle of nerves, I added a finger.

She pulled her knees higher. "Oh yes. Don't stop."

My mouth found her again as I slowly pumped my fingers in and out. I could eat her pussy for hours if she'd let me. She was close, and I would do anything to taste her orgasm.

"*Ahí, papi.*" Lost in pleasure, I had no idea what she was saying but *goddamn* was it sexy as hell.

After another swirl of my tongue, I increased the pressure, and she exploded around me. Spasming waves of pleasure stroked my fingers as I lapped up every drop of her.

Visions of surging inside her took over. I stood, causing the stool to topple loudly behind me. Leaning forward, I untied the leather strap from her wrist, gently massaging the tender skin. Val's hands immediately flew to my arms, pulling me closer.

"Yes. I need to feel your hands on me." My voice was thick with need for her.

"You feel too good. Kiss me." Val pulled my face toward hers, deepening the kiss as she tasted herself on my tongue. One delicate hand stroked my cock, and I broke the kiss to unfasten and unzip my pants. I pulled them just low enough to get my dick out and ready, reaching for the condom stashed in my pocket.

"Let me." Val sat straighter, plucking the condom from my hand. She made quick work of opening it but unrolled it down my cock achingly slow. Once it was on, she squeezed the thick base and cupped my balls. My hands flew to her hips, dragging her closer to the edge of the island table.

I hooked my thumbs under the straps of her thong and slowly trailed it down her legs, careful not to rip the delicate fabric.

I want those panties later.

Still slick, I rubbed the head of my cock against her folds. I was swollen and twitching to push inside her, but I wanted to make it last. To feel how her pussy milked my cock and took every inch of me deep inside her.

Inch by inch I went deeper, holding her hips steady and spreading her open. Together we watched as our bodies connected and met, hip to hip. Once fully seated, I paused, overwhelmed by how tight and wet Val was.

Together our breathing was ragged and shaky.

Val spoke softly. "Is it supposed to feel this . . ."

"Destined?" I dug my fingers into her hair as I pulled her close for a searing kiss and pumped in and out of her. Her nails scratched my back as we climbed higher and closer. I palmed her breast, rolling and pulling one nipple between my fingers.

The soft flutter of her walls around my cock was too much, and after another full, deep thrust, I stilled and poured myself into her. I came long and hard and clutched her closer with every spurt. Several moments after I'd finished, I still clung to her.

My thumb brushed across the slight sheen of sweat at her brow. She gulped, and the buzzing in my ears quieted. I stared at her for a long while, trying to give voice to the words that threatened to tumble out of me.

When I said that we were destined, I'd spoken the first word that came to me, and it was a simple truth. There was something more than Val and me meeting by chance. I felt it in my bones. I didn't care that I was nothing more than a reformed criminal and she was an officer.

There has to be a way.

"My whole body is tingling." The humor in her voice broke me from my thoughts, and I looked down at us, still connected. I grabbed the condom at the base and slid from her, immediately hating the loss of her around me.

"It's never been like this for me." My eyes pleaded for her to see the truth there before I moved to the sink to clean up.

Her impossibly long lashes floated down as she wrapped her dress closed. "You're too much."

Quickly closing the distance between us, I pulled her to me. "I don't fucking care if I'm too much, because I can tell you this: I will never get enough of you."

A smile played at the corner of Val's mouth, and I kissed her in that exact spot. She hopped off the table and shimmied into her panties before tying the wrap on her dress.

Without looking at me, she spoke and moved toward the door. "Okay, well . . . I'll just . . ."

"Where do you think you're going?"

She motioned toward the door. "I mean . . . I guess I just thought—"

"You thought wrong." I'd cut her off as my strides ate up the distance between us. "This isn't just a meaningless fuck." Irritation rolled through me.

How had I not shown her what she was doing to me? How she shredded my insides and I'd happily come back for more.

I smoothed her hair away from her face and tipped her head, forcing her to look at me. "I know the simple fact that I want nothing more than to take you back to my place means you should probably leave, but I can't let you go. Not yet."

Val's eyes fluttered closed, and I pulled her into me. I knew I needed to tread lightly. If this was going to work, Val needed to lead, and I didn't want the big feelings taking root in my chest to scare her off already.

"A few more hands," I continued, turning us away from the door. "Just hang out with me. Let's finish our wine, and then we'll go."

The smile that slowly spread across her face eased the tension in my shoulders. I kissed the top of her head. "Besides, maybe I'll let you win a hand and tell you about the time I stole a car."

"Stop it!" Laughter was back in her voice as she plugged her ears and walked back to the island table.

My laughter was true and easy.

"All right, big guy. Deal 'em up."

TWENTY

VAL

Even days later, if I closed my eyes and stilled my breathing, I could ignore the musk of the hay barn and still feel the pulse of Evan as he finished inside me.

"Someone has a secret!" Gemma's giddy, singsong voice cut through my fantasy.

My eyes flew open, and a faint buzzing in my ears deafened me to the room as panic prickled at the base of my skull.

She knows. Shit. Shit!

"Sorry. I didn't mean to startle you." Gemma's brows drew together, darkening her crystal-blue eyes, her hair half-swept up in a little messy bun at her crown.

"Hi." I cleared my throat. "Uh, yeah. It's okay."

Gemma finished climbing the ladder to the top of the hayloft and plopped down onto a bale, crossing her slim legs. Her eyes glittered, and her wide smile was radiant. She really was a beautiful girl.

"So," I said, ready to face the truth of being caught. "I think it's important you know—"

"I'm moving out!" Gemma's excitement bubbled out of her, cutting my confession off midstream.

I stared at her as her leg bounced and creaked the old floorboards. "Oh, come on!" She planted her hands on her hips. "I thought you'd be excited for me!"

"Wow, Gem. Yeah, no, I am. I'm just confused. Moving out?" Relief mixed with newfound confusion. Were Evan and Gemma leaving the ranch? A sharp and disconcerting pain pinched behind my breastbone at the thought.

"Yes! My *own* place. I can't *even* right now! They finished renovation work on one of the small cottages. It's closer to the lodge than our place now, and I buttered Ma up—told her I wanted to take some classes at a nearby community college and needed somewhere I could study, listen to the online lectures, that kind of thing. But you can't tell Evan yet. Ma's going to help me break the news."

"No, I wouldn't say anything, Why would I say anything?"

Gemma flicked her wrist in dismissal. "I know you guys are like, whatever."

I continued cleaning and sweeping the loft, but I couldn't meet her eyes. "I'm not sure what you mean. Your brother and I aren't . . ." I shook my head with a dismissive laugh, the lie dying a bitter death on my tongue.

"Yeah, okay. Whatever, I don't care. I just *had* to tell you!"

I frowned. I thought Evan and I had been doing a pretty good job at keeping outward appearances, but Gemma definitely seemed to have her suspicions.

Who else has noticed?

I steeled myself against the reality that I would have to be diligent in making sure that any interactions between us were strictly friendly.

No. Cordial.

Aloof? Fuck, I don't know how to do this.

"A place of your own. Wow."

"Maybe one day I can even get my own apartment off the ranch. But this is something."

"How do you think Evan will take the news?" I tamped down my errant thoughts and tried to muster up the excitement Gemma deserved. This was a big step in regaining her confidence and her independence.

She rolled her eyes. "He'll freak out. Sometimes I think he forgets that this isn't just a cattle ranch. The place is literally *crawling* with federal agents. I'll be fine."

She had a point.

I smiled a true, genuine smile for my friend. "I think it's a big, exciting, important step! Lots of girls your age go to college and live on their own."

"Exactly. Plus, I won't have to worry about seeing Evan walk around in a towel after his shower. Yeesh." She exaggerated a shudder, and I couldn't help but laugh with her. I also tucked that fresh, steamy image of Evan in a towel away in my mind for later.

"It really is a big step. I'm proud of you."

Gemma walked over to hug me. "What about you? You don't have to stay in the lodge. There are plenty of cabins you could claim as your own. Ma wouldn't care."

I squeezed her back but continued with my chores. The truth was, I hadn't really thought at all about moving into the little homes. Those were typically reserved for the long-term residents. Federal cases could drag on for years, and the cottages allowed a more homey space during that time. I had never planned to stay in Montana that long.

"My room is fine. It's got everything I need."

"Is it because you're going back?"

I offered her a sad smile, but nothing more.

"Ugh. I hate that. I'll miss you so freaking much. But I totally get it. I miss the city too."

Changing the subject to something that didn't make my heart feel so bruised, I asked, "Have you finished your chores yet?"

She smiled a playful grin and pinned me with a glare, but descended down the ladder. "See. You're even starting to *sound* like him."

My laughter filled the hayloft, and in Gemma's absence, I breathed in. Here in Montana, it was like you could smell the sunshine. Even the dank, musky smells of the animals had grown into a comfort of sorts. Gemma was taking a step forward in her life, and pretty soon I'd be able to do the same.

Why does that thought make me want to cry?

"Will you dance with me?" I sneaked Evan a playful grin as we walked toward the Tabula Rasa.

"Absolutely not." His jaw was flexing and tense.

We hung back, as the group of us from the ranch took up nearly the entire sidewalk.

I looked at his hard expression and couldn't help but poke the bear. Just a little. "Is it because you're a horrendous dancer? Do you do the white-man overbite while you only move your shoulders? It's okay. You can tell me."

Evan's face twisted in disgust. "I'm an incredible dancer. How dare you."

I covered my laugh with my hand and tried to settle the giggles that threatened to draw attention our way. "Fine. Be a stick-in-the-mud."

Evan subtly leaned into my space and lowered his voice. "There's no way in hell I could have you in my arms and everyone not see what's between us." The penetrating rumble of his words soaked through me.

Delight danced in my veins. Getting under his skin was half the fun of our interactions. "Oh, I felt what was between us the other night," I joked, lifting an eyebrow to glance at the front of his jeans.

He feigned shock and clutched his imaginary pearls. "I feel so . . . used." The giggle that erupted from me finally drew the attention of a few from our group, so I refocused my attention forward and quickened my pace, putting a few extra steps between us.

Evan Walker was funny, but sensitive under all that dirt and denim.

I could love him.

The thought was there before I could stop it—barreling through my mind like a freight train. In my heart, I knew it was a simple truth. In another life, I could love Evan Walker. He was a broken boy, grown into a man who'd pieced himself back together. He deserved someone to hold the leftover pieces that didn't quite fit.

Protect those precious bits of him no one else appreciated.

As we approached the bar, Evan held the door for me but didn't lose his playful grin as he growled, "Get inside."

Our group of ten gathered around two wooden tables, pushed together and tucked in a darkened corner. You'd think celebrities had shown up at the Rasa and not a few dirty cowboys. Delighted smiles and whispers floated through the crowd. A few men walked over, shook hands, and returned to their seats as our server appeared.

We ordered food and drinks, and my tummy rumbled in

delight at the thought of a greasy cheeseburger. Evan purposely sat across the table and several seats down, and I had to will myself not to gawk at his chiseled jaw or the way the corded muscles of his forearms made his tattoos come alive.

I wasn't the only one who'd appreciated his appearance. He'd caught the attention of several women in the bar, and I fought the pang of jealousy that reared its head. I hated that if he'd wanted to, Evan could take any one of them on a date. A *real* date—hold her hand and spin her around the dance floor and kiss her good night without having to worry about a damn thing.

I grumbled to myself, sinking lower in my seat and watching the crowd slowly gather on the dance floor as the band played a mixture of classic rock and country music. I surveyed our group too. After a few moments, it became obvious which of us were actual marshals and who was there for a burger and a good time. Maybe it was because of my training at the academy, but the most obvious tell was how their eyes never stopped scanning, and there was never an instant when they were completely relaxed.

Of our ten, I was fairly certain three were definitely on duty.

Thinking of them and my own training, I felt rusty. Had my instincts really gotten so far off? Thank god for the opportunity to spar at the gym or I would have really regretted my lack of practice and training. I needed to refocus. Get serious. It had been weeks since I'd even thought about my police work in the city. Sure, I missed parts of it— the nights when you knew you made a positive impact for someone or the camaraderie of the guys—but the grueling days of manual labor on the ranch, followed by stealing heated moments with Evan, consumed my days.

I thought of Eric and made a mental note to see if there was a way to check in on him. Knowing him, he was partnered up with someone who was driving him up a wall, maybe even actually making him work instead of nap, and likely the batteries were dead on his Taser.

A steaming basket of fries and my cheeseburger were a welcomed reprieve from my thoughts. Throughout dinner, conversation ebbed and flowed, people danced and laughed and listened to the band roll from one song to the next.

"All right, folks. It's the third Thursday of the month, which means it's open mic for the next two hours. Sign-ups are at the corner of the stage."

My eyes swooped across the table at Gemma. She didn't look at me but sank lower in her chair. I gently kicked her foot under the table, forcing her eyes to meet mine. I raised my eyebrow and tipped my head toward the stage. On a few of our rides into town, Gemma would roll down the windows and turn up the radio. That girl had a set of pipes, and if I could sing like that, I would have jumped at the chance to sing for people.

She looked at me in disbelief and mouthed, "No."

I mouthed back, "Go on." But she only tightened her arms around her front, pulling her sweater higher up her collar, and looked away.

Between songs, a few residents of Tipp sang karaoke—a trio of college-age girls sang Reba McEntire's "Fancy." One old cowboy sang an offbeat rendition of Tim McGraw's "Real Good Man" to his darling wife, who clapped and swooned in the front row. Even Al the bartender shocked me when he got behind the mic to swing his hips and rock out a popular Ed Sheeran song. When he leaped off the stage and walked back toward the bar, I caught his eye. He tipped his head in recognition and winked.

Unbelievable.

In this town, nothing was as it seemed. It was quirky and odd and hilariously different from any place I had ever known. The enthusiasm was infectious, and I tapped my foot to the beat. Together we hooted and hollered for anyone brave enough to get up on stage and sing.

My carefree laughter felt foreign but electrifying. Every week there were fewer and fewer faces I didn't recognize. I even started getting waves and making small talk with strangers on my trips into town. It was an odd sense of belonging. In Tipp, no one knew your history, because no one asked. Once you proved your mettle, you were woven into the fabric of the town, much like a patchwork quilt whose pieces didn't match and shouldn't have gone together but kept you warm all the same.

After a few more songs, our collective group agreed that it was time to call it a night. We shook hands, gave hugs, and waved our goodbyes to the friendly faces at the bar. The ten of us walked in twos, my arm looped through Gemma's, back to the trucks. When Evan's rig wouldn't start, I looked around, unsure of what to do.

Scotty offered the first suggestion. "We could shuttle back and forth. Between the two trucks we can squeeze in all but a few. Come back and get the rest?"

Evan nodded, but worry creased his forehead as he popped the hood of his truck to inspect it.

"Val and I can stay back with Evan," Gemma suggested. Scotty turned to her and nodded.

Ray tapped an impatient foot. "Just call Uber."

"We have Uber here?" I was amazed that this small town would have the service.

"No. *Hubert.* He's always home and can swing by and gather y'all up."

The sheer absurdity of it forced a barking laugh to explode out of me. Gemma and I clutched each other and laughed like a couple of loons. It even got a small laugh from Evan, lightening his grim mood.

"Thanks, Ray. I'll give him a call." Evan pulled out his phone, and the three of us, plus an agent, Hank, waved goodbye. The remaining two trucks carried everyone back to the ranch while we sat on a bench and waited for Hubert.

A few short minutes later, Hubert pulled to a stop in front of us. His maroon minivan was rusted and squealed when he used the brakes. "Heard you had some trouble? Hop on in!"

Gemma stepped in front to take the middle seat, followed by Hank. Evan and I moved forward at nearly the same time.

"After you." I hoped his deep voice would always send that tingle down my spine.

I risked a wink. "Such a gentleman."

As I stepped into the van and moved toward the back, a firm but gentle hand held my hip and guided me up. A tug pulled at my belly and warmth pooled. Evan's touch was fire against my skin. I tucked myself into the back corner of the van. Evan's sheer mass took up most of the room and was an easy excuse to touch him.

I stared straight ahead as Hubert made small talk, pointing out various things in town and making off-color jokes. He really was Tipp's very own Uber. I kept my eyes from peeking over, steadying them out the small back window.

Evan's large hand found mine. In the privacy of the back seat under the cover of darkness, he tucked my hand in his and placed it possessively in his lap. I bit the inside of my lip to keep the smile from exploding across my face. I wanted to sigh and lean my head against his strong shoulder. Instead, I moved slowly so my fingers brushed against the bulge in his jeans.

Evan shifted subtly and tried to ease away. Undeterred, I stroked the outline of his cock and felt it grow beneath my hand. The interior was dark, and I chatted with the rest of the group as I continued my covert assault on Evan. I could barely see his nostrils flare as his hips gently pushed upward, letting me feel the stiff length beneath my hand.

I stroked and teased. The thrill of getting caught had my heart fluttering. Gemma and Hubert were in a friendly debate about the merits of popular country music. I added my opinion here and there but continued to squeeze and tease Evan's cock.

"Don't you think, Evan?" I smirked in his direction.

He cleared his throat. "Yeah. Sure." He had no clue what I was talking about and I stifled a laugh. His jaw tensed and he swallowed hard.

When we pulled onto the dirt path that led to the lodge, I hopped out of the van on my side, waving a friendly goodbye to our transport.

I turned to our group, smiling brightly. "'Night, Gemma, Hank. Good night, Evan."

Fire danced in Evan's eyes, but I bounded through the door of the lodge and up to my room.

TWENTY-ONE
EVAN

"WELL, it's all going to hell now." Ray's snarl was clear as he spat on the earth beside our boots.

My shoulders were heavy from the grueling Friday morning I'd worked through. In the early hours of the day, a heifer from the naturally bred herd was found birthing, but it was not going well. After what felt like hours standing in a pasture in the spitting rain, our attempts to figure out why she was struggling were in vain. The calf was stillborn, and its mutated form caused one younger ranch hand to get sick right there in the pasture.

The calf was born a conjoined twin—one body, but its head was almost split in two, causing stress on the mother during birth. We'd be lucky if we didn't lose her too. Occasional calf loss was a real but unfortunate reality of life on a cattle ranch. But this was more. Genetic abnormalities were not a good sign for the health of the herd nor the reputation of the quality of cattle we produced—another reason the managers were pushing for artificial insemination.

And, according to Ray, a seriously bad omen.

Though ranchers were more superstitious than most,

they believed with such conviction that it rattled me too.

If it is an omen, what the hell is coming?

I tried to ignore him and his perpetual bad mood as I scrubbed the dried blood from my hands, but it was tough to shake.

I was little more than muscle on the ranch and wasn't in charge of making any real decisions, but I had come to care about the ranch and what it stood for. Protection for those who needed it. A fresh start for some. Redemption, or at the very least, the beginning of the path toward it.

My thoughts turned dark as Parker's face filled my brain. Ever since the farmers market, I'd found myself more on edge and suspicious than normal. A deep, irrational side of me wanted to kidnap Val, tuck her away kicking and screaming. Keep her and Gemma someplace safe where Parker and his army couldn't find us. Trouble was, Val was supposed to be nothing more than a friend.

I was proud of myself. The entire time at the bar I hadn't looked at Val more than three or four times. Even then, I made sure to make my glances quick and not let my eyes catch on the curve of her ass or how her throat bobbed when she laughed at something that she found truly funny.

But the proximity of her in Hubert's van had me coming apart at the seams. Val had teased me and her playfulness was addicting. I looked over, and Ray was still staring at me like I was something he'd stepped in. I was certain he could read my thoughts, so I buried them deep.

"I'm gonna tell you something, kid." I glowered in his direction, but Ray kept talking. "Do what's right, not what you want to do."

I furrowed my brows, not understanding his meaning. Ray's piss-poor attitude kept most people at a distance. Why he was suddenly feeling chatty was a mystery.

When I stayed silent, he continued, "You're gonna throw away a second chance on a piece of city ass. Damn shame."

I straightened to my full height, enraged that he'd referred to Val like that, fists clenched at my sides when I understood his meaning.

He knows. Fuck.

All I could do was stare at his back as he limped away.

THE DAY WENT from bad to spectacularly shitty as it wore on. I had been summoned to Ma's office, and she looked pissed. Gemma sat in a chair and refused to make eye contact with me.

I looked between the two women. "What's this about?"

"We need to have a conversation."

I breathed through the panic and flexed a muscle in my jaw to steady my nerves. "I'm listening."

Ma's voice was soft but controlled. "You know that here on the ranch, we do more than hide people away until their day in court."

"Of course."

"When the idea for this place came to me, I dreamed of giving second chances to people who deserved them. People who needed a leg up when life was busy pushing them down and beating the piss out of them. You of all people know what opportunities we have. Doors we can nudge open."

A sickening self-loathing laced through the words that sneaked past my gritted teeth. "I'm well aware of how lucky we are to be here."

Ma rounded my chair and placed a gentle hand on my

shoulder. "There's no need to give yourself a coronary. I simply want you to understand why I do what I do."

I looked at her but stayed silent, ready to hear that I'd royally fucked up. Gotten caught and was no longer welcomed at the ranch.

"Gemma is ready to walk through one of those open doors."

My head whipped up, and my eyes pinned a worried-looking Gemma. "What does that mean?"

Gemma swallowed hard but found her voice. "I'm moving out."

My brain blinked off after she spoke. I could only stare between the two women as I struggled to find my words.

This has nothing to do with Val.

Instant relief was replaced with confusion as Gemma's words began to sink in, and my heart pounded harder.

"Move out? Like fuck you are." I was on my feet, rounding the chair and pacing between the door and the desk.

Ma stood, the air in the office crackling with tension. "Ace." She shook her head. "She is a young woman. She can make her own choices. She'll be taking residence in one of the empty cottages."

"She needs protection. To be safe."

"She'll have all the protection she needs while having the space and autonomy to grow as a woman. Gemma has decided to enroll in a few college courses. This is a *good* thing. It's what we do here."

I scoffed an angry puff of air out of my nose and rolled my eyes. "She's a kid and you're going to get her killed."

At my tone, Gemma stood. Her tiny frame took up hardly any space, but she came toe-to-toe with me, lifting her chin and jutting her finger hard against my chest. "I'm smart and I can learn new things. You may look at me and see her, but I will be more than our mother. I wasn't asking for permission. I'm moving out."

Tears welled in her eyes as she stormed out of the office, rattling the keyboard as the door slammed behind her.

I sank back into the chair.

Dammit.

My skin felt too tight. I dragged my hands through my hair, feeling like a piece of shit. "Was this your influence?"

Ma laughed. "Hardly. You don't give her enough credit. That girl hasn't discovered it yet, but she's got fire in her."

I rubbed the spot in my chest where Gemma had poked me. "I know she does. But she's so young, she needs . . ." I had no fucking clue what she needed. All I knew was that *I* needed to feel like she was safe. That she was protected from anyone who wanted to hurt her and that she wouldn't get carved up in someone's basement because I couldn't help her.

"She needs her big brother to support her and love her." Ma's hands found my shoulders. "Part of you loving her is letting her make her own mistakes. She can't get into too much trouble here. The cottage is within walking distance of yours, and we'll be sure to make extra rounds if need be."

I growled at her logic, hating that she was right. "She'll be taking classes?"

"The community college in Chikalu Falls has online offerings. She can stay safely here and earn credits."

I relaxed slightly. It was an easier pill to swallow, knowing she would still be at the ranch and not moving farther than a few hundred yards away. Still, it felt like everything was shifting and changing beneath my feet.

"Okay. It's fine."

A burst of laughter startled me into looking at Ma. "Oh,

sweet boy. Gemma was right—neither of us was asking your permission." I rose as she wiped tears of laughter from the corner of her eye. "You are a stubborn, protective soul. Off you go."

Ma ushered me out the door as the conversation rattled around in my skull. I needed to track down Gemma, apologize for being an asshole, and see what I could do to make things right between us.

Then I was finding Val.

"You actually helped her pack?" Disbelief dripped from her voice as she looked at me across my small kitchen table. It was still a mindfuck to see her sitting in my cottage.

I nodded and sipped my beer. "Yup."

"I'm proud of you." Val's smile and words tightened the vise that resided in my chest whenever she was around.

Or I smelled her shampoo on the air.

Or simply thought of her.

"I don't think there's anything to be proud of. My hands were pretty tied."

"I'm proud because you could have thrown a hissy fit. Instead, you supported her. I'm sure that means more to her than you realize."

It was a strange and almost uncomfortable feeling to know someone was proud of you. In my years in Chicago, I inspired fear, respect, and intimidation, but never pride.

"Hissy fit? Me?" I lowered my brow and growled as I pulled her chair toward me, scraping it against the floor. I leaned in, breathing in her scent and trailing soft kisses up the column of her throat.

Her head tipped back, and her eyes moved across the

room, taking in the small space, washed in a warm glow. She leaned toward the little cork board, pausing to look at the few pictures I had on it. Val glanced at me, skepticism evident in her squinting eyes. "I never took you for a senti-mental guy."

I shrugged and buried the hot coal that burned in my chest. "A few pictures are all I have left." I reached across her to point one out. "That's Mom."

Val lifted the corner of the picture to get a closer look. My mother was young in the photograph. Her face was slightly away from the camera, a cigarette hanging from her fingertips. She was partway through a good laugh—a sound I wished I could remember. She looked happy and exactly how I wanted to remember her.

"God, Gemma looks just like her." Val set it back down and pointed at another—three rough-and-tumble, dirty kids. I was young, grinning up at the camera, flanked by two older boys. A muscle worked in my jaw. "Is this you?"

I could feel my smile, a tiny tug at the corner of my mouth. "That's me, my brother, Parker, and that's Michael."

The way Val's deep caramel eyes glittered at me over the dim lighting in my own kitchen churned something deep within me.

Maybe if I could keep her look of adoration, it could erase the memories of who I used to be. I reached forward, grabbed her ass, and hauled her into my lap. Her strong legs straddled me as I ran my hands up her back, eliminating any space between our bodies.

I ran hot, hard kisses up her neck, slowing at the sensitive spot just below her ear. My cock thickened at the low, needy sounds that purred in her chest. She felt it and tilted her hips to grind against me.

"I can't believe you're here. It's unreal." I felt like I had swallowed rocks, my voice grating against her delicate skin.

"I'll be wherever you are." If I wasn't already sitting down, with Val's legs locked around me, her breathy words would have knocked me on my ass. Even if I could have her for only a little while, I was going to worship her.

I stood, carrying her weight against me and not releasing my tight hold as I walked through the small cabin toward my bedroom. When my knees found the bed, I lowered us both to the mattress, covering her body with mine. Her sensuous moans made me feel ravenous, but I took my time, dragging my fingertips achingly slow down her rib cage.

Since the moment I'd seen Val at the bar and then later discovered she was the officer from Chicago, I'd been drawn to her. A surprising dichotomy of hard lines and supple curves. I wanted to explore and treasure every one of them.

I paused, forcing her eyes to meet mine. Hardworking, funny, resilient. I placed my hand at her temple, brushing my fingers in the soft hair that framed her face. I was lost in her. Nothing mattered but the feel of this woman in my arms. I would ruin my whole life for her and beg to do it again.

"I . . ." Dangerous words were recklessly close to pouring out of me.

Val was everything I never deserved and more than I could have ever hoped for. I knew, if I could never say the words, I could show her. My fingers wound around the hem of her shirt as I peeled it up, burning a path with hard, wet kisses. I teased her nipple through the thin fabric of her bra and was rewarded with a quick intake of her breath.

"Take off your shirt. I need to feel you." Val's hips tilted forward as she pulled at my T-shirt. I pushed my hips farther into her, pressing my hard cock against her clit. I sat on my heels to remove my shirt but quickly covered her body with mine and grabbed a handful of ass.

Val's hands smoothed over my bare shoulders. She stopped at the angry scar and feathered her fingers over the small, uneven circle.

Her brow was furrowed. "You were shot because of me."

I kissed her forehead where it wrinkled. "I was shot because of my own shitty choices."

Her beautiful brown eyes met mine. "You saved my life."

Now you're saving mine.

I smothered the thought with a kiss, and I moved my hands to unbutton her jeans and pull them down her thighs, along with her lacy panties. I moved slowly, taking my time to appreciate her soft skin, how her breasts moved higher with every soft gasp.

I kissed her shoulders, dipped my tongue into the valley of her collarbone, and sucked on the pulse point that hammered in her neck. As I traveled down the curves of her body, I slipped her bra down, exposing the rigid tips of her nipples. My tongue dragged across them, one by one, sucking and teasing gently with my teeth.

"You're going to fucking kill me."

I chuckled at her words. I was determined to take my time with her. She was here, in my space, and nothing was going to rush me. Val's sensitive skin prickled, and I used my body to give warmth to her. I sank my teeth into the inside of her hip bone, and my cock pulsed at how she bucked beneath me.

Farther and farther down, I moved my mouth over the valley of her thighs as I inched lower. My tongue dragged a wet line across the thin skin. Val was exposed to me, in every way, and I had never seen anything more stunning. My rough palms traveled back up her inner thighs as I pushed them apart and nestled closer. My hot breath moved over her, and I moaned the second my tongue felt her slick heat.

I pressed a firm kiss at her clit, nestling my face into her. Her hands tangled in my hair, and I knew exactly what she wanted.

I lavished hot, open-mouthed kisses across her clit, teasing and sucking it into my mouth. I dipped my head lower, licking her pussy with the gentlest touch. Her hands pressed into my hair as her hips lifted to meet me.

"I know what you need, baby girl. I won't even make you say it this time."

I drove my tongue across her, wide and flat, the sound of her strangled cry muffled by her strong thighs pressing against my ears. My head moved upward in slow, languid strokes.

"Your pussy tastes so fucking good."

Val's hands clutched the sheet beneath her as she moaned.

"I've got you. You don't have to be quiet here. Tell me."

"Yes, Evan. Holy shit that feels good." Her pussy pulsed around my tongue as I dipped it inside her. I wanted to taste her as she came. I moved upward. I licked my lips and sucked her clit into my mouth again, teasing and sucking and flicking it with my tongue.

Val drove her hips farther into me, a hot ball of pleasure tightening my back. On a cry, Val's pussy clenched, and I moved lower, drawing out every pulse and spasm.

My kisses turned light again as she came down. She was limp on the bed, and pride tugged a smile as her thighs still quaked. Her arm was flung over her eyes, and as she relaxed, she peeked at me from under her arm.

"You are a dangerous man."

"Yes, ma'am." I palmed my cock, desperate to drive into her and feel her pussy wrap around me. Val watched in appreciation as I stroked the outside of my jeans.

"Pull that cock out."

I lifted an eyebrow at her command.

"You heard me." Val pulled herself to her elbows and smirked. "Last time you insisted I tell you what I want. I want to feel your cock in the back of my throat."

I stood at the side of the bed, unbuttoned my pants, and slid down my black boxer briefs. Val scooted off the bed and kneeled in front of me. The sight of her looking up at me, her mouth slack with desire, was enough to almost finish me. I swallowed thickly.

Val gripped the base of my cock with a firm hand as she dragged the flat of her tongue up the underside of my cock, teasing the vein that ran its length.

I released a deep, throaty moan. Val sucked and stroked, her soft lips stretched around the thickness of my cock. I watched her beautiful face as she sucked me to the back of her throat and swirled her tongue. As her fingertips teased my balls, she worked the muscles in her mouth and throat to pulse around me, and I nearly came undone.

I pulled her from her knees and gripped her ass, lifting her off her feet. I needed her—*now*—to be buried so deep in her I couldn't remember anything but her wild black hair and her body wrapped around me.

"Evan, there's one more thing I want."

"Anything, baby girl."

"I want to feel you. I'm on the pill. Clean. Please let me feel you."

My jaw ticked. I had never fucked without a condom, but with Val, I didn't want anything between us either. I looked deep into her eyes. "You're safe with me."

Hovering over her—her on the bed, my feet planted on the floor—I lined the head of my cock to her entrance and pushed in, just the first inch. With quick pulses, I teased her, reveling in how hot—how wet—she was for me. Unable to take any more, I surged forward, bottoming out as her legs wrapped around my hips. Together we bucked and moved as I pumped into her.

I watched with reverence as we moved together. My hand planted against her ribs, the other teasing and rolling her nipple through my fingers. I was spiraling out of control, chasing my own release.

"I'm close, baby. Can you come with me?"

"Yes, Evan." Val bucked harder as I moved my hand lower to find her swollen clit. "*Más duro.*"

"Tell me, baby. Tell me what you need."

"Harder." Her ragged, needy breaths pushed me over the edge.

A few slow presses of my thumb as I pumped into her, and her pussy clenched and throbbed around me. Pressure built until I was right there with her, releasing everything I had as I continued to move in and out.

My hands dug into her hair at the base of her neck as I deepened my last thrust and held her onto me. The cabin was silent, our panting breaths the only sound that filled the air. I moved again, my cock hypersensitive to every flutter of her pussy around it.

I released my grasp on her hair and slid my hand down her throat and settled it on her chest. Val's heart pounded under my palm.

She gulped in a breath. "That was . . . intense."

No better word could describe my feelings. I could only nod in response. Easing back, I took a deep breath to steady myself. Val sat up, her long legs dangling on the edge of the bed, and looked around. I was usually the one who reminded her that we needed to be cautious, but in that moment, fear danced over me that she would stand up, gather her clothes, and slip into the darkness.

"Let's get cleaned up. Take a shower with me."

Val lifted an eyebrow but didn't object. After leading her to the bathroom, I let the water get as hot as we could stand before pulling her close and letting the water run in rivulets down her back. I held her, stroked her back, and stayed silent. My heart thumped hard in my chest, and I knew she could hear it. Her contented sighs released the tension in my shoulders. I took care in washing her hair and letting my soapy hands caress the contours of her hips.

It was getting hard to do the right thing.

Instead of getting dressed and saying our goodbyes, I crawled into bed and lifted the sheet and comforter, nodding toward the empty space beside me.

"Hop in."

"Evan, I . . ." Val toyed with the inside of her lip. A sick part of me loved that she was just as torn as I felt.

"Just for a minute. I'm dog-tired."

Without another word, Val slipped into bed beside me. The smell of my body wash on her skin caused a tingle in my spine as I breathed her in. I curled into her, tucking my arm beneath her head and lifting my knees, molding her to me. Val relaxed into me, the entirety of my front formed to her back from chest to toes. I wrapped my arm around her, pulling her even closer.

Her soft voice broke the silence. "Did you ever want to quit?"

My lips pressed together as I struggled to find the right words. In my silence, Val rolled to look at me, her dark-brown eyes serious in the dim light. "I thought about it a thousand times. Every day. But thinking like that will get you killed."

In her silent understanding, I found the bravery to keep going. "I learned to bury it so deep no one could see it. I held on to the things that made the life bearable—food, clothes, money, power." I faltered on that last one, but I'd promised her nothing but the truth, and I was stripped bare.

"Do you miss it?"

I exhaled heavily. "I miss a good hot dog."

Val pushed against me. I pulled her closer.

"I don't know. I don't miss hurting people. I don't miss watching my brother change. I don't miss worrying that my best friend will put a bullet in me one day. That's what's funny. I know right now I have a target on me, and I feel safer than I ever have."

"You are safe. I can protect you."

I smiled, pulled her close, and kissed her forehead as she nestled in closer. In our quiet bubble, I could pretend that this was real. That this thing between us didn't have the power to absolutely destroy me.

Propped on my elbow, I spent entirely too long memorizing the lines of her face and the swoop of her eyelashes. I kept the conversation light despite the thunderous thoughts pounding in my skull. Eventually Val drifted off to sleep.

I gently kissed the curve of her bare shoulder. "I know you should leave, but if you go now, you'd be taking my heart with you."

TWENTY-TWO
VAL

THE FOUR A.M. walk of shame from Evan's cabin was anything but shameful. Though my heart squeezed when the door clicked behind me, I had never been so sated in my life. Everything felt deliciously sore. Like a teenager, I sneaked in the back door of the lodge, avoiding eye contact and giving Scotty a terse nod as he drank a cup of coffee in the kitchen. Maybe there really was something good about having your own cabin. There were a lot fewer eyeballs watching your every move when you had your own space.

Bone-tired, I slogged through my Saturday morning chores. I'd hoped to spend the day with Evan, but he was called away to help with another project on the ranch. The quiet gave me plenty of time to think about the intensity of the night before.

Evan and I had had fantastic, toe-curling sex together, but last night there was something different about the way we moved with one another.

Dangerous.

Hard as it was to admit, there *was* something dangerous

about Evan. Not just his former life, but in what he was doing to my insides. Thoughts of him were muddied by future thoughts. Thoughts I shouldn't be having when I knew that we could be only temporary.

By the time afternoon rolled around, I needed a nap. My boots felt like a thousand pounds as I dragged myself through the lodge toward my room.

My foggy brain registered Ma's scratchy voice when I passed her office door. "Hey, Val. Do you have a minute?"

My eyes were dry, and it took effort to not crumple from exhaustion.

"You are dead on your feet." She eyed me from boots to nose. "I won't keep you. Just wanted to give you this. Agent Walsh would like you to call him back."

She handed me a piece of paper, and the tiny hairs on my neck stood up. I stared down at the black numbers against the stark white of the paper, my mind uneasy. "Thanks. I'll give him a call."

"I'm heading out. You're free to use my office if you'd like. Just close the door on your way out."

I nodded. "Yes, ma'am." I continued to stare at the slip of paper. "Thanks," I said weakly at her back as she walked away.

In the empty office, I pulled the phone toward me. I chose a seat in front of the desk rather than behind it. Even though she wasn't around, it still felt inherently wrong to sit in Ma's chair. I dialed the numbers and waited, my heart thumping in my ears.

"Special Agent Walsh."

I cleared my throat and hoped it hid the wariness in my voice. "Hello, Agent. This is Val Rivera, returning your call."

"Ah, yes. Officer Rivera. Thanks for returning my call."

I picked at the seam in my pant leg and waited for him to speak again. Nerves rattled my insides.

"I'll get straight to the point. You passed your psych. Congratulations."

My throat squeezed and my eyes burned. I had no words. A swirl of excitement, relief, elation, and dread rioted in my stomach. I tried to recover as quickly as possible. "Thank you, sir."

"So how has it been? Life on the ranch."

Exhausting.

Thrilling.

Confusing.

Sexy as fuck.

"It's been fine, sir."

"Interesting. You're the first and only person we've placed at the ranch that wasn't an agent or a witness."

"Yes, sir." *What the hell is he getting at?*

"Strange little town, Tipp. Isn't it?"

"I still find the whole concept a little mind-boggling. Sometimes, I think everyone's clueless—that they really are hiding in plain sight—but then I'll walk down the sidewalk and someone will give a knowing nod or a little smile, and I get the feeling they *know.*"

"Dorothea knew what she was doing when she opened the ranch. How was your experience with the witnesses under our protection?"

Oh shit.

I hoped he couldn't use his secret agent lie-detector skills over the phone as I fed him as much bullshit as I could.

"A lot of people keep to themselves, which I understand. Those I have interacted with have been friendly."

"Friendly." He paused as though he was considering

something. "Good. That's good. Well, next steps for you will be to get you home."

The room felt wobbly and my stomach roiled.

"Yes, sir." My voice was tight and barely squeaked out of me.

"There's a debriefing process, and these things do take some time, but we'll get the ball rolling. I'm sure Chief Dunleavy will be thrilled to hear from you. I'll be in touch."

I choked out a goodbye and hung up the phone. Hot tears pooled in my eyes and burned my nose. I've wanted nothing more than to leave Montana since the day I arrived.

Why the fuck do I feel like crying?

I'm going home.

Despite not knowing when, the fact remained—my time in Montana was over. I didn't have the heart to call Chief right then and there. My fingers hovered over the keys, and the dial tone rang in my ear. My throat was thick when I swallowed, and I forced myself to key in the numbers.

The hollow ring was deafening. When the receptionist answered, I stated who I was and asked for Chief Dunleavy and waited on hold.

"Rivera!" My partner Eric's voice boomed on the line. "Where the *fuck* have you been?"

My chest pinched tight but I forced a laugh. "Aww, you miss me."

"Shit yeah I miss you. I miss my naps."

I rolled my eyes and felt my muscles relax. "I was looking for Chief."

"He's out, but Mary Lou said you were on the horn. I couldn't believe it."

Eric and I slipped into easy camaraderie as he filled me in on all I'd missed at the station. I ended the call but didn't ask him to take a message or remind him to tell the chief I'd called. Something just . . . stopped me.

I was drained. I dragged myself up the stairs to my room and collapsed on the squeaky, lumpy bed. I closed my eyes and readjusted, remembering how plush and warm Evan's bed was. How warm it was in his arms.

How safe.

I pulled my arms around myself and fought the incessant thoughts tumbling through my head before I finally succumbed to sleep.

"WHAT'S WITH YOU?" Gemma pulled her cropped hair away from her face.

"Nothing's with me."

"Hmm." Her stark blue eyes flicked up and down, skepticism written all over her face. Together we walked through Tipp's local library. The warm, musty smell of old books reminded me of my grandfather. "We should grab a coffee and head back after this."

I agreed, and we wound through the stacks at a casual pace. I recognized a few friendly faces and offered a small smile and wave. Everything about Tipp, Montana, had changed since I first arrived. Once cold and unfriendly, it had somehow transformed to quirky and warm and protective.

Gemma studied the back of a few novels, and I walked away to flip through true crime stories before deciding that soon enough I'd be back to living through the horrible things described in those titles. When I found Gemma, she had four books piled in her arms.

"You're not getting anything?"

"No, I couldn't figure out what I was in the mood for."

"Here." Gemma balanced her books in one hand and flipped the top book in my direction.

I caught the book in the air and flipped it over.

"A romance?"

"Don't you dare make a face. These books are amazing."

I turned the book in my hands. "There's not even Fabio on the cover. My grandmother would be so disappointed."

"Well, let me tell you this. I can guarantee your grandma hasn't read a book like this." She pointed at the book. "That's no bodice ripper. Romance novels nowadays have everything from reverse harems to full, open-door sex scenes."

My eyes widened, and I gave the book the attention it deserved. "Really."

She grinned. "Really. Since I'm stuck here with *literally* no available guys, these are the perfect replacement." She pointed to the book she'd tossed at me. "You'll love that one. It's got a grumpy, damaged hero. The heroine is tough. She's a horse jockey and she works for him. The tension is *so hot*. Plus, I didn't see the big twist coming, which adds major points."

I turned the book over. I had my own hot hero on the ranch, but with all the downtime, escaping in a book wouldn't be terrible.

We made our way to the counter before I realized I didn't hold a library card. "Hey, can you check this out for me? I'll be sure to return it on time."

Gemma's face crinkled up. "Sure, but why don't you just sign up for a card? It takes, like, five seconds."

A lie was sour on my tongue. I didn't have the heart to tell her that I wouldn't be here long enough to get much use from a library card. I also couldn't tell her before I let Evan know about my call from Agent Walsh.

Stuck, I smiled and stepped forward. "You're right. That makes sense."

While I waited for my card from Emily, the surprisingly young and stylish librarian—growing up, all my librarians were elderly and smelled faintly of powder and dusky roses —I scanned the local Tipp bulletin board.

Cars for sale, a missing dog, notice of a neighborhood-wide yard sale. It was all so charming and hometown. I moved closer to read a poster that was partially tucked behind the high school musical flyer.

Try Tipp—See How It Feels
56th Annual Barn Party

"Is this for real?" I held the paper out for Gemma. "Did they actually make a *just the tip* joke?"

"Yes! Johnny was telling me about this. Isn't it hilarious?"

"What is it? A town party?"

"Exactly. The locals put it on for charity, and it's got music, dancing, all that. It's this Saturday. Do you want to go?"

The thought of dancing with Evan and a night of laughing with Gemma sounded perfect. "Think they'll let us?"

"We'll have a tail, for sure, but Ma can't really tell us *not* to. Besides, she's pretty cool about stuff like this."

"I guess I'll need to find some dress boots."

"Yes! The Boot Barn!" Happiness radiated from Gemma. I hadn't seen her this excited in weeks and, to be honest, the thought of a small-town barn party had my insides vibrating with excitement.

I grabbed my freshly made library card from the librarian, still warm from the laminator, and pressed it into my palm. For the time being, I could ignore the sting of disappointment in leaving and experience a small-town party for myself.

TWENTY-THREE

EVAN

"How the fuck did they talk you into this?"

Scotty walked toward me as I leaned against the large kitchen island in the lodge. He was dressed in a white pearl snap shirt, and his boots were as freshly oiled as mine.

"You covering us tonight?"

"Shit no. Last week Gemma told me about the barn party. I'm going." His grin spread across his face as we shook hands. "Your tail is Rodriguez and Miller. Waiting on Gemma?"

"Yeah. She ran up to grab Val. We're all going to head up there. I think a few of the guys plan to stop in too."

"It's a fun day. Nearly everyone from town will show up eventually. All right, man. Find me and we'll have a beer. Stay safe." He shook my hand again and swaggered off toward the back door. I ran a hand down the front of my black pearl snap. I grabbed my dark denim with the fewest stains on them and oiled my work boots. It was a far cry from the tailored suits I'd gotten used to in Chicago. Tonight I'd almost considered adding a belt buckle.

Almost.

After an eternity, I could hear Gemma and Val's laughter float down the hallway, and my chest got tight. They rounded the corner and my eyes crawled up Val. Starting at her boots, pointy toed and high heeled, the supple brown leather stopped midcalf. The dress was long but had a high slit that showed off her curves as it nipped in at the waist. Her long, tan legs went on forever until they met the bottom of the flowing dress with large embroidered flowers that barely covered her thighs. The low V neckline had my mouth going drier than the desert.

In Gemma's presence, I recovered quickly. "You ladies look lovely."

Gemma curtsied. Her short denim dress was cute, with long sleeves and a high neckline. It even had a Southwest-style belt around it that made a tinkling sound as she moved. "Such a gentleman."

I held out my arms to them both. "Shall we?"

They slipped their arms into mine, and Val gave my biceps a quick squeeze. Pleasure hummed through me as I led them to my truck.

Gemma hopped in the back, leaving the front seat for Val. As she sat, the slit in her dress rode high on her thigh, and my palm itched to touch her. I flexed my hand at my side to keep from reaching across the bench seat and feeling her smooth skin. Thankfully, the girls kept the conversation going, and I focused on getting us across the county to the party.

As we approached, even I was shocked at how big of an affair the town of Tipp had put on. A large gate was deco-rated in twinkle lights and led to a long gravel driveway edged in pine trees. My truck bounced along the path, and I kept my eyes laser focused on the road in front of me and not on the way Val's chest bounced along with it. Down the winding path, cars and trucks began to pull to the sides and park. The entire field was filled with rows of vehicles. A large barn had both doors swung open, and the deep bass of music poured out. Laughter and whoops and hollers filled the air.

I parked and hopped out, circling the hood to help Val. I gave her a wink and enjoyed the slow blush that crept onto her cheeks. Once Gemma and Val were ready, we headed toward the barn. Rodriguez and Miller weren't far behind. I gave them an acknowledging nod, which was ignored. They melted into the crowd but never strayed too far from sight.

"Isn't this wild?" Energy radiated off Gemma as we walked into the barn.

I took care of the cover charge, and my hand found the small of Val's back as we walked into the barn. The dance floor was already flooded with people, all in step and doing the same line dance. A large stage at the front of the room had a full band setup. The name Colin McCoy and the Dirty Pidge Boys was scrawled on the bass drum.

Val leaned in close to talk over the music, and I let her citrusy shampoo wash over me. "We're going to make a lap before we decide where to sit. Maybe get a drink. Sound okay?"

"It's perfect."

I grabbed two beers and a Coke for Gemma as I watched them lace through the crowd. They passed tables and waved to people, pointing and taking it all in. I noticed how the men in the room also appreciated the view, and a possessive grumble rattled in my chest. Val snagged an open table, and I headed their way.

Before I could sit down, Val grabbed my hand and tugged me toward the dance floor. "Come dance with me."

"Not happening." I dug my heels in further.

"Come on, spoilsport." Val bit her lower lip and shimmied her shoulders in what I assumed was her version of the bad white-man dancing she'd teased me about before.

"You're not the kind of woman to hear 'no' often, are you?"

She smiled, knowing she had clearly won. "Nope."

She tugged me toward the dance floor as the music shifted to a slow, bluesy song.

Damn, that dude can sing.

I spun, pulling Val closer and settling my mouth just outside her ear. "That's fine. I like giving you what you need." My fingers dug into the fabric of her dress at her lower back.

Val melted into me as I led her around the dance floor. I loved the way her body moved with mine.

We fit.

I leaned my head toward hers, breathing in the fresh citrus of her hair. "I could go a thousand lifetimes and never forget how good you smell."

Val leaned away, and her honeyed eyes looked into mine. No one had ever *seen* me the way it felt like Val could. I couldn't imagine this kind of unwavering acceptance from anyone else. I pulled my forehead down to hers and made a silent vow.

I will be the man you deserve.

Val sucked in a delicate breath and tightened her arms, as though she'd heard my thoughts. We were so different, but I had to find a way to make this work.

When the next song picked up, I carefully transitioned us to a two-step. Her eyebrows shot up, and her bright smile crinkled at her eyes. "Smooth moves, cowboy."

"I've picked up a few things. Growing up in Montana

and all." I winked at her. When I fumbled a few steps, we both laughed and I shrugged. "It's a work in progress."

Val shimmied and twirled with impeccable rhythm, and when someone asked to cut in for a dance, I shot him a murderous glare—tensed and ready to go.

Val simply rested a hand on my chest. "Sorry. I'm here with someone."

That's right, asshole. She's here with me.

"I like the sound of that," I said, pulling her into me again. Not caring who was around and tired of keeping secrets, I lowered my mouth to hers. Tentative at first, I teased the corner of her mouth.

Val's eyes searched mine, and I brushed a strand of hair from her face. "I can't pretend anymore."

"Pretend?" Her voice was light but urgent.

"I can't pretend that when you walk in the room, the temperature doesn't shoot up twenty degrees. Or pretend that the ache in my chest isn't from watching you walk away."

"Evan, you can't say things like that."

"I can and I will. You deserve to know."

It was Val who pulled me into her, crashing her mouth to mine. I pulled her close, my hands gripped at the back of her dress. She opened for me, her tongue sliding over mine, confirming I wasn't the only one tumbling.

No connections to your former life.

I ignored the warning bells. The only thing that mattered was that Val was there, in my arms. I knew when she left, she'd be thousands of miles away, but I'd still be tethered to her.

When the song ended, we broke apart. I brushed a thumb over her cheekbones, memorizing the flecks of caramel and brown in her eyes. I led her back to our table to catch our breath. Gemma had wandered off and was a table over, deep in conversation with the guy who ran the little shop she loved.

Val perched on the stool, letting her knee rest against the outside of my thigh. My arm draped possessively on the back of the chair as we both looked around the large barn.

"Did you know places like this *actually* existed? It's like a movie."

"Very different from Chicago."

Val clinked her bottle against mine, but a look I couldn't explain swept across her features. "About Chicago—"

"Guys!" Gemma nearly crashed into the table as she leaned across it. "You have to come outside! They're doing a lumberjack competition. Ev, you have to do it!"

"A what?" Val's laughter floated across my skin.

"No." I crossed my arms and planted my feet wide. No fucking way.

"Dude, come on," she whined. "First prize is a whole spa package, but it includes goat yoga!"

My face twisted. "The fuck is goat yoga?"

Gemma rolled her eyes. "It's yoga, *with a baby goat*. Oh my god, it's all over Instagram. Do it for me. Do it for *charity*!"

Val bit her lips to keep from laughing and tipped an eyebrow in my direction. I knew I was fucked.

When I sighed, both women cheered in unison.

Gemma clapped her hands. "Yes!"

"You got this, big guy." Val patted my back as we walked toward the exit and out into the warm almost-summer air.

TWENTY-FOUR
VAL

I couldn't believe Evan was actually doing it. Gemma had that man wrapped around her little finger, and he didn't even realize it. The Tipp, Montana, Axe of Kindness was, in fact, for charity. The money collected, along with the wood they split, went to local families who'd fallen on hard times. Men of all ages, sizes, and strength lined up to show off their skills in a relay race–style wood-splitting competition.

Spectators could also bet on their favorite competitor, all of the money going to the families in need. Scrawled on a large dry-erase board were nearly twenty names with dollar amounts next to them. I proudly put fifty dollars on Evan and watched on the outskirts as he stood behind a large stump. He dragged his hands down his thighs, and I squeezed my own together.

Fuck me, that man is sexy.

The announcer of the competition spent a few minutes talking with the competitors, ensuring they knew the rules and expectations. She then turned to the crowd. "Let's hear it for them!"

The crowd roared in appreciation of the men. She introduced each person in the competition, and the donation totals continued to steadily rise. Evan was a clear favorite, the dollar amount next to his name going higher and higher. Other men had fans as they laughed and flexed, getting into the fun of it all.

When she got to Evan, he introduced himself and was rewarded with whoops and hollers as he lifted a hand to wave. I cupped my hands around my mouth. "Take some of it off!"

Gemma burst out laughing, and Evan hammered me with a death stare. A ripple of laughter pinched my sides. With some added encouragement from the announcer, Evan finally smirked and shook his head. The crowd went crazy as he slowly unbuttoned his shirt and peeled it off. Hard, rippling muscles flexed, and I had to press my tongue to the roof of my mouth to keep it from wagging. His tattoos snaked up his arms and molded onto his back. Even the way he stood oozed sex appeal. He adjusted his belt and jeans, and I thought I was going to combust.

Donations for Evan shot through the roof. I clapped and bounced on my toes, shouting him words of encouragement. He lifted his chin to me, and Gemma grabbed my arm. A ripple of excitement ran through the crowd as the men readied themselves. The announcer raised an air horn as Evan's long fingers flexed at his sides. The strong muscles in his back tensed as he watched and waited.

With a blast of the air horn, they were off.

～

"Here's your goat yoga." Evan tossed the envelope over his shoulder to Gemma, who sat in the back seat of his truck. "Are you happy?"

He tried to sound annoyed, but his voice was tinged with laughter. Gemma danced her feet in the back seat as she held the certificate to her chest.

"Yes! This is so amazing. You *killed it* out there."

A smug smile tugged at the corner of his mouth. I slid my hand across the bench seat and settled it on top of his. With a squeeze, I said, "You were very impressive."

He turned his head and winked. "Glad you enjoyed it."

"Enjoyed it? Val dropped fifty bucks on you!" Gemma leaned back against the seat in pure satisfaction. Evan had more than killed it. He'd crushed the competition. Once the air horn sounded, he'd torn off like a wild man toward the first stump and the pile of logs. In single swings, he split the wood, sending large chunks flying, before moving onto the next pile. It hadn't even been close.

He looked at me and my breath hitched.

"What? It was for charity."

I settled into my seat. A warm, melty feeling spread through me. Gemma's laughter, Evan smiling with his hand on mine in the truck—I couldn't imagine a more perfect night.

I watched the flats of Montana speed past me as the fading summer sun sank lower behind the mountains. Evan's warm palm pressed into mine, and he rubbed small circles with his thumb. The drive was quiet, peaceful. I couldn't remember a time where my mind felt so quiet. Every so often I'd catch Evan looking at me instead of the country road, and I wondered if he felt the same surprising comfort I did.

~

A WARM MONTANA breeze pushed my hair from my face as I sipped my iced coffee and waited for Gemma to meet me at Brewed Awakening. We'd made plans to work out again today. Behind her perky facade, I could tell her anxiety still simmered just below the surface, but every day she was getting stronger and more confident. The self-defense lessons I was teaching her seemed to help her shed some of the guardedness that settled between her shoulders.

Sitting at one of the outdoor tables, I flipped a page of another novel Gemma had convinced me to check out.

Holy hotness.

I'd started off with what Gemma called a *spicy romance* but quickly found myself eyeballs deep in everything from blue aliens to minotaurs to rodeo cowboys with an attitude. There was truly something for everyone, and I was, Here. For. It.

Glancing up, I saw Gemma approaching with Johnny in tow. I slid my bookmark between the pages.

I'll show Evan that little trick later.

I smiled at them as they approached. "You working out with us today?"

Johnny looked at me over his lowered eyebrows. "Ew. No. I just had a little something for Gemma."

She lifted a small brown bag, and a tentative smile pressed her lips together as she glanced away.

"I'm off. Bye, gals!"

We said goodbye, and my eyes shifted to whatever it was Johnny had given her. Gemma tucked it into her gym bag. She caught me looking at it and zipped her bag closed. "He ordered some specialty scar-treatment cream. Thought

I might want to try it." Her voice was thick as she fought against her emotions.

I stood, pulling her into me. "There are good, kind people here, aren't there?"

She only nodded. I released her and tucked my book into my bag, then walked my empty cup to the garbage.

I bumped my hip into her playfully as we walked. The gym was only a few blocks away, and my muscles enjoyed the warm-up.

Gemma was quiet on the walk, still lost in her thoughts. "He's a good guy."

"Johnny? Definitely."

"You know he said something today. It's probably nothing, but something about it feels weird."

An acute prickle tugged between my shoulder blades. "What was it?"

Nervous energy radiated off Gemma. "Johnny joked about having the hots for someone new."

"New?" My eyes whipped to her, and my hands clenched the strap of my bag as we walked.

"Someone he said he's noticed around town. I think he was only half joking about how cute the guy was. But I guess this man showed up around town a few times, asking some weird questions. He told me to keep a heads-up. Do you think it's weird no one knows who this guy is?"

I steadied my breath, alarm bells shrieking between my ears. Gemma didn't need me freaking out.

"People pass through Tipp a lot. It's small, but not that small, you know?"

She nodded, unconvinced. "Yeah."

"Hey. No worries. We're probably safer here than anywhere on the planet." Her eyes met mine, and I tried to give her an encouraging smile, but it felt a little more like a grimace. I pulled open the door to the gym. "Let's go kick some ass."

~

GEMMA and I worked out for over an hour—some cardio, light weights, and a little sparring and more self-defense training to finish off. The entire time I couldn't stop thinking about what Johnny had reported to Gemma.

It was probably nothing. Just some guy who was passing through and had caught his eye.

Some guy who was *asking some weird questions.*

That bit stuck with me as I pulled the Silverado across the bridge just outside of the ranch. I couldn't let it go, and the niggling feeling stayed with me. Something wasn't right about it. Johnny wasn't a gossip and wouldn't have mentioned it had it not alarmed him too.

It had been over a week since Agent Walsh had informed me that I'd passed my psych review, and there still hadn't been any word on when I was cleared to go back to Chicago. Though he said it could take some time, I had no idea if that meant a few days, a week, longer? May was creeping closer to June and I was still left waiting.

What if he calls and tells me it's time—that I need to pack up and leave? I'd have no time to say goodbye.

No. That couldn't happen—definitely not if something odd was happening in town and there was even the tiniest chance that Evan and Gemma could be in danger.

Maybe I was overreacting. Maybe I was just looking for any excuse to have a little more time. It didn't matter. My gut was telling me something major was off. I pulled into a space outside of the lodge and marched toward Ma's office. I raised a hand to knock.

Her head lifted, and a friendly smile greeted me. "Val, how are you, dear?"

Energy bounced on my insides, and I tried to stay calm. "I'm fine. Good. I was wondering if I could use your phone? My cell still doesn't get any service out here."

She immediately stood. "Of course. I'm surprised you haven't switched carriers yet, but you're always welcome to use the office phone."

I lifted a noncommittal shoulder. Switching cell carriers would certainly make my life easier. As it was, I got good reception only when I was in town. Out on the ranch, it was nearly a dead zone. But that felt big. A step toward permanent.

Ma shuffled a few papers before rounding her desk. She stopped in front of me and smiled. "Evan came to see me this morning. He mentioned that his relationship with you has somewhat changed."

Panic laced through me. Things had certainly shifted from sneaking around to public displays of affection at the barn party yesterday, but we hadn't talked about it yet. Evan and I still needed to discuss whether that was a mistake, a fluke, or our new normal. I understood exactly why we should probably keep things quiet. An integral part of your protection was that there were no ties to your old life. None. I was a direct link to the night Gemma was taken and Evan was shot. If someone outside of Tipp were to find out their real identities, they'd be able to directly link us to each other. That information in the wrong hands could mean serious trouble for Evan and Gemma.

"Yes, ma'am." I lifted my chin and steadied my breathing.

She nodded and paused. "He is building life here. Are you?"

I could only blink.

"Just know this," she continued. "If you hurt that boy, you won't be dealing with Agent Brown—you'll be dealing with Ma."

Stunned, my mouth dropped open.

Me? Hurt Evan?

Dismissed, I moved toward the door but cleared the burn in my throat when she reached the doorway. "If either of us are coming out unscathed," I said, "it's him."

Ma didn't look back. Tears pricked at my eyes as I watched her walk away. I couldn't let anything happen to the people I cared about. Being linked together was a risk we were willingly putting ourselves in, but I also couldn't force myself to walk away from him.

My gut was screaming at me that something was brewing in Tipp, Montana, and I had to do something about it.

If I called Agent Walsh and requested my return to Chicago be expedited, I would sever the link between Evan Walker and me forever. That also meant that if there *was* someone asking questions around town, I wouldn't be here to protect them. Evan would have laughed his ass off at the thought of anyone protecting *him*, but the truth of it was I had the training. I was an officer and a damn good one. Until we knew for sure who the mysterious stranger was and whether he was a threat, Evan was no longer safe here. Neither was Gemma. I steeled myself against the fear that slammed against my ribs.

If I stayed, I would have more time with Evan, but anyone looking to cause trouble would find all three of us in one convenient location. Nausea bubbled up and threatened at the back of my throat.

It should have been an impossible choice.

I dug through my purse and pulled up his contact information. My fingers flew over the numbers, and I tapped them on my thigh as I listened to it ring.

"Neil Walsh."

"Agent Walsh, this is Val Rivera. I have a proposition for you."

TWENTY-FIVE
EVAN

I DIDN'T DESERVE this kind of happiness.

Soft, early-morning light filtered through the curtains and spilled over Val as she curled into my bed. The sheets were a tangled mess, wrapped around her legs. My heart shifted in my chest as I took in the oversize black T-shirt she wore as a nightgown.

My shirt.

Everything inside me screamed *mine* as I watched her sleep in my bed. I moved carefully, trying to get a better view of her gorgeous face. As if she sensed me, Val shifted, draping one long leg across me. I nuzzled her closer and did my best to gently rearrange the tangled sheet, but I managed to get only a small corner for myself.

Fuck it.

I slid my arm around her, palming her ass and pressing her into me. Keeping her tucked in close, I breathed in her scent and committed every soft sigh to memory. Val would leave Tipp, and one day the memory of her would be all that was left.

The ache that rolled across my chest squeezed tightly,

and heat burned behind my eyelids. Once she went back home, she could no longer exist. I couldn't need her, and the last thing I wanted was someone needing me. It didn't matter that she looked at me without judgment. I had one purpose—testify in order to put the men responsible for harming Gemma behind bars. Even if that included my own brother.

Also, to keep Gemma safe. And now Val.

And if someone threatened that, I'd rip his fucking throat out.

Freezing my balls off because Val had alligator rolled in the middle of the night and stolen all the covers proved more than worth it to wake up with her tangled in my arms for however long I could keep her.

The feel of her pressed against me, along with the soft moans of her waking up, had my dick rigid and ready to feel her. I pressed my face into her neck and teased her with soft, wet kisses.

I rolled her onto her back and looked deeply into her eyes.

Val bit her lower lip, sleep still thick in her voice. "Every time you give me that look, I can't help but think how dangerous you are."

"Baby girl, I'm not the dangerous one."

My rough palms moved from her ample hips up to her ribs, taking the T-shirt with me. I pulled the shirt over her head and marveled at how her tits bounced. I lowered my head, sucking one perfect nipple into my mouth. It hardened as I laved and swirled my tongue around it. My dick was heavy as it hung between my thighs and pressed into her. I pinched one nipple as I teased the other with my mouth.

Her breath came in short pants, and her hips moved

upward, increasing the pressure against my cock. I ached to be inside her. I wanted nothing more than to feel her walls squeeze my shaft and milk my orgasm from me—to be connected to this woman, no barriers, no secrets, as I poured every part of myself into her.

Precum leaked from my tip and onto her hip bone. I needed to slow down, savor every second with her if I expected to last more than a few thrusts. I sat back on my heels, dragging my fingertips down her body and hooking them into her smooth black underwear. The small wet spot at her opening had me stifling a groan as I peeled them down her legs. I balled her panties into my hands and brought them to my face. Val's eyes went wide as I held her gaze and inhaled her delicious scent.

"Holy—"

"I can't wait to taste you, baby."

Shifting my weight, I lay on my back, pulling Val on top of me with one quick motion. I pulled her hips up, and she braced her hands on the wall above my head as I settled between her thighs.

"Give me that pussy, baby."

Val hovered above me, desire darkening her gorgeous features as she watched me through the curtain of her dark hair. I could smell the sweet scent of her arousal, and I needed to taste her. I looped my arms around her thighs and pressed her lower.

"I don't want to suffocate you."

"You won't." I tilted my head upward to lick a slow path across her pussy.

"Oh shit." She lowered, only fractionally. "I don't want you to die."

I scraped the scruff of my beard against the delicate skin

of her inner thighs, and they quivered. "Baby girl, if I die with your pussy on my face, it would be an honor."

I tightened my grip on her thighs, and she finally—*finally* —sat all the way down on my face. Her heat tore through me. Her taste had a growl clawing from my chest. She moved her hips gently, and I grunted in encouragement. As much as I wanted her to feel incredible, eating her pussy was also for me. My cock throbbed as I teased and sucked her clit.

"Evan. Evan, I want to feel you."

Val twisted her torso to reach behind her. She gripped my throbbing cock and my hips twitched upward, thrusting my shaft in her grip. My hands found her round ass, and I spread her open, licking and sucking as her walls throbbed around me. She was close, and I wanted to drive into her, staking claim on her in as many ways as possible.

As I kneaded her ass and tilted her hips, Val shifted back, holding the wall. She swiveled her hips as I devoured her. On a cry, her thighs tensed as her orgasm tore through her. I continued my assault on her pussy as it soaked my face and chin. Nothing had tasted better. Her ragged breath matched the pounding rhythm of my heart. She eased up, staring down at me, dazed and sated. I grabbed her hips, guiding her downward. Her thighs met the outside of my hips as my cock bobbed in anticipation.

I reached for the condoms I'd purchased and stashed in my nightstand. Val's hand gripped my forearm. "If you think I'm going back to having something between us, you're fucking nuts." Pleasure thrummed down my spine, and my cock twitched again.

"Yes, ma'am."

Val purred and shifted, centering her entrance over me. "Oh, I like the sound of that."

Slowly, achingly slowly, Val lowered herself onto me. "I want all of you."

"You've got me, baby girl. Every part of me is yours."

Together we moved and moaned as her hips rocked against mine. "That's it, baby. Ride this cock until you come."

I shifted, helping her get the perfect angle so the base of my cock rubbed against her clit. Her walls tightened. It was a fucking miracle I could hold on. I was close, so close, but I could tell she was hurtling toward a second orgasm, and I'd be damned if I wasn't going to help her get there.

"Goddamn. You feel so good. I love the way you move."

I reached a hand up, teasing her nipple as she rode me hard. The other hand gripped the back of her neck, pulling her mouth to mine. We crashed together, her hips grinding against me as I deepened our kiss.

Small, desperate groans escaped her as she used my cock to ride out the waves of the orgasm that crashed over her. As her inner walls pulsed around me, heat gathered at the base of my spine, and I exploded, filling her.

We were both breathless as Val slumped against me. I pulled her as close to me as I could manage. My voice was scratchy and ragged. "How do you do that to me?"

"Mmm." She snuggled closer as I stroked a possessive hand down her back.

I love her.

I need her.

Those thoughts should have scared the fuck out of me, but for once, I couldn't find it in myself to feel anything other than bliss.

∾

My eyes cracked open, only vaguely aware that we'd fallen asleep. "Stay here. Let me make you a cup of coffee."

I shifted, placing a gentle kiss on the strong slope of her shoulder before tucking the disaster of a sheet around her. Val's eyes fluttered closed as she snuggled deeper in the bed. I threw on a pair of sweatpants and padded into the kitchen and flipped on the coffee maker.

As it warmed up, I looked around the small but tidy space. I was grateful to have a space of my own, and as much as I hated the idea at first, I think it was good for Gemma too. I thought about how Val fit so seamlessly into my life here. If it were up to me, she wouldn't spend another night in the lodge in her cramped, barren room.

Just as I was pouring Val her coffee, she emerged from the bedroom, looking like a perfect, rumpled sex goddess. Heat crawled across my chest. I couldn't get enough of that woman.

I stared at her.

Val hummed while she shuffled to the pantry cabinet. I tried to memorize every part of her.

"What?" she said around a mouthful of granola bar.

Goddamn. Watching her walk away is going to be brutal.

"Just enjoying the view." I thought about how quickly time seemed to be passing and scowled into my coffee. Val did a little spin and twirled her way toward me. I opened my arms for her, and she sat on my lap, looping her arms around my neck. "You're cute when you're grumpy."

"I'm not grumpy. Or cute."

Val pressed her thumb between my eyebrows, smoothing out the crease that had formed there. "What's this, then?"

I pulled her closer to me and nuzzled into her neck. "Just enjoying this while it lasts."

Val's hands found my shoulders as she tipped back. I couldn't read her face, but it was full of questions. I stood, gently setting her on her feet, and went to move toward the bedroom before remembering her coffee.

"I guess we should get this day started," she said.

"Go on a date with me."

Val reached across the table and scooped up her coffee. "A date?"

"Today. Right now. We'll take the horses out and go for a short ride. There's someplace I want to show you."

She cocked an eyebrow as she sipped her coffee, but I could see her trying to hide a smile. "Okay, cowboy. Let me get a coffee and a shower in first."

As Val turned to head toward the shower, I slapped her ass.

It was going to be another incredible fucking day.

TWENTY-SIX

VAL

Wiping the sweat from my brow, I looked out onto the pasture of Redemption Ranch. It had officially been my home for over four months. Summer warmth was already waning to cooler days as we approached September. In the distance, the very tips of the trees were losing their bright green and giving way to muted yellows. It wouldn't be long until fall swept in. Sometimes fall in Chicago was pretty, with golds and reds splashed across the trees, but more often than not we took a nosedive into winter and everything just looked brown and gross.

Here, it was easy to see how the canary, burnt orange, and red would slice across the mountain, making its way up to the peak. I made a note to plan a picnic with Evan down by the creek once the leaves had fully changed.

Waking up tangled in Evan's arms was definitely something a girl could get used to. He was strong and warm and always smelled like fresh laundry and a hint of woodsmoke.

Delicious.

This morning Gemma had swung by for breakfast, and once she'd left, instead of hurrying out, Evan and I took our time getting ready for the day. We eventually got side-tracked, and he propped me up on the counter to tease kisses down my neck. Two orgasms later, my limbs were pleasantly heavy and my body delightfully sore.

Around town, posters advertising Tipp's Apple Knocker Festival started popping up, and the idea of another small-town event tucked into Evan's side made my insides glow. At the library, my list of books on hold was growing and growing. I'd long given up the worry that I'd be called to leave any day. I'd made my arrangement with Agent Walsh. It was settled. There was plenty of work to do on the ranch, so I busied myself with manual labor and buried any complicated feelings that went along with the decisions I'd made.

I'm doing what needs to be done.

The days were filled with hot looks across the barn, aching muscles, and tired feet. Now that I wasn't a total newbie around the ranch, I could have a little more say in how I spent my time. Stalls still needed to be mucked out, and the daily grind never ceased, but I also got to spend most of my days with the horses, which I'd fallen in love with. While the backbreaking work on the ranch toned and sculpted muscles I never knew existed, my nights were always spent with Evan.

Every morning I went back to my lonely room at the lodge, feeling downtrodden and miserable, so I'd finally decided to pack up my clothes and stay at the cabin with Evan. We didn't put a label on it, but a month or so ago, when Evan had referred to it as "our place," my heart had fluttered against my ribs, and I hadn't corrected him.

"You gonna stand around all day?" Ray's scratchy voice snapped me out of my daydreams and back to the reality of mucking out barn stalls.

"Morning, sunshine!" I'd decided the *kill him with kindness* approach was going to be my best defense in dealing with his surly attitude. It rarely worked. A sneer in my direction was all the kindness I got most days.

Unfazed, I pressed on, sweeping my arm in the direction of the pasture and the buttes beyond. "How can you not see this and think, 'Holy shit, this is amazing'?"

Ray swept the concrete floor behind me. "Seen better," he grumbled. Never once had Ray talked to me about anything even remotely personal. I considered this a tiny victory.

"Oh yeah?" I didn't look at him, but I kept up with my chores and hoped he'd elaborate.

"There ain't nothin' like a bayou in Natchitoches."

I studied him as the old man shuffled the broom in rhythmic sweeps. He was a mystery. Surly and crabby and dismissive, but also hardworking and generally respected on the ranch. He'd clearly had a disdain for police officers, as evidenced by his wintry demeanor toward me.

"Home?"

He paused on his broom. "Long time ago."

"Do you miss it?"

He thought for a moment, not looking at me but out across the pasture. "Don't miss the heat. Goddamn, it got sticky."

"Family?" I pressed.

He grumbled to himself. "Only one person worth missing."

Then it hit me.

Ray was a witness under protection.

His entire life had to be left behind in order to testify and be protected from any repercussions from that testimony. He made no attempts to start a new life here. He simply *existed* as the shell of the man he used to be. An irritable old man riddled with regrets of one person he missed. I couldn't help but wonder if it was a woman or a child he missed so badly.

His eyes sliced to me and narrowed. He likely hadn't meant to reveal so much, and once he came to his senses, he scowled.

"And now you've got family here." I tried to sound light, hopeful.

His snarl curdled my stomach as he walked away. "No one here is family. But at least I ain't spreading my legs, pretending like anyone here gives a shit about me."

A hot lance of resentment tore through my belly, and tears pricked my eyes as he ambled away. The rational part of me knew he'd lashed out because I'd hit a nerve, but fuck. He left me feeling like I'd been slapped in the face.

Something dark and oily spread through me.

Who else felt that way? Maybe I don't really belong here.

The camaraderie, nights around the bonfire, family dinner—was it all bullshit? Was I nothing more to these people than a cop biding her time until I could go back to Chicago? I shook the dark thoughts from my mind. I couldn't let one rough conversation with a bitter old man shake my resolve. I *was* still a cop. I had a job to do, and I needed to remember that.

There hadn't been another word about anyone asking questions around town, but I couldn't help but feel like Evan and Gemma were still in danger. If I was going to protect them, I couldn't let fear or insecurity stand in my way. I closed my eyes to fight back tears, gritted my teeth and steadied my quivering breaths.

"Hey, Val!" A ranch hand trotted by on a horse and offered a wave and a friendly smile.

I swallowed hard and did my best to smile back and fight a fresh wave of tears.

"Smokehouse skillet, eggs over easy, and a coffee, please."

Our server had a youthful face, skin tanned from the summer sun, and hot-pink lipstick. Her black hair was pulled tight into a ponytail, and intricate tattoos swirled up one arm. She scribbled down my order with a smile, grabbed our menus, and walked away. Gemma sat across the booth and smiled at me.

"Fall classes start in a few weeks, right?"

Her cheeks pulled tight with a huge grin. "Two weeks and the fall semester starts. I'm registered to take online classes for now, but I can't freaking wait."

"What'll you go for?"

"I'm not sure yet, mostly just getting my gen ed classes out of the way. Then I can decide." Gemma flipped a coffee creamer, trying to get the landing to stick as we waited for our food.

"What about something with music?"

She shot me a bland look.

"I'm serious! I've heard you sing in the truck. You're amazing."

"No. No, no, no." Her blonde crop swayed as she shook her head. "Definitely not."

"I think you've got the talent."

Gemma fiddled with the collar of her chambray shirt, pulling it tighter over her scar. "Belting one out in the car is different. I could never get in front of people and sing."

The punky waitress derailed our conversation, dropping

off Gemma's orange juice, then filling my mug with steaming black coffee. I dumped in two creams, tasted it, and decided it required a full packet of sugar.

"How's life in cohabitation?"

My cheeks immediately flushed. "Gem . . ."

"Oh, whatever." She swatted at me. "It's not like it's a big deal."

"Yeah, but it's your brother. That's . . . I don't know. Weird."

Gemma rolled her eyes. "Well, whatever you're doing, keep it up. He hasn't harassed me about my chores in weeks, and it's glorious. Apparently, all he needed was a good lay in order to stop being such a crabby old man."

I nearly choked on my burned-tasting coffee. "Okay. New topic."

Gemma tapped her lip to hide her grin. "Fine. Be boring. Do you want to go to Apple Knocker? It's supposed to be like a carnival, but there'll be bands and lots of food. I heard there's bingo with some major prize money too."

"I haven't been to a carnival since I was a kid." We continued rambling on, talking and making plans.

Midway through our breakfast, Gemma's eyes unfocused, and the color drained from her face. Her blue eyes went wide, and she was frozen in place, staring at the wall above my shoulder. Her lower lip began to tremble, and I looked around. No one else seemed to notice she was in the middle of a total silent meltdown. I had never seen her like this.

I scanned her face. She was stark white and completely still. I looked around the diner. Children giggled, waitstaff cleared plates, a man behind us was paying at the counter, pulling bills from his wallet and making small talk with the cashier.

"Gem," I whispered. "What's wrong? Gemma!"

A tear slipped from her eye, but she didn't move. I reached across the table to grab her shoulder. "Hey. What's going on?"

My ears pricked. Something was happening, and I couldn't understand what had caused her to freak out. I moved from my seat, digging out bills from my purse to drop on the table, and I pulled her from the booth. She went with me, her eyes still wide and dazed. I hurried her out the door and pushed her toward the parking lot to her truck.

She sagged against me as I tore the door open and shoved her inside the truck. By the time I rounded the hood, Gemma was curled in on herself, her knees to her chest and her head between them. I tore out of the parking lot and headed toward the ranch, my attention split between the dusty country road and Gemma's heavy panting.

"Deep breaths. You're going to hyperventilate."

Ragged breaths scraped out of her and showed no signs of slowing. I stomped on the accelerator, pushing the old truck past its limits in an effort to get back home. Get to Evan. He knew her better than anyone, and she trusted him implicitly. Maybe he could get her to talk.

The truck bounced across the wooden bridge that led to the entrance of Redemption, jostling us in the cab.

"Fuck. Hang on, Gem. We're home."

The brakes squealed in protest as I slammed my foot down and threw the truck in park. I had no clue where Evan was, but I needed *someone* to help her.

"Gemma, can you walk? Come on. We can get help." Panic raised in my voice. Typically controlled in stressful situations, my excessive worry over her spontaneous melt-down had my system bouncing out of control. I had moved toward the door of the truck when Gemma's hand grabbed my shirtsleeve. My eyes whipped to hers.

"Don't leave me. Don't leave me. Don't leave me." She pulled my arm closer to her.

I reached across the cab, pulling her close to me. "I'm not leaving. I got you."

Sobs racked from her, and she clawed her arms around me.

"What is it? Gemma, what happened?"

"The man." Her voice was broken over the tears she shed. Her eyes were wild and unfocused. "Paying at the counter. It was Parker."

TWENTY-SEVEN

EVAN

"Stop dragging your dick and let's go." Scott's voice had me flipping him the middle finger before I took one last glance around the cottage and closed the door. It had changed since Gemma left—fewer clothes scattered on the floor, and her shoes weren't haphazardly thrown in front of the door. It was quieter. My shoulder ached as humidity hung in the air, and I pressed my thumb into the ridges of my scar, a constant reminder of what we'd been through.

We'd both endured that night, but I had chosen to step in front of the gun. Gemma wasn't given a choice, and instead, she was disfigured simply because grown men were afraid of what a kid had overheard. I never wanted her to feel fear like that again. The men responsible also hadn't counted on inciting my hatred and me choosing Gemma over the life. Over Parker. I thought of her again and how she looked so much like our mother.

I'd choose this kid again in a heartbeat.

I ambled toward Scott. The windows were down in his truck, and he draped one arm over the steering wheel.

"Where to, Agent?"

"Ma wants us checking on fence posts around the north pasture. A few need replacing."

I nodded as I climbed into the cab. Scott was a born-and-bred Montanan. His transition to the work on a ranch was seamless—you'd never know he was actually a federal agent and had seen some gruesome shit in his lifetime. More and more it seemed, at Redemption, we were all battle weary and had pasts we wanted buried. With Scotty, it was easy for me to let the past go.

Same with Val.

Even thinking of her made my chest feel tight. She hadn't mentioned anything more about her fitness for duty evaluation or her leaving Montana in weeks. I couldn't help but think about it, and a few times I almost asked, but then decided to say *fuck it*. I was more than happy to pretend it didn't exist and go on living the lie that we could stretch out whatever was happening between us. As long as Val was working on the ranch, she fit perfectly into the new life I was building.

"We gonna get ahead of those clouds?" I nodded toward the ominous black clouds rolling in.

"That's the plan." Scotty pulled onto the dirt road and headed out toward the pasture. We spent the next hour in near silence, checking each post, reinforcing ones that were salvageable and marking ones that weren't and could be replaced later.

"How's Gemma liking her new place?"

I eyed Scotty.

Why the fuck is he asking about Gem?

"She loves it. Like any *nineteen*-year-old loves their free-dom." I'd been sure to emphasize and remind him about her age. I didn't give a fuck how much I liked Scott, Gemma was off-limits.

Unfazed, he continued, "That's great. Good for her. Everything else fine?"

I knew he was prodding. It was no longer a secret Val and I were sleeping together, and though everyone knew it was temporary, no one talked about it. "Yep."

It wasn't fine. As recent days wore on, I was fixating on her evaluation more and more. The less she mentioned it, the more I waited for the other shoe to drop—for her to breeze in, pack her shit, and move on to bigger and better things. A few times I'd almost slipped and told her how I felt. That I fucking loved her more than I ever thought I was capable of loving, and it scared the shit out of me. But nothing was tying her to Montana once that evaluation was cleared, and I wasn't about to be the weight around her neck that dragged her down.

She would move on from here. They'd be fucking idiots to not snag her for the ATF, and she'd be gone. Somewhere far from Montana where she would kick ass and lead the life she had always wanted. Val Rivera would cease to exist at Redemption Ranch.

Except I knew that was total bullshit. Val was the type of woman who left a brand. My fingers grazed the scar on my shoulder. In her case, I would carry my very own reminder on my skin. Even after she left, I knew I would think of her every day for the rest of my life. I'd reach for her when I slept. I'd hear a stupid pun and want to share it with her just to hear the tinkling of her laugh.

She would haunt me.

I pounded the final post harder than I intended, shoving down dark and dangerous thoughts with every thwack.

"If you're done beating that post to death, let's go. Rain's coming."

~

OUTSIDE MY CABIN, I held the water hose to my lips. The rain held off, doing nothing but spitting and making the warm air thick and charged. After washing the mud from my boots, I let the cool water ease the burn in my throat. The clouds hung heavy and low. Before long rain would wash the film of dust off the day. Down the dirt path that sloped toward the main cabin, I saw Val running toward me.

Heat bloomed in my chest. Excitement tittered in rippling waves under my skin. Her black hair blew back as she ran toward me like a fucking movie.

Then I saw her face.

Panic.

Fear.

I dropped the hose and tore off toward her. My boots slammed into the gravel and dirt.

"Evan!" I could see my name on her lips before I could hear her.

"Val!" I screamed back at her. I needed her to know I saw her and I was coming. My lungs burned as dust and dirt choked me. Adrenaline pumped through my veins. I finally —*finally*—reached her, and Val slammed into me.

Her breath was ragged as she sucked in air. "Gem." Her eyes were huge, and I could barely understand the words. Her arms gripped mine. "It's Gemma."

Razors sliced at my gut. "Where? What happened?"

I'd started to pull away, to run the rest of the way toward the main lodge, when Val's grip tightened. "Evan. Look at me."

I did, but I couldn't focus as panic and worry took over. "She's safe. She's at the lodge with Robbie and Ma." Val pulled me toward the lodge, and we started walking as fast as our feet would take us while talking. Her legs were long, but she trotted behind me as I barreled toward the lodge.

"What the fuck is going on?"

"I don't know. Something happened at the diner. She had a panic attack or something. One second we were talking about school and classes and the next, she . . . I don't know. She freaked out."

I slowed my feet so Val could catch up, relaxing just a bit, knowing Gem was at the lodge and safe. "Gemma's had panic attacks before. Just after we got here. She still has nightmares sometimes, but I think those have gotten a little better."

Val nodded, and her hand gripped my forearm. "Ev, there's more. She's saying she heard Parker."

My head whipped to her. "Heard? What do you mean *heard*?"

"I mean, she said she didn't see him, but heard him at the counter of the diner. His voice. I don't really know."

When I reached the door to the lodge, I nearly ripped it off its hinges. Sitting in the living room, Gemma was in a chair, silent tears streaming down her face, and Ma was next to her, rubbing slow circles around her back. One look at me and Gemma dissolved into a fresh round of sobs. I stormed up to the chair and sank to my knees, pulling her into me.

"He's here. He's here. He found us." She was clawing at my back. Panic rolled off her in waves as untethered rage whipped through me.

I'd promised her this was over. That she was safe. I sold my soul to make sure this would never happen again.

I held Gemma's shoulders and forced her eyes to mine. "No one will hurt you. I'll take care of it."

Straightening, I turned to leave and met a wall of agents. "Get the fuck out of my way."

Scott tried to reach out, but the glare I shot him had him lowering his hand. "Slow down. We'll take care of this. Get the details. We don't even know if it was, in fact, your brother."

Gemma's small voice floated over my shoulder. "It was him." She hiccuped as she tried to even her breathing. "I'd know his voice anywhere. I know it was him."

"Scott's right," Val said. "We need to investigate. Follow protocol."

I studied her face, only then realizing she was standing with the agents. "We? What do you mean, *we*?"

"I'm here. Helping. All of us are helping. We'll figure this out."

"Scott. Give me your keys."

"Can't do that, man. Sorry."

"Evan, I can drive you home." Val's warm brown eyes pleaded with me. "Ma will take care of Gemma, and we can figure out what to do next."

My breathing was heavy, but she was making too much sense to argue, which pissed me off even more. I didn't need Gemma to see me lose my shit either. I stalked toward the door, found the truck, and slammed the door to the Silverado. The short drive back to my cabin was in heavy silence. The entire ride I thought of all the ways I was going to find and murder my brother.

TWENTY-EIGHT

VAL

FIERCE, protective Evan was a major part of his sex appeal, but the man in front of me was something more. Something unrestrained and aggressive.

Dangerous.

Evan stormed around his cabin, and rage poured through him as he fought for control. The tension in the cabin was palpable. I followed him to his bedroom as he grabbed a duffel from his closet and began shoving clothes inside.

"What are you doing? Where are you going?"

A large vein pulsed in his neck, and he spoke through gritted teeth. "I'm handling it."

"You heard what Scott said—*we're* handling it. Let the agents figure it out."

He ignored me as he continued to throw items in his bag. The calm, rational man I knew was nowhere to be found. I stood my ground in his bedroom—*our bedroom*—as he seethed. Evan disappeared into the closet, shoving storage boxes and clothing to the side. A small black safe I didn't know existed was nestled into the corner. Evan pressed his thumb to the center pad and with a quiet *beep beep* and a green light, the small door swung open.

From the safe, Evan pulled a handgun. He didn't look at me but checked the magazine before loading it.

"Whoa. What the hell, Evan?" My voice raised, and he finally looked at me.

"Parker found us. It's time I go remind him who the fuck I am."

A reminder. A criminal.

His eyes were hard. I took a step back. The funny, kind-hearted, warm man I had fallen in love with had slipped behind a mask of blind fury. Crystal clear, I could see Evan Walker transform back into Evan Marino, Mafia criminal who would use brute force to get any job done.

His breathing was erratic as he moved through the cabin. He dragged his fingers through his hair. "Someone must have leaked it. How else would he have been able to locate us on a ranch in the middle of goddamn nowhere Montana?" His anger flowed over me, swallowing me whole.

I suppressed my uncertainty. I knew in my bones he would never hurt me, but I barely recognized the man in front of me. "Leaked it? Who would do that?"

"Anyone. Anyone looking for a payday. Someone gave us up." He straightened and pinned me with a look. Tension pinched his shoulders back as he stared down on me. "You."

I lifted my chin. "Me? What do you mean, me?"

"Have you talked to anyone in Chicago?"

Denial was on my lips when I recalled my conversation with my partner, Eric. The blood drained from my face. "I called my chief but he wasn't there. My partner, Eric, got on the phone. He couldn't believe it when I told him I'd been holed up in Montana."

Evan reached me in two long strides. "You told him where we are?"

"No. Not exactly." I moved to place my hand on his forearm, but he pulled back as though my touch would burn his skin. "I didn't give him any details. He doesn't know anything about the ranch or what goes on here, just that I was halfway across the country and how different it's been for me." My throat was dry, and every swallow felt like nails raking down the inside.

"Yeah, fucking great." Evan tucked the pistol into the back of his jeans. "You told him where we were. You gave us up."

My eyes went wide. When I'd talked with Eric, I'd joked about the *nothingness* of the ranch and how someone like me, someone who'd never been exposed to rural living, was practically limping my way through the day-to-day. I searched through my memory. I had mentioned the ranch in nonspecific terms and lamented crappy takeout from Uncle Mao's—but that was before. Before meeting Evan changed everything.

He stood in front of me, breathing hard. He closed his eyes. "Val." It was clear he was warring with himself. "Move."

I raised both hands in the air. "Eric isn't a great cop, but he's not dirty."

"All cops are dirty!" Evan threw his arm in the air toward me, clearly lumping me together with that statement, painting all police officers with broad strokes of contempt and mistrust.

Anger bubbled inside me. "How dare you. I've done nothing but stay here and try to help. To protect *you*!"

Realization dawned on him as the words tumbled from my lips. "That's what you meant by *we*, isn't it?"

My brows drew together.

"Earlier when you said 'we're handling it.' You're not just helping. You're working."

My mouth popped open, but no sound would come out. I'd had every intention of telling Evan about the deal I'd made with Agent Walsh. Once the threat was gone, I was going to tell him everything. The pain that crossed his face was a brand on my heart. I lowered my shoulders and fought the tears that choked my voice.

"Evan, I passed my evaluation weeks ago. Special Agent Walsh and I worked it out that I could remain here on the ranch. My job was to quietly gather any information if it were pertinent to the investigation, but, overall, to help keep you and Gemma safe."

"You've been lying."

"No, I . . ." I took one step forward, but the fire in his eyes stopped me.

Evan's voice was cold and hard. "No, I get it. You've got your big promotion, and wouldn't it look great if you helped save the day. Close a big case."

He moved to walk past me, and I finally found my voice. "Do not walk out that door."

"I'm leaving. You can arrest me, or you can get the fuck out of my way." The door slammed behind him and echoed in the hollow of my bones.

I STOOD IN STUNNED SILENCE. The metal door to Evan's truck banged closed, and through the window, I watched his truck tear down the dirt road, kicking up dust in his wake.

The last hour was a blur of chaos and heartbreak. The bone-chilling fear in Gemma's eyes was familiar—it was the same wild-eyed, frantic expression I'd seen on the faces of gunshot victims. Women who'd suffered abuse. Children abandoned by their parents. It was a look of pure terror that you wouldn't wish on your worst enemy. Fear rattled Gemma to the core, and she'd been inconsolable.

Gemma was certain Parker was in town, and I prayed the marshals would find him before Evan did something epically stupid to get himself hurt, or worse. I had to move, to do *something* other than recall the way Evan's blue eyes had turned dark and hard.

Unease snaked through me. He'd slipped so easily into someone I barely recognized. All his warmth was zapped from his body, and only his cold, hard exterior remained.

But under all the anger and determination was something he couldn't hide from me.

Panic.

Evan was truly afraid, and he'd lashed out because of it.

In the echoing silence of the cabin, I wasn't feeling as confident in my decision to strike a deal with Agent Walsh. I hustled toward the lodge. If Evan thought he could hurl himself headfirst into the fray without backup, he was wrong. I didn't care how hardheaded he was—there were plenty of people in his corner now.

I gathered my resolve and made my way back to the lodge. Inside, Gemma was curled on the couch, her legs tucked under her and the wool blanket high under her chin. Scotty hovered over her, two fingers touching the slope of her shoulder as they spoke. She nodded once, fighting back tears.

I walked into the center of the room and cleared my throat. "We've got a problem." My thoughts warred against each other. My instincts were screaming at me to tell everyone that Evan had left in search of his brother—gather backup and haul ass out of there to help him.

Your gut told you to stay and look at the mess you've made with him.

Uncertainty clouded my thoughts. I wasn't one to stress over difficult decisions. In the past I'd always listened to my intuition, and it had always, *always* worked out. This was different. I couldn't separate my head from my heart, and it made everything seem unclear.

Ma stepped up. "What is it, Val?"

I stalled. I didn't know if telling her Evan had left with a gun in search of Parker would get him in more trouble. I searched her face. Ma's kind eyes were looking at me expectantly, her mouth in a firm line. The rest of the agents turned toward me, ready to leap into action.

These people care about him. They're his family.

"Evan is about to do something reckless."

TWENTY-NINE

EVAN

I wanted to smoke. To beat the shit out of someone for no reason other than that was my job.

Simple.

Nothing about the way I felt about Val was simple. The way I'd spoken to her made me feel like a piece of shit. Deep down, I knew Val thought she was doing the right thing. She was built to protect the people she cared about, so making arrangements to stay on the ranch made sense to her. I'd always known that Val was too good for me, and the fact that I could have no ties to my former life cemented the reality that what we had could only ever be temporary.

Trouble was, it had started to feel awfully permanent.

I had convinced myself that I could actually have a new life. Evan Marino was dead, and Evan Walker had eagerly stepped into his place. Only the old me, the real me that I'd shoved down so deep and buried beneath swagger and charm and warm smiles, came clawing to the surface frighteningly fast. I hated myself for how easily I slipped back into the man I'd tried so hard to leave behind.

Val had seen it too. I saw it in her eyes—the shock gave way to the realization that I was not a good man.

My leg buzzed with energy as I sped down the highway toward town. In a place like Tipp, Montana, a swaggering city boy like Parker Marino would be hard to miss. Once I raised the flag, it would be only a matter of time until I found whatever rock he'd been hiding under. It had been weeks since Johnny had reported a stranger in town, asking questions, but that didn't mean he was gone.

Gemma heard him. He's still here.

I pushed through the heavy wooden door of the Rasa, and low country music poured out of the building. Al was standing sentry behind the bar, and his head whipped up as I stalked toward him. Families were scattered, laughing and enjoying their lunches. I scanned every face, looking for my brother. A few unfamiliar patrons sat, idly chatting or eating and enjoying their beers. My boots pounded on the wood floor toward the bar.

"What's got a hair up your ass?" Al's deep, raspy voice showed signs of daily smoking and a lifetime of interesting choices.

"Looking for someone." I continued to scan the patrons of the bar. "Tall, muscular build. Johnny Porter told Gemma and Val a few weeks ago that he was sniffing around."

"Yeah, I seen 'im. Though not for . . . maybe two, three weeks now. He was asking questions. Looked a little too slick to be from around here. I guess my warm-welcome stare scared him off."

Fuck.

I did not have a good feeling about this.

I dug through my pocket and unfolded the small picture. I had to be sure. "This him?"

Al grabbed the photograph and dragged his skinny, wrinkled hand down the wiry length of his beard.

"I've seen him around. What's he to ya?"

Unease rose from my gut, and my heartbeat pounded like a drum between my ears. "My brother."

"You say the word, and we'll rally the troops if someone's giving you trouble, Evan."

I couldn't help a sad chuckle. Tipp, Montana, was nothing if not loyal to one of its own. It was yet another reason I needed to protect my place in this town. I raised my hand to him, and he gripped it in a firm handshake. "Not yet. I just need to have a conversation first."

"Look on your face doesn't seem like he's gonna get a warm family welcome."

A noncommittal grunt passed through me, and I saddled up onto a stool, tossing the faded photograph on the bar.

Al poked one finger down onto it. "I recognize him, your brother. Though he wasn't the guy asking questions. That'd be the one to have a talking to." I looked down to see Al's bony, weathered finger held right between Michael's eyes.

An hour later I was no closer to finding Parker.

Or Michael.

I had walked up and down Main Street, stopping in every shop, office, barber, and grocery store to ask if anyone had seen either man. Most people recognized Parker's dark hair and light eyes.

Mrs. Sanford remembered he did some light grocery

shopping on Tuesdays, but only ever enough food for two shopping bags. Mostly organic.

Mr. Vega owned the Mexican restaurant and recalled Parker had sat in the back corner and shot the shit with the bussers in Spanish.

Mabel at the diner claimed he was a great tipper and smelled nice.

Fucking great.

Parker was one charming smile away from fooling this entire town, and Michael was a ghost. Other than giving Johnny the creeps and Al serving him a whiskey neat, no one else recognized him or recalled seeing him around Tipp. I pulled the pistol from the small of my back and laid it on the truck seat next to me. Dragging both hands through my hair, I emptied my lungs.

In an afternoon, things had gone completely sideways. The glass castle I had built around myself had come crashing down around me. The only way to get out of this mess was to find Parker—talk to him and see why he'd come to Montana—and find out what he knew about Michael.

Defeated, I drove back to the ranch. No doubt Ma would be pissed I'd gone rogue, and there'd be hell to pay. I'd find her and explain myself. If my reckless behavior had gotten me booted from the ranch, I could beg her to allow Gemma to stay. Then I had to find Val. I owed her some sort of an apology. I swallowed the rocks in the back of my throat. Getting close to me was a mistake, but I never meant to hurt her.

I pushed through the back door of the lodge. The kitchen light over the island illuminated the small space in a soft glow. One agent eyed me warily and tipped his head in the direction of Ma's office. When I came to her door, my heart stopped in my chest.

Sitting in the chair in front of her was Parker.

When I caught their attention, both stood. Parker took a step toward me. "Little brother. It's been a long time."

THIRTY

VAL

"Whoa. Where do you think you're going?"

Gemma's face twisted as she walked toward me. "With you."

I stopped her with my hands on her shoulders. "Gem, no."

"You said that Evan was looking for Parker. If he's in trouble, I have to go. I'll go crazy staying here, and I don't feel safe alone." Her eyes pleaded with me. "Please. Please don't leave me here by myself."

I chewed the inside of my lip. The only thing we were doing was driving around Tipp to see if we could find Evan and talk some sense into him. Maybe he'd even listen to Gemma.

I weighed the options and sighed. "Fine. We're just looking to see if we can find Evan. Talk him out of doing something stupid. That's it."

"Yeah. I'm good with that." Gemma grabbed her coat and headed toward the Silverado. Once we were settled into the cab, we pulled out onto the highway and headed toward town. "Where do you think he'd go?"

I shrugged, energy radiated down my arms, and I forced myself not to speed. "He's angry and worried about you. I'm hoping he's just in town asking around." The quick drive through town produced nothing. I pulled into a parking spot near the Rasa.

"Maybe they've seen him." I tilted my head toward Gemma, signaling her to follow me. We walked into the bar, scanning the crowd. I went straight to Al, who was wiping down the bar.

"You just missed your boy." Al barely looked at us as he continued cleaning.

"How long ago? Do you know where he was headed?"

He nodded. "Not sure. He was looking for his kin, but I'll tell you what I told him. His brother ain't the one to be watching out for."

Gemma took a step forward. "What do you mean?"

Al raked a hand through his wiry beard. "It wasn't him that was asking the questions, but another dude. Tall, skin had scarring on it." Al looked at us, his mouth grim. "No soul behind his eyes."

"Was it acne scarring?"

Al considered. "Coulda been."

Gemma gripped my arm. "That's Michael. He grew up with Evan and Parker. He and Parker were pretty close, I think. They did a lot of jobs together."

Michael.

Evan had told me about their childhood friend who'd also been brought up alongside the Mafia. Clearly, no lost, impressionable boy was safe around the Chicago Mafia. They gathered them, providing safety, security, and power. Evan believed he was full of darkness, but I knew in my heart it was more shades of gray. Michael, on the other hand, had become ruthless. The few stories Evan had shared had turned my stomach until I couldn't stand to know more.

"The other man, Michael. He was here?"

Al pointed between the two of us. "He's the one who'd been asking around about you three. Up to no good if you ask me. He wasn't welcome here."

I leaned across the bar and pulled Al into a quick hug. "Al, thank you!" I tucked my arm into Gemma's and moved toward the door. "We have to go. Thank you!"

Gemma ran with me back to the truck. "You think you know where he's at?"

"I don't know. Not really, but there's got to be somewhere around here an outsider can go and not be noticed."

WE DROVE for what felt like forever, winding down endless country roads. Cell service was spotty, per usual, so attempting to use the maps was practically useless. I crisscrossed through the county, using the looming mountain to get my bearings.

Old farmhouses. Abandoned buildings.

He could be anywhere.

Doubt crept in. Gemma stayed silent and stared out the window. My gut was screaming that Michael was here. Close. That the people I loved were in danger, but I had no proof except for a sinking feeling in my stomach. My whole life I'd trusted that feeling. I couldn't stop now. If I could find places where someone like him would hide—*something* —maybe it could help Ma and the other agents look into it.

Farther down a county road, Gemma grabbed my arm. "There!"

I looked to the side of the road but didn't see what she

was pointing at.

"Tire tracks in the mud. They turn and go down that little dirt road."

I slowed, seeing the tracks Gemma had noticed. They veered off the highway onto a dirty road that disappeared beyond the trees. My ears pricked and goose bumps erupted on my skin. I turned the truck onto the road, bracing myself against the bumps of the uneven surface. I looked again but couldn't see anything but road and patchy forest.

This is stupid.

"Okay, Gem. We can let everyone know. Let's turn back."

She gripped her arms and nodded. I continued forward, looking for a place to turn around, and spotted a clearing. An old church was long forgotten in a patch of dying grass.

"You see that, right?"

I nodded at Gemma. A newer-looking car was tucked under the awning at the side of the building.

Illinois plates.

My heart beat a war drum rhythm. I pulled out my cell phone.

Please have cell service. Please, please.

"Do you have service?" Gemma pulled out her phone but frowned. I pulled up Scotty's number.

Me: *Went driving to find Evan. No luck but found something odd. An old church building, Cedar County Baptist? Looks abandoned but there's a car here. It may be worth checking out. We're heading back.*

With the message, I tried to drop a pin to my location, but the little bar at the top seemed to stall. I prayed the message had gone through. It wasn't worth getting killed over, so I slowly shifted the truck to reverse to back down the dirt road.

Movement at the window caught my eye at the same time Gemma said, "Did you see that?"

Fuck.

If this was Michael and he was hiding out, there was no doubt he'd seen us. If we'd spooked him, he'd be gone.

"We need to go. I need to get you back home."

"Val, what if he leaves? Or what if he has Evan tied up in there or something?"

I clenched my jaw. That was highly unlikely, but now that she'd spoken the words, I couldn't get it out of my head. Our window of opportunity to question this person was rapidly shrinking.

I pointed at Gemma. "Stay in the car. Lock the door behind me. Keep trying the phones to get through to anyone on the ranch. Tell them where we are. I'll make a loop around the building, and if I don't see anyone, we're leaving."

She swallowed hard and nodded. I reached into the glove box and pulled out the service weapon and handcuffs that I'd gotten since being back on duty, and her eyes went wide. I reached across to squeeze her hand. "Back in two minutes. Keep calling."

I quietly got out of the truck, checking my surroundings and creeping slowly toward the old building. The white structure stood stark against the cloudy afternoon sky. Its gray shingles were peeled at the corners, and the north side of the roof was covered in slick, emerald moss. The paint, once a vibrant white, had long since faded to a dull, smoky alabaster and was peeling on every side. The windows that were broken had plywood on the back. It had been ages since this building had been loved.

I watched for any movement inside the church, but there was only the swaying of the trees. I listened, the sounds of the forest and leaves rustling at my feet. I crept forward and sent up a silent prayer that this didn't end in disaster. I would have given anything to have backup—Scotty, Ma, even Evan—anyone to watch my back and Gemma's, but that wasn't an option. I would rely on my training to investigate any possible threats and get the hell out of there.

I glanced at Gemma, who gave me one curt nod as she clicked the locks on the truck. I straightened my shoulders and moved quietly around the side of the building. The car was poorly hidden under the sagging awning, but the entire building was sheltered from the main road. It was a desolate, abandoned church. The perfect place to hide. A cursory glance showed the inside of the car was spotless. I placed my hand on the glossy black paint of the hood.

Still warm.

The cool fall breeze kicked up, and I could smell overpowering cologne just before a large frame stepped forward and grabbed me from behind. One arm was tight around my neck, and the other wrenched the gun from my hands. I watched in horror as it bounced away in the grass and dirt.

"Stop! Police!"

I had startled him, and he tightened his uneven grip around my neck. I turned my face just enough to see a smirk play on his lips. His face was calm as he struggled to hold me. As Gemma had recalled, it was riddled with small pockmarks, likely from years of acne. Another scar ran down the side of his neck, definitely not from acne. It was jagged and ugly. His eyes were green and reminded me of a serpent. Evil rolled off him in waves.

"Can I help you with something?" His cocky smirk turned darker as he glanced over my shoulder. I shifted my weight to block Gemma from his view.

"You are under arrest." My voice was hard and commanding despite the hold he had me in.

"Doesn't much look like it to me." Humor danced in his voice. "For what charge, sweetheart?"

"Stalking. Obstruction of justice in a federal investigation. You're being brought in for questioning. Let me go and I won't add assaulting an officer to the list." It was total bullshit. At this point I was making it up and praying he didn't know the law well enough to see right through me.

I assessed his hold on me. I needed to break free to control this situation and get Gemma the hell out of there. Using my training, I reared my hips back to make him unstable. I slammed my foot down on top of his. The surprise loosened the grip around my neck, and I flung myself forward toward the gun. My head reared back, and stars exploded behind my eyelids as I was yanked backward by my hair.

"Fucking bitch!" Michael roared as he dragged me closer to the building by my hair. He tipped my head up, the cloudy afternoon sun blinding my eyes. Gemma's scream had a newfound source of energy pouring out of me. I hooked my leg around his in an attempt to make his grip unstable. He was too fast, too strong.

I watched in horror as Gemma, being lifted by another man and fighting to get free, came around the corner. Tears streamed down her face, black mascara running tracks down her cheeks. She kicked and screamed as the man moved her toward us as though she weighed nothing.

"Bruno, shut that bitch up!" Gemma continued to struggle, and Michael added, "Tell me where he is."

"Go fuck yourself." I pulled and fought to be free.

Michael rubbed his face down mine, his breath hot against my cheek. "Well, that's not very nice."

I knew we were in trouble. The men didn't have guns on them, or at least they couldn't access them. If they had, they would have used them already to intimidate or shoot us. There had to be a way to break free. My eyes met Gemma's, and I willed her to calm down. She needed to understand what I was trying to communicate to her.

You can do this. You know how to break free.

Over and over, I sent those thoughts to her, and I watched as her breathing slowed. With a gulp and a slight nod, I knew it was time. "Now!" I shouted and tried to wrench myself free.

Gemma lowered her stance and lifted her arms. The swift action threw Bruno off-balance, and she almost got away. I struggled against the hold at my waist. The man grabbed Gemma's wrist, his grip so strong his knuckles turned white.

Just as we'd practiced, Gemma dropped in the horse stance. She gripped her fist with her hand and jerked up, popping her arm free.

"Run!" My voice was raw with emotion. She had to get away. I could handle myself, but Gemma needed to get to safety. Instead of running toward the truck, she lunged forward toward the tree line. "Gemma, run!"

She bent into the grass and stood, the gun that had been tossed aside in her shaking hands. "Let her go." She was so brave despite the waves shaking her entire body. If she tried to shoot Michael, there was a good chance she'd miss and hit me instead.

The crack of a single shot rang out and I flinched, waiting for the pain. I kept struggling.

"Consider that your warning shot. I won't miss next time. Don't think I won't shoot you in designer clothing."

Johnny?

Another shot rang out as Al sidled up beside Johnny, a shotgun at his shoulder. "Already been to prison and don't mind going back. Health care sure was cheaper."

In a stream of cars and chaos, plumes of dirt rose down the path leading to the main road. Michael still held me. Bruno was stunned into silence as he held up both hands. A vehicle skidded to a stop, and Scotty launched out of it, weapon drawn.

"Let her go. You damn well better believe I will let them shoot you."

"Lots of places to hide a body in the mountains." Al's grin spread across his craggy face. Johnny tipped his chin in solidarity.

Scott moved toward Gemma as other agents filled in, surrounding the group. Cars continued down the dirt road as more and more familiar faces from town exited their cars. Each had a weapon, from guns to baseball bats to shovels. They surrounded the group like a ragtag band of outlaws. Adrenaline coursed through my body. Gemma's arms were still raised, the gun shaking in her hands. Scotty gently placed his hand over hers and lowered the weapon.

With nowhere to go, Michael released me as he was brought to the ground by a marshal. I sank to my knees. "How did you know? My texts wouldn't go through." I sucked in ragged breaths as my skittering nerves started to settle.

"Al put the call out that he thought you girls were going to run into some trouble. We were all out looking when your text location finally came through."

I stood, wrapping my arms around Gemma.

Al leaned against the butt of his shotgun. "What did you expect? This is Tipp. When one of our own is in trouble, we come running."

THIRTY-ONE

EVAN

Ma stood behind her desk as I stared at my brother, fury rising in my chest. "Do not kill each other. Blood's a bitch to get out of the carpet." She rounded her desk, and the door closed behind her.

Parker shot to his feet and we were at a standoff, both with our arms crossed and feet planted wide. I broke first. "Don't fucking tell me you're an undercover agent or some bullshit."

Parker's barking laugh filled the office. "You know better than that." His eyes raked down me, snagging on my work boots as though he couldn't believe I was wearing them. He finally looked back at me and shook his head. "Never thought you for a rat."

My fist connected with his face with a satisfying crack. Heat radiated up my arm. I held my hands up, ready for the fight.

"Fuck!" Parker swiped the back of his hand over his lip, smearing blood across his forearm. "I forgot how much that goddamn left stings." He pinched his nose and shook his head.

"You may not have thought me for a rat, but I never thought you'd kidnap our sister. Guess we were both wrong."

"That wasn't my call. Ow. Fucking dickbag."

I took one step forward, ready to lay it down again. "The fuck you say to me?"

"Gemma. That wasn't my call. But she'd overheard some shit—weapons trafficking and the location of the drop. It made Michael jumpy. I told him I'd take care of it."

A disgusted scoff pushed through my nose.

"Jesus, Evan. I was going to *talk* to her. Make sure she understood that she couldn't tell anyone what she'd heard. Ever. Apparently, Michael was worried a conversation wasn't enough. He had her snatched." I lowered my hands and watched my big brother, looking for any signs of him lying. "Word got around that he'd nabbed her. I was looking for her, too, you know."

I could only stare at the stranger in front of me. For years I'd watched him slowly morph into someone I barely recognized. Controlled. Darker. I hated to admit that I had been changing too. I'd used Gemma's abduction as an excuse to leave the life, but in reality, I'd already had one foot out the door.

"Looking for her? You didn't want anything to do with her."

Parker lifted his chin and stared me down. "Can you blame me? She's the spitting image of Mom. I didn't need the walking reminder. That doesn't mean I want her dead."

My nostrils flared. I was at war between protecting my sister and believing the bullshit my big brother was trying to feed me. I gritted my teeth. I had to know. "No bullshit?"

A smile cracked across his features as he reached out his hand. "No, man. No bullshit."

I stared down at his open hand. The ruthless man that he'd become still held traces of the protective brother he used to be. I hated myself for even considering forgiveness. Instead, I held my ground, my eyes level with his. "I need answers first. Starting with what you know about Michael and how the fuck you found us here."

The conversation with Parker left me drained. I now had more questions than answers. Park still had his secrets, the biggest being the tiny blonde with owl eyes he'd dragged in with him. When Parker left, she rose from the couch and scurried behind him without a sound. I chose to tackle that mystery another day.

I was dog-tired and needed a shower. I hated myself for how I'd spat venom in Val's direction. I would have got on my knees and begged for her forgiveness if I thought that would make her stay.

Selfish.

Val didn't belong here.

I braced myself on the kitchen island of the lodge and hung my head. My shoulders ached and my head throbbed. The lodge was quiet, and I could feel the long-ass day tug at the muscles in my back.

Commotion from the hallway caught my attention. Robbie came barreling down the hall, Ma and two other agents at his heels. "What's going on?"

"Val found Michael. They ran into some trouble, but the truck's pulling in now."

I immediately straightened and moved with them when Ma stopped in front of me. "Absolutely not." She pointed to the chair near the island. "Sit down."

"No." My fists clenched at my sides.

"Had you been there and it'd gone sideways, it would have put yourself and Gemma at risk. Val was smart. She tried to get out of there at the first sniff of trouble. He got the drop on her."

I clenched my jaw. I had to see her for myself, to know that she was okay.

"She needs to speak with me. I need to debrief and then she's all yours."

Over Ma's shoulder, Scotty walked in with Gemma tucked under his arm. When she saw me, she rushed forward. I caught her in my arms as she cried against my chest. I murmured words of comfort but kept my eyes pinned to the door, waiting for Val.

She walked in. Other agents were slapping her back and offering congratulations. She gave only a small smile. Robbie walked with swift steps, leading her down the hallway to Ma's office.

Our eyes met and my chest hitched. She was messy and dirty and the most gorgeous woman I had ever seen. I'd brought her into this mess, and because of me, she'd been put in danger. Even here, I couldn't keep her safe.

I tracked her movements until she disappeared behind the door.

"I've been removed from any further investigation." I lifted my head to see Val's shoulders back, chin raised. The defiant glint in her eye was so damn gorgeous I wanted to pull her into me. I turned toward her but my feet stayed planted, and I ignored the pit aching in my middle. I didn't respond. "Agents Brown and Brown felt that I was too close to the investigation and my involvement with you was a conflict of interest."

"You're leaving, then?" I felt sick. My insides were screaming to go to her, comfort her, but she was guarded. She stood with her arms clamped across her chest. Scott had kept me company and told me what had gone down at the church. After what she had been through, I was afraid to touch her and make it worse.

"Final arrangements have been made. I'm only waiting to be debriefed, and then I'll know my next steps." Val took a tentative step forward, and I stiffened. One touch and I'd crumble.

She let out a breath and looked at me. "I understand you're angry, but I want you to know that I made the deal with Walsh because I thought it would protect you and Gemma. I *wanted* to stay. With you. I couldn't stand the thought of leaving. I should have told you."

Losing her would destroy me. Val was the best thing that had ever happened to me, and I was the anchor tied around her neck. A life with me would mean giving up her dream job at the ATF, her life in Chicago. If protecting her from me meant that I had to live without her, I'd willingly suffer through it.

"You should have left." My heart had been carved out of my chest, and I held the knife. I closed my eyes and tried to swallow the bile that threatened the back of my throat. I gritted my teeth to get through what needed to be said. "Listen, we both knew what this was."

Val stared at me, her dark eyes serious and unwavering. "What this was . . ."

She was going to make me say it.

Fuck.

"Yeah. Fun. Temporary, until it ran its course or you

went back to Chicago." The words burned in my mouth. The warmth in her eyes was gone, and I knew I'd never feel them warm my skin again. She would never look at me like I was something more than a lowlife. A criminal.

"This isn't who you are."

I turned away from her. It was too painful to hear the hope in her voice. I couldn't hold on to the hope or I would destroy us both. "You're wrong. I know exactly who I am. You just didn't want to believe it. Don't put that on me."

"You are unbelievable," she whispered, shaking her head, her jaw set.

I realized that I needed her anger. I couldn't stand the idea of making her cry. Anger was better. Anger wouldn't rip my insides to shreds, but the tears that clung to her lashes would bring me to my knees.

"Gemma and I have started over. You're a threat to everything I'm trying to build here." She knew. Val knew what going into witness protection and adopting a new identity meant for us. We would never get the chance at a fresh start again. "This is the one chance I have at giving Gemma the life she deserves."

"What about what *you* deserve?"

A humorless laugh huffed out of me. "I know I'm getting exactly what I deserve." I had never spoken truer words.

Val took a long, shaky breath. When she moved toward the back door, the relief I'd hoped for was replaced with a skittering of panic. My body was screaming to turn around and move forward, stop her and somehow make it right.

"It didn't have to be this way, Evan. Whether you can admit it to yourself or not, we both know this was more than just some casual fling. Yes, it was complicated and unconventional, and it would have taken some hard conversations to figure out how to make it work, but it wasn't impossible."

Her words, so empty of hope, gutted me. Somewhere between trying to be someone I'm not and falling in love with her, I had lost control. "You said it once yourself. I'm too much. This is too much. You were right about that."

Her anger flared. My beautiful, spitfire goddess. "You may make a habit of twisting words, but I refuse. I know exactly what this was, and when you'd told me that you would never get enough of me, I was stupidly hopeful enough to believe you."

I couldn't think straight, not with a hundred warring emotions coursing through me. I sucked a ragged breath in through my nose. I knew the facts. "You're a cop, and I'm a criminal testifying in a federal case. How did you think this was going to play out?" I took a deliberate step away.

Val turned the handle to the door, but at the last moment, I surged forward, gripping her arm and pulling her into me.

I love you so much, and it's fucking killing me.

She melted against me, her chin lifted so her eyes could meet mine, and a ripple of disgust ran through me for getting hard against her. Knowing this was the last moment I would hold her in my arms ripped my heart from my chest.

Her unshed tears were replaced with cold indifference as she wrenched herself free. "Goodbye, Evan."

IF LOOKS COULD FREEZE HELL, Gemma was about to become Ice Queen of the Underworld. She sat on the small porch of her cottage, and I carefully lowered myself into the wooden rocker next to her. My eyes dipped to the bruises that colored the inside of her wrists. I tried to lay a comforting hand on hers, but the look she shot me stopped my hand midair. Somehow, in the forty-eight hours since her panic attack and confrontation with Michael, Gem had stuffed her fear and anxiety so deep that it had forged into blind rage.

She. Was. Pissed.

"Come on, Gem."

"Don't 'Come on, Gem' me. None of this makes any sense."

I breathed deeply. "I know."

"Parker is *here*. Why hasn't he been arrested?"

"I don't know."

"And he brought a girl?"

I dragged a hand through my hair and expelled a breath. "Yeah, it's fucked up."

"People are saying they're married. You know as well as I do that's complete bullshit. Parker was a total skank."

I scoffed at her relatively accurate description of our brother. We hadn't been close enough for me to know, but he didn't come across as the kind of man who was looking for commitment. I shrugged and let my hand slap against my thigh.

"And what about Val? You screwed that up royally. She's *leaving*, Ev."

Tightness shifted in my chest. "Yeah. She's going home."

"Are you going to tell her not to?"

"Why would I do that?"

She blew out a disgusted little noise. "You're a coward."

Today I had managed to piss off two women I cared about, and there was nothing I could do about it.

Awesome.

To prevent further emotional beatdowns, I stood and walked in the direction of my cabin. The low *moo*s of the cattle in the pasture were an unwelcome reminder of the first time I'd kissed Val. Tension wound through my back. Voices ahead of me caught my attention. In the distance, I could see a car had pulled up next to one of the open cabins. Parker exited the car, rounded the hood and opened the door for the small woman.

Parker's deep voice floated across the open air. "I'll grab your stuff."

It looked like the woman was choking back tears, but when her eyes met mine, she paused, and I stopped walking. Her shoulders straightened, and she marched up to me as Parker stared after her in disbelief. "Hi! You must be Evan. I'm Sienna. Parker's wife."

My eyes shot to my brother, who scowled and stomped into the cabin.

THIRTY-TWO
VAL

I wasn't a violent person, but I really wanted to slap the fuck out of Evan Walker. Tears burned in my eyes as I glanced in the rearview at the Laurel Canyon Ranch gate. In my heart, it would always be Redemption Ranch.

I contemplated my long, depressing drive back to Chicago. Not even the mug full of Robbie's French press coffee was a comfort, though I didn't feel bad about snagging the mug from Evan's cottage. Not even a little. I glanced at it again. One quiet morning lying in bed, Evan had surprised me with it—a crafter at the farmers market had created it just for me. The black letters *So Fucking Zen* had a sad smile tugging at my lips as I recalled our first yoga class.

I shifted in my seat and gripped the steering wheel. It was time to go. Ray had fixed up my old car, and when I thanked him and moved in for a hug, the wad of chaw he spat at my feet was all the goodbye he offered.

He's a real charmer.

I adjusted in the seat, trying to find a comfortable position. Somehow the economical little car had become uncomfortable. Foreign. The seat wasn't broken in enough. It sat too low to the ground. I missed the crappy beat-up Silverado Ma had lent me. With the long drive ahead of me, I groaned internally. Twenty hours of driving was a long time to be alone with your thoughts. I could have turned left, wound around the mountains, and headed straight for the interstate. Instead, I decided to pull through town. Not saying goodbye to the people I'd come to love didn't feel right.

I stood in front of Rebellious Rose, rooted to the spot until Johnny must have seen me through the window. He pushed open the door and called to me. "I'm not doing it."

I looked at him, my face twisted in confusion as he stalked toward me.

"Gemma called. I'm not saying goodbye. I refuse."

I pulled my friend into a hug as his arms hung at his sides. "I am going to miss you." I gripped his face, squishing his cheeks together. "You're one of the good ones."

"I don't eben like you that mush." His words were garbled as I pushed his cheeks together, and we both laughed. Finally, his arms wrapped around me, and I hugged him back. "You're sure about this?"

I stepped back, nodding. "I'm sure. It's time to go home."

"You know, home isn't always where you come from." Fresh emotion burned in my lungs at his words, and I pressed my tongue to the roof of my mouth to keep from crying all over his black angora sweater.

After a few more minutes of a sad goodbye, hugging and rocking on the sidewalk, I turned toward my car. The swinging wooden sign for the Tabula Rasa called to me. It was my first stop when I'd arrived in Tipp, and it felt only right that it was my last on the way out.

The midday lunch crowd was sparse, and the smells of pizza and fried chicken wafted from the kitchen. I looked around the dim bar, and so many memories of Evan flooded back to me. Seeing him sitting in the shadows that first night. Our not-really-a-date date when we played pool. Karaoke night.

"The rumors are true, aren't they?" Al's scratchy voice called to me from behind the bar. The old bartender's face was hard, but his eyes were kind. I smiled and walked toward him.

I raised my palms and let them gently slap at my sides. "I'm headed out, but I couldn't go without saying goodbye first. Thank you for everything you did. It started with your frosty welcome. I was hoping for a warmer goodbye."

Al rounded the bar. "Ah, kid. You're gonna make me sentimental."

I looped my arms around his lean frame and squeezed. "I won't forget this strange and confusing place. It's a wonder no one's discovered what a gem it is."

Al's chest rumbled in agreement as he continued to hug me. "This place is special. I left my life with an MC with nowhere to go. No one to turn to. My bike broke down outside of town, and I've never left. The people here accept you. What more can you want?"

I stepped back from his arms.

"It's complicated. My job. Evan and me . . . there's just too much history."

"Do you know why I named my bar the Tabula Rasa? I had a cellmate who was always spouting off ancient Greek and Latin. Tabula Rasa means a clean slate. That's what you get in Tipp."

My chest pinched, the lump in the throat too hard to swallow around.

If only it were that easy.

I took a deep breath. "Thank you again."

"I'll see you soon."

Al winked at me, and I strode out into the blinding afternoon sunlight. I turned my car down Main Street and headed east toward home. I stared at the rearview as the town got smaller and smaller. I was headed toward a new future, but leaving my heart behind.

Montana—I thought of nothing but Evan and cried through the entire state.

North Dakota—I tried to forget about how good he smelled. How strong and warm his hands were.

Minnesota—I blasted power ballads until my throat was raw and I was convinced that I was born in the wrong decade. Michael Bolton really knew how to make you *feel* that heartache.

Wisconsin—I drowned my sorrows at the Mars Cheese Castle. It was a poor choice.

Chicago.

I walked into my apartment, and the musty, closed-up smell of being locked up for months was intense. I set the bag of takeout from Uncle Mao's on the counter and immediately threw open every window and let the cool fall air sweep through the house. My landlord had agreed to watch over the apartment during my extended leave, and the pile of mail on the countertop was overwhelming. I'd have to sort through all of that, along with the rest of my life, eventually.

I glanced down at my phone. Once I'd left the flats of Montana and got closer to more populated areas, I watched my phone expectantly. Maybe he would call. Or text. I knew even then that if he did, I would have turned my car around and sped back toward the ranch without a second thought.

He didn't.

Evan Walker was forever gone from my life, and the dull ache under my ribs had taken his place. My bag lay in a sad heap on the floor. I'd left my boots and ranch clothes with Gemma. We were nearly the same size, and I had no use for them in here.

Here, I was Officer Val Rivera. Tactical boots. Body armor. Handgun. That was the uniform I had chosen. The sooner I realized that it was the *only* choice, the better I would be. I had made my intentions clear to Evan. And he had made his intentions clear to me.

He didn't want me.

I steeled my heart and had no other option but to move forward. While I pushed the revolting vegetable medley around the take-out container, my phone lit up. A wild flutter tingled my insides. I glanced down to see an unknown number, and the butterflies flapped wildly.

"Hello?"

"Is this Val Rivera?" Disappointment coursed through me when I realized it wasn't Evan on the other line.

"This is she."

"Officer Rivera, Special Agent Walsh. Do you have a minute?"

"Of course." I pushed the takeout away from me and stood to pace the room.

"I've been communicating with Agents Brown and Brown. Heard you ran into a little excitement down there. They sang your praises regarding your work and time on the ranch."

A warm glow heated my cheeks. I was relieved to hear they weren't upset at how I'd left things at Redemption. Hope bloomed in my chest as he continued to tell me the wonderful things Ma and Robbie had told him about my time there.

Did they want me back? Was that even a thing?

Agent Walsh's voice cut through my tumbling, incoherent thoughts. ". . . which is why I'd love to offer you the position at the Chicago Field Division of the ATF."

Disappointment, longing, sadness. Emotions I couldn't reconcile with the news he'd just delivered.

This is everything you've worked for.

"Seems like I've rendered you speechless."

A small laugh escaped me as I cleared my throat. "Uh, yeah. That's, wow." I took a deep breath and got my shit together. "It's an honor, sir."

"Glad to hear that. You've earned this. Don't get too comfortable there in Chicago. Next stop for you is Glynco for the Academy."

My mind was spinning. "Yes, sir."

Agent Walsh droned on about the procedures and when to report for training. I took notes on the back of an envelope and hoped I'd gotten all the information down correctly.

I'm leaving again.

The ATF National Academy in Georgia meant academic and legal courses paired with physical and specialty training. After that, I would finally be a special agent.

Everything I'd worked for.

If only my heart would get the memo.

THIRTY-THREE

EVAN

To: Val Rivera

From: Unknown sender

Subject: Open this. It's not spam.

Dear Val,

Please hear me out—I got Scotty drunk and then swindled him in poker in order to get your email address. He paid a guy who paid a guy to get it. Emily, the one librarian you called "funky," is apparently some kind of tech genius, and she showed me how to email without it getting tracked. You can reply to this address and it gets bounced around the world, but it'll get to me. Apparently, it's not exactly legal, but I don't feel bad about that. I think there's always going to be a part of me that gets off on skirting the law. You should probably know that up front. You should also know that I didn't mean the hurtful things I said to you. Also, I'm an asshole (*that* you probably figured out for yourself).

I know we called it quits. That I pushed you away. I thought I was doing the right thing. I'm not sure what I expected, but I sure as hell didn't expect this. I'm tired. I'm tired of rolling over in bed and reaching for you and the emptiness that follows me around all day once I realize you're really gone. I'm tired of replaying our last conversation over and over with what I should have said and done. I'm tired of trying to convince myself I did the right thing. So fucking tired.

There are so many more important words that I should have said to you. Three in particular. I hope one day I'll get the chance to say them.

Yours,

Evan

To: Val Rivera

From: Unknown sender

Subject: ghosts

My dearest Valor,

Do you believe in ghosts? Today at the last farmers market of the season, I swore I saw you in the crowd. I nearly lost my mind. There's nothing new around the ranch, and the days are long. The nights without you are even longer. We had a few new calves born, and I thought about the day you helped with AI. I would have laughed if everything didn't hurt so damn much. I wanted to name one of the new babies Val after you, but then Gemma reminded me that honoring a woman with a *cow* was (and I quote) "the least romantic thing on the planet." In my head, I call it Marian instead. Every time I see that goofy cow I think about the first time I kissed you under the stars, in the pasture. I knew, even before that moment, that you were different. Real. I know I made you think otherwise, and for that I will always be sorry.

I'm sorry. I'm sorry. I'm sorry.

Love,

Evan

To: Val Rivera

From: Unknown sender

Subject: A promise

Everyone in town hates me. The gossip mill spread quickly about why you left Tipp, and no one seems too thrilled with me at the moment. I've lived here nearly a year, and suddenly my coffee orders are getting fucked up and I can't get Al to serve me a beer to save my life.

Family dinner is a lot quieter too. Whenever someone mentions your name, a weird and uncomfortable silence falls over the table. My chest hurts so bad I have to leave. Usually I take a walk around the pond or sit on the dock and worry. I worry that you're not safe. I worry that you'll never know how deeply you changed me for the better. I worry that you haven't heard a pun lately that made you laugh.

Here's one: the new hapkido instructor at the gym said he was pulling out a new move from his "kicktionary." I thought you might like that one.

More than anything, I worry that I made you feel like doing the right thing was wrong. I know you had the best of intentions and I couldn't see that. I worry I made you doubt your instincts. But mostly I worry that one day people will stop mentioning you.

I promise to say your name every day.

Love,

Evan

≈

To: Val Rivera

From: Unknown sender

Subject: restless

Waking up without you is painful. My bones ache from the minute I wake up until I lie in our bed and stare at the ceiling. I miss you stealing the covers. It's too fucking hot in here anyway.

Love,

Evan

≈

To: Val Rivera

From: Unknown sender

Subject: family secrets

When I was a kid, Parker and I were left alone a lot. It's strange seeing him here on the ranch. Gemma avoids him altogether. He and I don't talk much yet—it's a work in progress. The looks he gives that wife of his are full of secrets that I don't fully trust. If you were here, I'm sure you would have already figured out what the deal is with those two.

Seeing him again brings up a lot of painful memories I tried to forget. My mom was unreliable at best, and the men she brought home were violent and frightening at worst. I learned early on that the people who were supposed to love you sometimes didn't. That's a hard lesson for a kid to learn. When we got older, Parker kept me on the outskirts, never letting me get too close.

When you were here, it felt like family is supposed to feel. I know there is darkness inside me, but you had a way of finding the light.

I miss your laughter and your light.

All my love,

Evan

To: Val Rivera

From: Unknown sender

Subject: desperate

Stalking is a criminal behavior, right? I let it slip to Gemma that I was emailing you and she called me a "psycho." She misses you, too, but she's made sure I know the blame lies fully on my shoulders. She's happy to mumble *asshole* under her breath whenever she gets the chance, so it's pretty clear she agrees. I let her know that I don't even know if you're getting these emails. If it's painful for you, I'm sorry. I can't help it, and according to Gem, I'm "too desperate" to stop. I can't bear the thought of losing the only connection I have to you. Fuck, I hope you're getting these. Please say something. Tell me what a dick I am. Tell me you hate my face. Anything.

Love,

Evan

To: Val Rivera

From: Unknown sender

Subject: what if

Dear Val,

Most nights I lie awake and think about how different things should have been. Last night I wondered what it would have been like if we'd met in Chicago. The reality hit me that if we would have met in Chicago, it probably would have been because I was in the back of your squad car. You deserve so much more than a man who lived to break the rules. I know this. I'm working on it. I've convinced myself that if I can be the best version of myself, the semblance of a man worthy of your love, you'll find your way back to me.

Option two is to make you arrest me, but that's probably not a great idea.

Let's go with option one.

Love,

Evan

THIRTY-FOUR

VAL

Late fall was as brown and dreary as I'd remembered. Only weeks after Agent Walsh's phone call, I resigned from my position at the Eleventh District Police Precinct, paused the lease on my apartment again, and boxed most of my belongings for storage. The strange and uncomfortable feeling of not having a home nagged me constantly.

I thought of Tipp, Montana, every single day.

Training was grueling and intense. I learned more about procedural law enforcement than I ever thought possible. Tactical training made my muscles ache. As a woman, I had to work twice as hard to prove that I was capable. Proving I was more than my exterior was exhausting and demanding, but it left little room for anything else. Whenever Evan and our time together threatened to surface, I refocused and shoved it down.

At night, in the quiet moments before I let sleep take me, I ached for him.

The day I logged in to my email, I stared at the full inbox. I read his first email twenty times.

Shock.

Sadness.

Elation.

I warred with the emotions that coursed through me. The emails from the unknown address came every single day. I couldn't stop myself from reading them. Night after night, I curled up on my couch in my shitty dormitory and stared out the window after reading them. Over and over, I read them and pictured Evan as he wrote them. My view was the brick wall of the neighboring building, and I missed the wide-open spaces, the towering indigo mountains of Montana.

A thousand times I almost wrote him back, but stopped. There was no place for me at Redemption, and Evan needed to move on with his new life. He deserved it and so did Gemma.

After my return to Chicago, Chief Dunleavy and Agent Walsh congratulated me. My time at the ranch was considered an extended interview, which I'd passed with flying colors. The ATF National Academy was grueling, but fascinating, and because I'd spent all my energy trying to *not* think about Evan and the people I'd left behind in Tipp, I did nothing but study and learn. As a result, I was the newest member of the Chicago Field Division of the Bureau of Alcohol, Tobacco, Firearms, and Explosives. Spanning northern Illinois, northern Indiana, and eastern Wisconsin, we were responsible for investigating armed violent offenders, career criminals, gun traffickers, and gangs.

Mostly I pushed paper.

At a glance, I had everything I had ever wanted, and I couldn't be more miserable.

My skin felt too tight. Nothing seemed right despite the fact that professionally things were finally clicking into place. Trouble was, there was a hole inside me that couldn't be filled. I would be hollow forever.

On my lunch break, my mother called. I debated letting it go to voicemail but knew pushing it off was only a detriment to Future Val. I sighed and answered her call.

"Hi, Mom."

After a disapproving cluck of her tongue, she continued the conversation in Spanish.

"It wouldn't kill you to call me for a change. A mother worries, you know."

I rubbed my weary eyes. "It's been busy."

"You should never be too busy to call home, *mija*. You work too hard."

"It's a tough job."

"Work like that is no place for a woman. Why can't you get a job that doesn't require a gun and those ugly pants? You could have been a schoolteacher. Settled down and started a family."

I sighed. She still didn't understand that I wanted to be so much more than the roles society and our community told us were appropriate.

"I know." Over the years I'd learned that it was easier, and faster, to agree with her disapproval of my life choices. Mom's mention of a family had me immediately thinking of Evan. Did he even want kids? My tan skin and his blue eyes would have made some beautiful children.

Fantastic. Now I have something new to obsess over.

She prattled on, doubling down to tell me all the adorable things my sister's children were doing. They lived in the suburbs, and Graciela took after my mother and had decided to stay home to raise her kids. I loved that for her, but I needed something *more*. I was built for more. I thought clawing my way up the ladder was going to be what fulfilled me, but I was slowly learning that I still felt empty.

"The work I do is important."

"There is nothing more important than love, *mija*. Remember that."

My MOTHER's words clanged around in my head.

There is nothing more important than love.

I had filled the lonely hours with work since I left Montana, but no matter how I filled the days, it still hadn't left me. I thought about Evan and Gemma, Ma and Robbie, even Ray, every single day.

I couldn't stand not knowing what they were up to, despite the emails that came. I only read them every few days. My heart couldn't handle more. Scott had told me how genuinely shocked Evan looked when his brother, Parker, showed up at the ranch. He was even more stunned that Parker had a wife in tow. Apparently, that was new and altogether unexpected.

Michael had been arrested. Bruno, his hired muscle, had squealed on him the moment he was interrogated. Apparently, in Chicago, no one had been able to find Evan. He'd been a ghost. Michael had also been keeping tabs on Parker in hopes he'd lead him to Evan. When Parker found out that Evan was in Montana, Michael had followed him out west.

But something was off.

My intuition was humming and I couldn't let it go.

How did Parker know Evan was in Montana?

I needed to talk this through with someone—see what theories I could shake loose. My fingers opened the contacts on my phone, and I was dialing my old partner Eric's number before I could second-guess myself.

"Rivera! How's life in the ATF, Agent?"

I did my best to infuse as much fake happiness as I could muster. I swallowed hard. "It's great. You know, getting to know the ropes. It's a lot more procedural than I was expecting, but I'm sure it'll get busy soon."

My friend gave a noncommittal grunt.

I could feel his judgment through the phone. I had to change the subject. "So the reason I'm calling . . . I, uh, was going through some old case files and came across some information. Thought we could run through it, for old time's sake."

"'Course. What do you got?"

"What do you know about a man named Parker Marino?" I chewed my lip as I waited for him to answer.

"How do you know that name?"

"I can't tell you that. But you have to trust me. Please. Who is he?"

Silence rang in my ears for a few beats. Finally, he spoke again. "Parker Marino fell off the face of the earth a couple of months back, and we've been looking for him. He was my informant."

VAL

To: Unknown sender
    From: Val Rivera
    Subject: I need to know.
    No bullshit?
    V

VAL

I WORRIED my thumb as I stared at my computer screen, refreshing my email for the thousandth time. Sending the email to Evan was stupid. He'd sent me messages for months, and I had ignored them. At least to him. In reality, I held my breath as I opened my email each morning, hoping to see a new one from him.

The minute I finally sent my reply, he'd gone silent. Maybe he realized I wasn't worth the work. Or maybe he needed something more from me, and my simple question in an email wasn't enough. Only an idiot would hold out that long and not get frustrated and move on.

God, I hope Evan's an idiot.

I refreshed my email again and let my heart sink. The empty, hollow feeling was consuming. I no longer had even that small connection with him. He was truly gone.

A knock sounded at my door, and I looked up. Agent Walsh stood in the doorway. "Got a minute?"

I stood and smiled, but I knew it didn't reach my eyes. "Yes, sir."

"There's someone who would like to speak with you."

Agent Walsh moved aside. A man, broad shouldered in a black suit that looked more expensive than my car, stepped in and filled the doorway. I'd know those shoulders anywhere. Evan stepped forward to stand in front of me. He looked so different. His face was clean shaven. Without scruff, his jaw was sharp, and my eyes trailed down the muscular cords of his neck before snapping back up. His blue eyes, the most gorgeous mix of navy and sky, held mine.

"I'll leave you two be for a moment." I stood, unable to move, as Agent Walsh stepped around Evan and closed the door behind me with a snick.

Evan's hands were in his pockets. It was easy to see how this gorgeous man could fit seamlessly into the Mafia. The suit molded to his body, and he wore it with confidence.

I finally found my voice. "What are you doing here?"

"I've got a meeting with the prosecutor. Michael is being arraigned here in Chicago. She claims my testimony can help put him away for a long time."

"And Parker?"

Evan's eyes held mine, his jaw tight as he shook his head. "He's still at the ranch. I won't be testifying against him."

My eyes widened, trying to read this stunning, complicated man. "You're covering for him."

"Things are far from good between us, but I've started to realize a few things. He looked out for me all my life—we would have starved or been lost in the system if it weren't for him. Later, he worked the high-level jobs, wouldn't let me in even when I showed interest. I thought he was freezing me out because he wanted the money and power for himself. I let my resentment and anger prevent me from seeing what was really happening."

My voice dropped as I thought about the scared little boys who only had each other. "He was protecting his little brother."

He nodded. "The less I knew, the better off I was—at least in his mind. When I thought he had ordered Gemma's kidnapping, it broke the last thread of trust I had for him. When I made my deal for witness protection, handing over Parker was a part of the agreement."

It made sense. But I knew the system—there was more. There had to be more. "Did you get my email?"

A small smile teased his mouth. "I did. It was nice to see you got mine."

My heart plummeted to my feet. I scrambled to find the words. To explain the warring emotions that kept me from reaching back out to him. Then I realized—he's here. He came to Chicago, only days after I sent the email. That couldn't have been a coincidence.

"You don't need to be present to make amendments to your testimony." I took one tiny step forward. Hope leaped in my chest as tears burned at the corner of my eyes. "Why are you in Chicago?"

"When you didn't reply to my emails, I knew I'd blown it. But the minute I got your email, I started making plans to come to Chicago. Turns out I left something here." He moved his hands from his pockets and swiped one hand over his face.

"What?"

"My light."

In one swift move, he covered the distance between us. His mouth crashed to mine. Evan wound his arms around my back and hauled me against his chest. His tongue swept against my bottom lip, and he moaned into my mouth. I arched up, pressing myself into him. He kissed me like a man who needed oxygen and I was the only source. Every regret, emotion, and shred of love I had for him, I poured into that kiss.

My hands gripped his arms as he pulled away. "Evan, I don't know what to do. I feel like I can't breathe without you."

He lowered his forehead to mine, surrounding my senses with his clean woodsmoke smell. "Come with me. Come home."

I searched his face. "I . . . I can't. How could I do that? I have my life, my apartment, my job. I can't just move to Montana."

He straightened. His jaw set. "Then I'll move back to Chicago."

"You know you can't do that. It's not safe for you here."

"Sure I can. Gemma is safe where she's at. She'll be protected there. I can move back. Be here with you. If you'll have me." I could see in his face he meant it. Evan would risk everything—his proximity to Gemma, the new life he was building, his safety—in order to be with me in Chicago.

But Evan would never be safe anywhere near Chicago. Everyone in his former circle knew he had turned. It would be a lifetime of looking over our shoulders and worrying that every phone call was someone calling to tell me he wouldn't be coming home. I paled at the thought. It wasn't the life either of us wanted. In Tipp, Evan had meaningful work, a community that accepted him with open arms, a family in Ma and Robbie and Gemma. Tipp brought out the best in him, and I wouldn't stand for anything less than the greatness he deserved.

"No," I croaked. My voice was scratchy and dry. Tears pricked at my eyes as my heart thrummed in my chest.

Evan looked at me like I was the most precious thing in

his world. He brushed the hair away from my forehead as he held my head in his hands. Sadness darkened his features. "You are the most exquisite woman I have ever known. Thank you for showing me I was worthy of your love." He would accept my rejection if he thought that was what I truly wanted.

Evan turned from me, heaviness weighing down his broad shoulders, and I quietly laughed. This noble, infuriating man. I straightened my back. "I'm coming with you."

His body stilled as though he was processing the words I had spoken.

"Evan Walker." He turned his tortured eyes to meet mine. "Let's go home."

Special Agent Neil Walsh stared at me over his crossed arms. Once Evan and I had made out for an inappropriate amount of time against the door of my office and on top of my desk, we found him in a conference room. I locked hands with Evan, lacing my fingers with his, and announced my resignation.

"I do not accept."

My mouth opened and closed, but no sound came out.

Can he do that?

Evan tensed but squeezed my hand, and I took a steadying breath. Before he could jump in, Agent Walsh continued: "Agent Rivera, you are smart, tenacious, and quick under pressure. Those are qualities you can't teach someone. They're a part of who you are. That's a tough thing to find—even harder to replace."

I steadied my shoulders. "I understand, sir. Unfortunately, I have also found something irreplaceable. No amount of work could ever replicate it." My eyes flicked to Evan, but I had to get through this. I couldn't get emotional. "I joined the police force because I wanted to make a difference. I also hoped it would fill a hole in me, a sense of community and belonging that I'd been lacking. When it did not, I assumed climbing the ranks and earning my position in the ATF would do it. Unfortunately, while I enjoy the work we do, it has not. The one place I have felt truly whole in my entire life has been in Tipp, Montana, with this man beside me. I can't explain it, and it hurts me to disappoint you, but this is the right decision for me."

He let out an exasperated breath. "I was afraid you'd say that." Agent Walsh moved to the phone, dialed, and murmured something into the receiver. A minute later the conference room door opened, and Ma Brown strode in. She had exchanged her jeans, boots, and flannel for a smart blazer and slacks. Her hair was styled, and she even had on low heels.

I rushed over and wrapped my arms around her in a fierce embrace. "Ma."

"We've missed you, honey."

She pulled me to arm's length, and I quickly recovered. "Shit. I'm sorry. I'm rumpling you. It's just so good to see you. Are you here with Evan?" I looked between Agent Walsh, Evan, and Ma, not quite understanding what was going on here.

"As I'm sure you've heard, Evan was making a few amendments to his testimony. I escorted him here for the meeting."

I nodded. When all was said and done, Ma was a federal marshal, and she would protect Evan during the trip back to his hometown. The trip he didn't really need to make.

For me.

"I think I've got a solution for you," Ma said.

My eyes leaped to Ma's, hope blooming in my chest.

"I agree with Agent Walsh," Ma continued, "you are far too talented to quit law enforcement. Have you ever given any thought to marshal service?"

Evan stepped forward, gripping my hand in his. I held it fiercely. "You mean, back in Montana?" I said.

"Yes. You did great work out on the ranch, and I don't just mean shoveling cow shit. When it came down to it, you trusted your instincts. It was the right call. If you want it, you have a job, as a marshal, protecting those who come to stay at the ranch. People who are in search of a second chance—redemption." She paused to smile at me. "Come home, dear."

"Yes! Yes, I accept!" My eyes flew to Agent Walsh, and dread pooled in my stomach. "That is, if Agent Walsh accepts my resignation and allows me out of my current contract."

Ma held one hand on her hip and pinned him with a glare. Special Agent Walsh stepped forward, his hand outstretched to Ma. "I was afraid you'd steal her from me, but I never could say no to you, Dorothea. You owe me."

She smiled, her kind eyes crinkling at the corners. "That I do, Neil. Thank you." She turned to us, looking at Evan. "We leave in ten minutes. Val, once your affairs are in order, we'll fly you home."

Home.

I turned to Evan, his strong arms holding me close to his body, his fresh woodsmoke smell consuming me. "I don't want you to go."

"I know, baby. But it'll only be a short while. You'll be back in my arms in no time." I squeezed him harder, burying my face in his chest. Evan reached into his pocket. "I have something for you. Something to keep you company until you're back in Montana."

He reached out his hand. In the center of his palm was a delicate necklace. The base of the chain held a geode, cracked open, the crystal center shimmering under the fluorescent lighting of the office.

"Evan. It's breathtaking." I held it in my hand and let it twirl at the end of the chain.

"I went back to that booth at the farmers market every week, looking for the perfect one. The crystals in this one match your eyes. I knew it was the one when I saw it." His large hands framed my face. "Just like I knew you were the one. It's something I felt in my bones the minute I laid eyes on you at the ranch. I love you."

I was lost. Lost in his eyes, in *him*. This man was everything. "I love you too."

THIRTY-SEVEN

EVAN

Two painfully slow weeks later, I was standing in the Montana sunshine, staring at the huge wooden door of the lodge as Val finished her meeting with Ma. I still couldn't believe she was back in Montana, that it had all worked out. When I'd entered the Witness Protection Program, I thought it would be a different kind of prison sentence. What had started out a prison of my own making ended up being the exact thing that freed me—from my old life, from the limits I put on myself, from every regret I had about the choices I had made.

I knew I didn't deserve a second chance. I sure as fuck didn't deserve Val, but if she said I was the man to make her happy, I'd spend the rest of my life making sure I could live up to that. She would have zero regrets when we were through.

"Looks like you did it." Scotty approached from behind, and I turned to shake his hand.

"Yeah." I sighed a breath. "Still can't believe I convinced her to come back."

"Nah. You deserve this." His smile was slow and easy. "Val does too."

"Thank you. For letting a piece of shit like me have a fresh start."

He nodded. "You're a good guy. Don't be so hard on yourself."

"Now you'll be working with my girl. Don't let her kick your ass."

His face shadowed. "Unfortunately, I won't have the pleasure. I've been reassigned."

I turned to face him. "Oh?"

"Voluntary transfer." His voice was thick and laced with something I didn't know him well enough to recognize. When Gemma came bounding out the door arm in arm with Val, his face transformed into a painful scowl as he walked away.

Huh.

"Are you not *dying* that you're home?" Gemma's bubble of excitement overshadowed any questions I had about Scotty and why it seemed to pain him to look at Gemma.

Val laughed and hugged my little sister. "It's unreal. I'm so happy." Val dipped her head toward Gemma. "I'm sorry I was an asshole and didn't call."

She shrugged. "Hey, I get it. It's all good. Hashtag Team Val." She bumped her hip with Val, and my chest warmed.

My family.

Work, friendship, family, love. Everything I needed I had right here in the strange little town of Tipp, Montana. I couldn't wait to bring Val to town and see Johnny and Al and everyone else that had been asking after her. They were going to lose their minds when they found out she's back.

"Hey, that one's mine." The deep rumble of my voice

had Val's head whipping up and her pupils going wide. Pleasure skittered over my skin. I fucking loved she reacted to me that way. I stood, my arms crossed over my chest as her eyes soaked me up from bottom to top. Fuck, she looked so good in faded jeans that hugged her muscular thighs and stretched across the curve of her ass. She looked damn good. My mouth went dry, and a heaviness settled between my thighs.

"Hey, handsome." She beamed at me. This was really happening.

"Sorry, Gem. I'm stealing her."

Gemma stuck out her tongue like a brat and waved as she walked away.

"Come with me." I bundled her up in the truck, and we headed toward my cabin.

Our cabin.

The short drive was full of tangled hands, neck kisses, and low groans. She couldn't keep her hands off me. Her hands slid over my thighs and squeezed. Her fingertips grazed the slices of muscle across my abdomen. My fingers flexed around the steering wheel, trying to keep the truck on the road as we made our way back.

I threw the truck in park and rounded the hood. I dragged Val from the truck and hoisted her up over my shoulder like a caveman. She squealed and pretended to fight it. With a smack to her ass and a squeeze, I carried her through the door of the cottage—our temporary home—with a hearty laugh. The sound was foreign to me, deep and rumbling and genuine. Val lit me up from the inside.

Heat flooded across my chest and my cock thickened. My hand rubbed and squeezed the back of her thigh as I stalked toward the bedroom. Once inside, I flipped her on the bed. She bounced and laughed, but her giggle was silenced when I covered her body with mine. Our mouths fused, and her hips bucked up to meet me.

I wanted to tear the clothes from her body. Rip them to shreds as I fucked her hard and deep. I needed to slow down. Savor every curve. My rough hands moved up her rib cage, taking her shirt with me. Val's full breasts filled her lace bra, and my mouth when dry.

"So fucking perfect." I bent to tease her nipple through the black lace. She sucked in a breath, and I clamped down harder. Her hands threaded through my hair on a moan. I ground my hips into hers as her legs wound around my waist.

My breath left my lungs as I look down at this gorgeous woman.

My woman.

I wanted to worship her. Fill her and pour every ounce of my love into her. I framed her face in my palms. "I love you."

Before she could speak, I laid a gentle kiss on her, trailing my mouth down her throat. My hand cupped the back of her neck and kneaded the muscles there. I wanted her ready, pliant, and aching.

I was hungry for her, but I forced myself to draw out the kiss. Slowly I peeled the clothes from her body. I reached behind my head to rip off my shirt and get rid of my pants and boxer briefs. On her back, Val parted her knees, revealing the glistening slick of her pussy. I dipped my head low, pressing the flat of my tongue against her from bottom to top.

Val gasped, raking her nails against my scalp, and hot tingles crawled down my torso. I could feel her getting close. I needed to bury myself inside her. I leaned back, one hand holding my cock and giving it a long stroke. Val sat up, leaned in, and took my cock in her mouth. The center of my chest was hot and heavy. The soft skin of the back of her throat flexed around the head of my cock, and I moaned. Her satisfied giggle vibrated through me, and I nearly came.

"Baby." I held her hair, and she looked up at me, her plump lips stretched around my cock.

Oh fuck.

It was brutal, keeping myself from surging forward. I leaned back and shifted her hips so she was settled on top of me. My cock teased the center of her heat.

"Yes, Evan. I want to feel you." She was breathless, waiting. Val's mouth met mine as I angled my hips and pulled her over my cock. Her pussy was hot and tight, and my cock pulsed at how perfectly we fit together. Val's legs wrapped around me. I held her torso flush with mine as we sat, wrapped in each other. She began to rock her hips, and I matched her rhythm.

She moaned as she used my cock to chase her release.

"That's it, baby. Grind that clit against the base of my cock."

Val's head lolled to the side, and I used the opportunity to kiss and suck the thin skin of her neck. Her pulse beat wildly out of control. I used my strength to pull her hips farther down my cock. Slow and hard and deep, I fucked the woman I love.

Val's arms wrapped around my head, and we both panted hard as we got closer and closer. The familiar pulse of her pussy sent a hot ball of pleasure racing down my spine. "You're close, baby. I can feel you. Come on this cock."

At my words, Val's heat exploded around me, and I couldn't hold back. My cock pumped, hard and rhythmic as I released into her. We rode the waves of our orgasms together. We were a hot, sweaty, sticky mess, but I held on to her. I couldn't let go.

Val shifted but I held her tighter. "Stay here. Stay here with me."

She leaned back to look at me. Her deep-brown eyes, heavy with pleasure, were the most gorgeous sight I'd ever witnessed. "I'm here."

⁓

THE GLOW of the clock illuminated the small bedroom. Nothing about the cottage was enough for what Val deserved. We'd spent hours making love, sleeping, rolling over to make love again. I was gentle, sure she would be sore, if she wasn't already.

The soft red glow illuminated her skin as I trailed my fingertips down her back. With my head propped on my hand, I memorized every curve of her body. Val was sleepy, her eyelids heavy, and a soft smile played at her lips.

"Tired?"

"Mmm." She was nearly asleep.

"This is everything. I want to give you everything you deserve. Thank you for coming home."

Val looked at me and smiled. "Thank you for not giving up on me."

My chest tightened. I would fight for this woman for the rest of my life. "Marry me."

Her eyes searched mine, her sleepy smile growing wide. "Really?"

"Be my wife. I'll make you coffee, tell you bad jokes, whatever it takes. I will be the man that gives you the life you deserve."

Val shifted, pushing me on my back. A curtain of her

hair cocooned us. "Yes." She planted a kiss on my lips. "Yes." Another kiss. "Yes." An elated giggle erupted from her as I wrapped my arms around her and tickled her side. We laughed and rolled around the bed. I felt brighter than I ever had, the darkness inside me dulled to a small, faded shadow.

My light.

EPILOGUE

Evan

My palms were sweaty.

When was the last time I felt nervous?

Probably when I'd stood in the ATF building in Chicago, hoping that Val wouldn't turn me away. It had been six months since then, and life couldn't be better. Though Val deserved so much more than the impromptu proposal she'd received, she said over and over that she wouldn't want it any other way. Just a month later we married in a quiet ceremony on the ranch. When Val rounded a corner wearing a white gown and flowers in her hair, I couldn't breathe. She was the most stunning woman I'd ever seen, and she had chosen me. I was a lucky bastard, and I made sure she knew it every day.

In that time I had also taken on more responsibilities at the ranch. What started as an opportunity to have a leg up and develop skills before entering the workforce had turned into a career I had never envisioned. Turns out I had a knack for management and solving problems. Ma called it a "way with people." It sure was a far cry from how I dealt with people in Chicago. In time, Ma and Robbie had talked with the other managers. They offered me a full-time position managing the day-to-day operations on the ranch.

The days were still sweaty and dusty, but the sense of accomplishment always overshadowed the blistered palms and aching back. I could also oversee different aspects of ranch operations and make sure things were running smoothly, efficiently.

Val was also thriving. She loved her role as a marshal on the ranch. If she wasn't on duty, she'd spend her hours working the ranch, usually with the horses she loved so much. We were still living in the small cottage that had given us our start—there were so many good memories under that roof.

"You sure clean up nice." I turned to see Gemma smiling at me, a cup of something warm between her hands.

I looked down to my boots, then ran a hand down the buttons of my shirt. I'd made sure it was pressed and tucked in. I still couldn't get myself to commit to a belt buckle, but I was relieved my attempt to look decent had hit the mark.

Today was special.

"Thanks, Gem. What are you up to?"

"Just grabbing a few things from Johnny." She gestured with her cup toward Rebellious Rose. "Val with you?"

I shook my head. "She's on her way. Once she's off shift, another agent is dropping her off, and we're snagging some of Irma's apple pie."

Excitement shone in Gemma's eyes. "Ohh. Get me a piece!" She leaned in for a hug, and I squeezed her tight. "Later, Ev."

"Will do. Bye." I watched my little sister cross the street, smiling and waving to a town full of friendly faces. She still wrestled her demons some days, but she was here. Safe and, I hoped, happy with her life in Tipp.

A low catcall whistle caught my attention. I whipped around to see Val smiling at me. "Looking good in those jeans, cowboy."

I tipped my imaginary hat. "Ma'am."

Val dissolved into a fit of laughter. She threw her arms around my neck, and I wrapped mine around her waist, pulling her into me. I inhaled the bright citrus scent in her hair and swallowed a groan as I kissed her neck.

"I missed you today."

She smiled at me. "I missed you too. Busy day. We have a new guest."

I tried to ignore the way my back stiffened. New guests meant a change in the routine. A possible new threat. "Everything okay?"

She smiled and nodded. One concession we had to make when Val became a marshal was that there were some parts of her job she couldn't share with me. As long as she could share her life with me along with everything else, I had made peace with that.

"Are you ready to *finally* have the world's best pie, Mrs. Walker?"

Val's plump bottom lip caught in her teeth. She loved when I called her Mrs. Walker. "Why, yes, Mr. Walker. Lead the way."

I snagged her hand and walked her toward the door to the Tabula Rasa.

≈

"Now I know why you kept the pie to yourself the night you followed me out to the parking lot at the Rasa." Val's satisfied smile was dreamy as she rubbed her full belly.

"Told you." I smiled at her across the cab of my truck. "I wasn't giving up Irma's apple pie. Even if I did think you were the most gorgeous and intriguing woman I'd ever laid eyes on." I pulled our entwined hands to my lips and kissed her knuckles.

The nerves were back. I was thankful that my truck was a stick shift, because the constant movement kept me from bouncing my knee. In a matter of moments, Val would know something was up as soon as I turned right instead of left toward the ranch.

Gazing out the window, she noticed. "Where are we going?"

I kept my eyes on the road. "There's something I wanted to show you."

Her eyes narrowed. "You're being weird. Is it a surprise?" Hope laced in her voice, and I knew right there she'd love it. My girl loved surprises.

I stayed quiet, letting the anticipation build. I couldn't look at her. If I did, I'd spill my guts and ruin the surprise that I'd been working on for months. Down more winding mountain roads, I finally reached the small turnoff. I eased the truck down the dirt road. Val had her nose to the window, taking everything in. She'd look over in question, but I kept my eyes forward.

After a slight jog to the left, the road opened up to a huge clearing. In the center of the clearing was a large, two-story farmhouse. It was white with black shutters—pretty, but simple. I put the truck in park and rounded the hood before I could look Val in the eyes. I grabbed her hand and pulled her in front of the house.

"This is gorgeous! What is this place?"

"Come on. That's what I wanted to show you." I walked across the lush green grass toward the wraparound porch. "Al had mentioned this place was going up for sale. We can't live in the cottage forever. Especially if we want to have kids."

"Kids?" Val's eyes were wet with unshed tears.

I nodded. My throat was tight and I swallowed hard. "I know we've talked a lot about kids. Knowing they could never know the truth about my past. But all my worries, my fears about passing on the darkness to them . . . it's quiet when I'm with you. I know that your light will fill them with goodness. Because it has for me. I want this for you. For us."

I pulled her into my arms and rested my forehead on hers.

"Evan, this is too much." Her heart hammered against my chest.

"I told you before—it's never too much if it will make you happy. I will never get enough of you. The seller has already accepted my offer, and the paperwork from the banks is ready to go. If you love it, it's yours. If you don't, I'll find something else. Just say the word."

Val leaned her head up to look me in the eyes. "It's perfect."

"Welcome home, Mrs. Walker." I planted a warm, wet kiss on her lips and deepened it because, fuck it, she was my wife, and kissing her was the greatest feeling in the world.

"Can we go in?"

I shrugged. "It's locked, but I can probably break in for you."

Val laughed and swatted my arm. "Stop it!"

I winked at her and tickled her ribs. She was so fun to tease. I grabbed her hand to give her the outside tour.

"You can see that it backs up to the mountain on this side. There are flower beds—they need a little work, room for a garden. Whatever you want. Anything you want and I will make it happen for you."

Val leaned against my arm as we walked around the property that would be our home. We'd raise babies here. Spend Saturday nights with a bonfire under the stars. Grow old together. Live a happy life.

Nothing could top the life I'd build with Val.

My name is Evan Walker. I work at Laurel Canyon Ranch. It was there I found redemption.

SNEAK PEEK AT THE ALIAS AND THE ALTAR

Sienna

"We have to leave. Now."

The words barely registered as I looked down at my shaking hands and tried to wipe away the streaks of blood across my knuckles. My heart was racing and my fingers numb. I couldn't stop staring at my hands. I started scooping up the overturned contents of my purse, smearing blood on the hard linoleum floor.

The man clasped my arm. His hand was so large it enveloped my biceps. His tug toward the back exit of the restaurant was gentle but insistent.

I looked up at him, my eyes going wide as the intense furrow in his brow deepened. I should run. I should be afraid of him.

"It's too late. They already know who you are," he insisted.

I swallowed hard and only nodded.

I trusted him.

After all, this was the man who came into the restaurant

every Tuesday and Sunday. He sat in the darkest corner of my section every time and offered little conversation beyond his order. Once I'd realized he ordered the same thing—a meatball sub, extra marinara on the side—his conversation skills plummeted to a series of grunts and nods.

That man had also just saved my life.

A twenty-hour car ride from Chicago to the middle of nowhere hits different when it's done in near silence.

I'd learned that my mysterious stranger was *the* Parker Marino. I'd only gaped at him when he'd reluctantly revealed his identity. Working in a sub shop in Little Italy, I'd heard plenty of rumors about the Chicago Mafia and the ruthless business they conducted. It was best for everyone if you didn't ask questions, so I never did. My schedule was flexible and tips were amazing, so no matter who came into the restaurant, I'd serve them with a smile. My gift in life was that I could talk about everything and nothing with anyone.

Parker was notorious in the neighborhood for being intense. Ruthless. Driven.

Everyone forgot to mention he's also hot as fuck.

I adjusted in the seat beside him, angling my body even closer to the door.

Was I being kidnapped?

I spared a glance in his direction. His sharp blue eyes were laser focused on the road ahead of him. The long trip had a little scruff across his sharp jaw, and my stomach tingled at the closeness of him.

No. I definitely went with him willingly.

As flats of tall grasses sailed past, I longed for the

familiar chaos of Chicago. I had never left Illinois, and as I looked out onto the horizon, I was overcome with the sheer *nothingness* of the landscape. In the distance, jagged mountains rose out of the golden plains, black against the riot of indigo and crimson that bled across the fading afternoon sky. I tucked my legs under me and wrapped my arms around my knees.

"Are you cold?"

Without bothering to wait for my response, Parker adjusted buttons and cranked up the heat.

Ignoring his question, I embraced his willingness to speak. "Do you know where we're going?"

He only nodded but I held my stare. Finally he continued: "I had a contact in the police department. I've been looking for someone, and it turns out we'll be safe where he's at."

It was more words than Parker had spoken to me in our entire relationship, and I still had no idea what he was talking about. I fought the urge to spew the onslaught of questions that bubbled inside me.

I gestured toward the window. "And where is that?"

Parker kept his eyes on the road and was silent for a moment. "Montana."

I looked outside again. The wide-open space started making a lot more sense. "Montana? There's *nothing* in Montana."

Parker shook his head, quietly mocking me with a gentle laugh. "Exactly."

Hours ago at a gas station bathroom outside of Minneapolis, I'd been tempted to run and hide. Find a way to leave Parker and never look back. Except I owed him more than that. I'd made a promise to a man I'd spoken only a few sentences to, but I wouldn't break my word.

Not after what he had done for me.

The sun sank lower beyond the mountain as small farm buildings gave way to larger ones. Soon we approached a town, and a faded sign that read Tipp, Montana greeted us. As we drove across the main drag, it looked quiet. Peaceful. A banner hung across the road, advertising a fall festival. Despite the early evening hour, it looked as though shop owners were dimming the lights and locking their doors.

Parker checked his phone and skirted around Main Street to a dingy motel a few blocks from downtown.

He put the car in park and gripped the steering wheel. "We'll stay here tonight. Then I'll find Evan and get this sorted out. It'll be fine, Ray."

"Sienna."

"What?" How he made one syllable sound both sexy and dangerous was beyond me.

I fumbled for my words. "My name is Sienna."

The crease between his eyebrows deepened. "Your name tag said *Ray*."

I turned my palms up. "Old family joke, I guess."

A grumbling sound rumbled between us. "Let's go."

I stared at the motel door in front of me. It was dirty and dark, the flickering overhead light not helping make it look any less murdery. I chewed the inside of my bottom lip.

Parker gripped the steering wheel so hard his knuckles went white. I tried not to stare at his left hand and the fact it was missing a pinkie. "I can sleep in the car. You can have the room to yourself."

My head whipped around. "No freaking way. You're not leaving me in there." I pointed toward the motel. "You're my bodyguard now, champ."

Parker didn't find me cute or funny. He only muttered as he exited the car and strode toward the office. I jumped out of the car and walked as fast as I could to catch up to him. Parker's strides made it nearly impossible to keep pace without breaking into a jog. When we got to the door, I was breathless.

"You might not have noticed, but my legs are a little shorter than yours." I had to look up to see his reaction. He only held the door open for me and tipped his head toward the cramped lobby.

After checking in, I reached into the back seat. Everything I owned was now stuffed into an oversize duffel bag. My heart sank at the thought. As I was hoisting it over my shoulder, Parker caught it midair and slung it effortlessly across his back. Panicked and heartsick when I packed, I had no clue what was in the bag. I only hoped it was enough clothes to get me by.

I stood in the doorway to the motel room. It was clean . . . in a *nothing here is ever actually clean* kind of way.

I closed my eyes and focused on the positive.

Just be thankful it doesn't smell.

I smiled a little to myself. Ever since I was a little girl, I'd had an uncanny knack for looking at the bright side of things. As a baby, my dad had nicknamed me Lady Radiance—Lady Ray for short, which had morphed into Ray, and the name followed me into adulthood. Even the name tag on my uniform touted the name *Ray*. My chest pinched at the memory. I stared back at my hands as I remembered my uncle's blood smeared across them. It had taken an eternity to get it all off, and sometimes when I looked down, I could still see it.

Parker stormed through the motel doorway and dropped our bags onto the small table under the window. Parker claimed the bed closest to the door, and I breathed a sigh of relief.

He stiffened at my side and looked at me, questioning my obvious relief in his choice of bed.

"Thanks," I offered. "I like the bed farthest from the door. It feels less *rapey*." I shrugged.

He stared at me.

Nerves tickled my throat, and I couldn't stop myself from continuing. "You know . . . if someone were to come in . . . I'd be farther away."

A muscle ticced in his jaw, and he turned from me.

Back to silence. *Awesome.*

Exhausted, I plopped down across the bed and flipped off my shoes. Soul-shattering tiredness swept across me. My eyes burned with fatigue, and I closed them just long enough to let the hum of the television next door lull my nerves.

Hours later, I jolted awake. The room was pitch black, and my eyes took a moment to adjust. I lay in silence, steadying my breath. Looking down, I noticed that while I was still clothed and sprawled across my bed, Parker had covered me with the top comforter from his bed.

A strange warmth spread over me at the thought of him covering my sleeping body to keep me from getting a chill. I knew—just *knew*—deep down there was more to Parker Marino than he was letting on. I tilted my head to get a better look at him. Next to me, his rhythmic breaths filled the small room.

I can do this.

No matter how long it took, I would honor the promise I'd made to myself. The men who'd attacked us, knew who I was. He could have ran, but Parker had protected me. Now it was my turn to protect him in any way I could. I would find a way to make sure that he wouldn't be punished for what he had done.

Parker's body was turned away from me. The silhouette of his massive shoulders rose and fell with every breath. His dark hair was inky in the low light of the motel room.

This man was a stranger.

This man was my protector.

This man was a murderer.

Read The Alias & the Altar free with Kindle Unlimited or purchase on Amazon!

SNEAK PEEK OF FINDING YOU

CHIKALU FALLS, BOOK 1

Lincoln

Three Years Ago

The jolt from the blast rattled through the truck, blowing out the front window. All of the doors flew open. Unlatched, I was ejected from the vehicle—thrown onto the open road. I slid before coming to a grunting halt against a nearby building.

I remember every second of it. There's no way to describe how it feels when you think you're going to die. No white light, no moment of clarity. The one thing that crossed my mind was that I wanted to kill the mother-fuckers who did this.

With so much adrenaline pumping through my veins, I couldn't feel a thing. The blast from the IED into the truck as we were leaving a neighboring village also meant that I couldn't hear shit. I knew from his anguished face Duke was screaming, writhing on the ground, but as I stared at him, I heard nothing but a low ringing between my ears.

Smoke swirled around me as I fought to get my bearings. My eyes felt like they were lined with sandpaper, and my lungs couldn't seem to drag in enough air.

Get up. You're a sitting duck. Get. The fuck. UP.

Dragging myself to my knees, I patted down my most tender places, and except for my right arm, which hurt like a bitch, I was fine. I looked back at Duke, whose face had gone still. Although I already knew, I checked his vitals, but it was pointless. Fanned out around us were eight or nine other casualties—some Americans, some villagers. One set of little feet in sandals I just couldn't look at.

Ducking behind another car, I drew my gun and swept the crowd. *Come on, motherfucker, show yourself.* Civilians were getting up, walking past like nothing had happened. Those affected by the blast were screaming, begging. It was a total clusterfuck. My eyes darted around the area, but I couldn't find the trigger man. He'd melted into the crowd.

I ran back toward the mangled, smoking remains of our Humvee. Fuck. It was a twisted mess of metal and blood. Crouching around the base of the truck, I moved to find the guys. Lying in the dirt, knocked halfway out of the doorframe, was Keith, hanging on by the cables of the radio, his left leg torn at a sickening angle. He was dazed, staring at the pooling blood staining the dirt around him and growing at an alarming rate. Without my med kit, I had to improvise. I ripped his belt from his waist and using that and a piece of metal, successfully made the world's worst tourniquet around his upper thigh.

Over the constant, shrill ringing in my ears, I yelled at him, "I got you! FOCUS. Look at me . . . We got this!"

His nod was weak, and his color pallid. He probably only had minutes, and that was not going to fucking happen. I grabbed the radio mic. The crackle of the speaker let me know we weren't totally fucked. Calling in a bird was the only way we were getting out of this shithole.

"This is Corpsman Lincoln Scott. Medevac needed. Multiple down."

"10-4. This is Chop-4. Extent of injuries."

"We've got a couple hit here. Ah, fuck, Wade took two in the chest. At least four down."

"Roger that. Let's get you men onboard."

Leaning back on the truck, weapon across my legs, I felt warmth spread across my neck and chest. The adrenaline was wearing off, and I became aware of the pain in my neck, shooting down my ribs and arm, vibrating through my skull. Reaching up with my left arm, I traced my fingertips along my neckline and felt my shirt stick to my skin. Moving back, I found a hot, hard lump of metal protruding from my shoulder and neck. It had buddies too—shrapnel littering my upper torso, arm, and neck. My fingers grazed the pocket of my uniform, and I held my hand there. I could feel the outline of the letter I kept in my pocket. Its presence vibrated through me. Touching my right forearm, I thought about my tattoo beneath the uniform. Looking down, all I could see were shreds of my uniform and thick, red blood.

Hold steady. Breathe.

My fingers explored. My vest was the only thing that kept the worst of the blast from reaching my vital organs. This neck wound though . . . damn. This wasn't great.

The cold prick of panic crept up my legs and into my chest.

Calm the fuck down. Stop dumping blood because you can't keep your shit together. Breathe.

I focused on Keith's shallow, staccato breathing next to me. I tried to turn my head, but that wasn't fucking happening. "You good, man?"

"Shit, doc. Never better."

"Hah. Atta boy."

We sat in labored-breathing silence. Listened for the medevac helicopters. As the scene around us came into focus, I realized how easily the lifeless bodies of the Marines around me could have been mine. I counted six members of my platoon killed or badly wounded. Our machine gun team, Mendez and Tex, had been among the dead. Mendez was only twenty.

Already struggling to breathe, I felt the wind knock out of me. Just last week, in a quiet moment outside our tent, Mendez told me he was afraid. He missed his mom and little sister and just wanted to go home to Chicago. Becoming a Marine was a mistake, he'd said.

"Doc, I don't wanna die out here, man."

In that quiet moment, he'd revealed what we all felt, but never spoke aloud. Instead of offering him some comfort, I'd stared out into the blackness of the desert by his side until he turned, stubbed out his cigarette, and walked back inside.

Leaning my head back, I let my own thoughts wander to Finn and Mom. His easy smile, her lilting laugh. I wondered what they were doing back home while I was slowly dying, an imposter in the desert.

When I walked off the plane, the airport had an eerie feeling of calm. I could smell the familiar summer Montana air over the lingering stale bagels and sweat of the airport. I hoisted my rucksack over my shoulder and began to walk toward the exit when a small voice floated over my right shoulder. "Thank you for your service."

My whole body shifted, I still couldn't turn my head quite right, and I peered down at a little boy—probably six or seven at most. "Hey, little man. You're welcome."

Then he clipped his heels together and saluted, and I thought I'd die right there. He was so fucking cute. I saluted back to him and dropped to my knee.

"You know, they give these to us because we're strong and brave and love our country." I peeled the American flag patch off my shoulder, felt its soft Velcro backing run through my fingers. "I think you should have it."

The little boy's eyes went wide, and his mother put her hand over her heart, teared up, and mouthed, "Thank you." I tipped my head to her as I stood.

"Linc! LINCOLN!" I heard Finn yell above the crowd and turned to see my younger brother running through baggage claim. His body slammed into me, and we held onto each other for a moment. I ignored the electric pain sizzling down my arm. Over his shoulder, I could see Mom, tears in her eyes, running with a sign.

"Damn, kid. We missed you!" Finn laughed, his sprawling hand connecting with my shoulder. I braced myself, refusing to wince at his touch. But Finn was huge, a solid two inches taller than my six-foot-one-inches. He'd definitely grown up, reminding me that he wasn't the same gap-toothed fifteen-year-old kid I'd left behind when I enlisted.

"Kid? Don't forget I'm older and can still beat the shit out of you. Hey, Mom." I engulfed my mother in a hug. Her tiny frame reminded me why everyone called her Birdie.

"Eight years. Almost a decade and now I get to keep you forever!" We hugged again, her thin arms holding onto me tighter, nails digging into my uniform. Mom was a crier. If we didn't get this under control now, we'd be here all afternoon with her trying to fuss all over me like I was eleven and just wrecked my dirt bike. But the truth was, while I'd been home for the occasional holiday leave, Chikalu Falls, Montana hadn't been my home for over a decade.

She finally released the hug, holding me at arm's length. "I'm so happy to have you home," she sighed.

"I'm happy too, Mom." It was only a small lie, but I had to give it to her. I was happy to see her and Finn, and to put the death and dirt and sand behind me. But I'd planned on at least another tour in the Marines. I was almost through my second enlistment when the IED explosion tore through my body. The punctured lung, torn flesh, and scars were the easy part. It was the nerve damage to my right arm and neck that was the real problem.

Unreliable trigger finger wasn't something the United States Marine Corps wanted in their ranks. In the end, after the doctors couldn't get my neck to turn or the pain radiating down my right arm to settle, I'd been honorably discharged.

I glanced down at the poster board that Finn scooped off the ground. "Oh, Great. You Somehow Survived" was written in bubble letters with a haphazard smattering of sequins and glitter. Laughing, I adjusted my pack and looked at Finn. "You're such a dick." I had to mumble it under my breath to make sure Mom didn't hear me, but from the corner of my eye, I could see her smirk.

"Let's go, boys."

It was a four-hour trip from Spokane, Washington to

Chikalu Falls, Montana—but only out-of-towners used its full, given name. Saying Chikalu was one way to tell the locals from the tourists.

The drive was filled with Mom's updates on day-to-day life in our small hometown. Finn eagerly filled me in on his fishing guide business, how he wanted to expand, and how I could help him run it. I listened, occasionally grunting or nodding in agreement as I stared out the window at the passing pines. Ranches and farmland dotted the landscape as we weaved through the national forest.

I was going home.

"You know, Mr. Bailey's been asking about you. He heard you were coming home and wants to make sure that you stop in...when you're settled," Mom said.

"Of course. I always liked Mr. Bailey. I'm glad to hear he's still kicking."

Finn laughed. "Still kicking? That old man's never gonna die. He's still sitting out in his creepy old farmhouse, complaining about all the college kids and how they're ruining all the fishing. I saw him walk into town with a rifle on his shoulder last week like that's not completely against the law. People straight up scatter when he walks through town. It's amazing."

Changing the subject, Mom glanced at me over her shoulder and chimed in with, "The ladies at the Chikalu Women's Club are all in a flutter, what with you coming home this week. You make five of our seven boys who've come home now." A heavy silence blanketed the car as her words floated into the air. No one acknowledged that three of the five who'd returned came home in caskets.

Clearing her throat gently, she added, "And you got everyone's letters?"

I nodded. The Chikalu Women's Club was known around my platoon for their care packages and letters. Without fail, every birthday, holiday, and sometimes "just because," I would get a small package. Sometimes because we'd moved around or simply because the mail carrier system was total shit, the packages would be weeks or months late, but inside were drawings from school kids, treats, toiletries, and letters. I'd share the candies and toiletries with the guys. We'd barter over the Girl Scout cookies. A single box of Samoas was worth its weight in gold. For me, the letters became the most important part. Mostly they were from Mom and Finn, young kids or other mothers, college students working on a project, that kind of thing.

But in one package in November, I got the letter that saved my life.

I idly touched the letter in my shirt pocket. Six years. For six years, I'd carried that letter with me. After the bombing, it was torn and stained with my blood, and you could hardly read it now, but it was with me.

"The packages were great. They really helped to boost morale around camp. I tried writing back to the kids who wrote when I could. Some of them didn't leave a return address," I said.

Mom continued filling the space with anecdotes about life around Chikalu. My thoughts drifted to the first time I'd opened the package and saw the letter that saved me.

In that package, there had been plenty of treats—trail mix, gum, cookies, beef jerky, cheese and cracker sandwiches. When you're in hell, you forget how much you miss something as simple as a cheese and cracker sandwich. Under the treats was a neat stack of envelopes. Most were addressed to "Marine" or "Soldier" or "Our Hero" and a few were addressed directly to me. I always got one from Mom and Finn. When I got the packages, I shared some of the letters with the guys in camp. The ones marked "Soldier" were always given to the grunt we were giving shit to that week. Soldiers were in the Army, but we were Marines.

On the bottom of this particular box was a thick, doodled envelope—colored swirls and shapes covering the entire outside. It was addressed directly to me in swirly feminine handwriting. Turning it over in my hands, I felt unsettled. An uncomfortable twinge in my chest had me rattled. I didn't like not feeling in control, so rather than opening it right away, I stored it in my footlocker.

I couldn't shake the feeling that the letter was calling to me. I spent three days obsessing over the doodles on the envelope—was it an art student from the college? The mystery of it was intoxicating. Why was it addressed to me if I had no idea who had written it? When I finally opened it, I was spellbound. The letter wasn't written like a traditional letter where someone was anonymously writing notes of encouragement or thanks. This letter was haphazard. Different inks, some cursive, some print, quotes on the margins.

It became clear that the letter had been written over the course of several days. The author had heard about the town letter collection and decided to write to me on a whim. It included musings about life in a small mountain town, tidbits of information learned in a college class, facts about the American West, even a knock-knock joke about desert and dessert. I read that letter every day until a new one came. Similarly decorated envelope, same nonlinear ramblings inside. A voice—her voice—came through in those letters.

There were moments in the dark I could imagine her

laughter or imagine feeling her breath on my ear as she whisper-sang the lyrics she'd written. Her letters brought me comfort in those dark moments when I doubted I'd ever have my mom's buttermilk pie again or hear Finn laugh at a really good joke.

Over the years, she included small pieces of information about who she was. Not anyone I'd known pre-enlistment, but a transplant from Bozeman. She'd gone to college in Chikalu. "The mountains and the river are my home," she wrote. Her letters were funny, charming, comforting.

The one I carried with me was special. News reports of conflict in the Middle East were everywhere, and she'd assumed correctly that I was right in the thick of it. She told me the story of the Valkyrie she'd learned about in one of her courses.

In Norse mythology, Valkyrie were female goddesses who spread their wings and flew over the battlefield, choosing who lived and who died in battle. Warriors chosen by the Valkyrie died with honor and were then taken to the hall of Valhalla in the afterlife. Their souls could finally rest.

Reading her words, I felt comfort knowing that if I held my head high and fought with honor, she would come for me. I carried her words in my head. Through routine sweeps or high-intensity missions, her words would wash over me, motivate me, and steady me. She connected with something inside of my soul—deep and unfamiliar. At my next leave, I'd gotten a tattoo of the Valkyrie wings spread across my right forearm so I could have a visual reminder of her. I could always keep her with me.

Glancing down now, I slid my sleeve up, revealing the bottom edge of the tattoo. It was marred with fresh, angry scars but it was there. My goddess had been with me in battle, and I'd survived.

Pulling into town, I knew I had to find her—the woman who left every letter signed simply: *Joanna*.

Finding You is available on Amazon!

ACKNOWLEDGMENTS

To my amazing husband, thank you for always cheering me on, letting me bounce ideas off you and not getting frustrated when I don't ever use them. I feel so encouraged and loved when I make you proud.

Leanne - there are NO words. I couldn't accomplish half of what I have without your support, tenacity, and encouragement. I've said it once and I will say it again–you are the ULTIMATE hype woman. We really are the #dreamteam and I am so thankful every, single day that we work together.

Chula Gonzalez, you are a GEM! You provided a thoughtful and very thorough sensitivity read. THANK YOU! Thank you for helping me share Val and her family with the world in a way that showcases how incredible and unique they are. I hope I've made you proud. Also, your Spanish dirty talk is on point. I'm still fanning myself.

Another special shout out to Elise & Amy, who not only give the best book recs, but are my daily dose of reality. I wouldn't make it in the book world without knowing we have each others' backs! Friends like are you are the best part of this business.

Jenn - forever and always my favorite cheerleader. One day we'll be in the same state and you're never going to be able to get rid of me!

To every reader who gave this book a chance, THANK

YOU! When I had the idea of a "mafia cowboy" a lot of people thought I was joking. Ha! Thank you for reading Val & Evan's love story. You are the reason I can write and bring love into this world. You are everything. 🩶

ALSO BY LENA HENDRIX

The Chikalu Falls Series

Finding You

Keeping You

Protecting You

The Redemption Ranch Series

The Badge & the Bad Boy

The Alias & the Altar

The Rebel & the Rogue

(coming Fall 2022)

Printed in Great Britain
by Amazon